SOUL SURVIVOR

James T. Wiley

S.A.W. Publications; LLC
Chicago, Illinois

Copyright © 2012 by James T. Wiley
All rights reserved
Second Edition 2016

Cover design by barronsteward.com
Layout/Typesetting by creative-ankh.com

James T. Wiley
SOUL SURVIVOR
Visit my website at www.sawpublications.com

Printed and bound in the United States of America. No part of this book may be utilized in any form or by any means, electronic or mechanical, including photocopying, record- ing, or by any information storage or retrieval system except by a reviewer who may quote brief pages in a review to be printed in a magazine or newspaper, without permis- sion in writing from the publisher. Inquiries may be addressed to the following:

Published by:
S.A.W. Publications; LLC
4601 S.Vincennes
Chicago, Illinois 60653 United States

ISBN-13 978-1-45078122-0

10 9 8 7 6 5 4 3 2 1

Printed in the United States of America Second Edition, Second Printing

ACKNOWLEDGEMENTS

I want to Thank God for moving on the hearts of those who inspired me to write: C. Fletcher from Baltimore you wanted to hear the real Chicago and wouldn't let up off me until I started writing, literally! My brother, partner and second mind Michael (One-Luv) Stubbs you kept me motivated in treating every project as though it were my first you are Cleveland's finest! Jason (J. Rock) Poole of "Larceny." Once you got signed with giving us the real of Washington D. C., I took off with Hope!

D. Waithe thanks for giving me the format on how to write a book. I never would've thought it could be so simple, yet hard at the same time. My book doctor Brian (Voodoom) Ashley thanks for bringing life out my story Milwaukee's Best! Markeeta Allen your editorial skills paid off from Chicago State University; Thank You for taking your time on this project regardless of you being a Mother of two; Gloria Franklin of "Today's Manners for Teens" I love you thank you, for keeping me encouraged when I felt I was just a write; you showed me that I'm an "Author" whose story has to be heard. Michelle Wright of "If All Men Are Dogs What About the Women Who Feed Them?" Thank you for leading me in the direction I needed to go with the production of this book. Which brings me to my publicist Barron Steward this is immaculate. You saw my vision all the way from Atlanta with assistance of Javin Foremen my Chicago Marketing Director, and last but not least, Lorraine Elzia my developmental editor, Thank you! I also thank Terri Woods of True to the Game and Vickie Stringer of Triple Crown thanks for the inspiration of your story's as well which made me produce my own project (God Bless)!

SPECIAL ACKNOWLEDGEMENTS

To my family, friends and relatives I wanted to name you all but that'll be a whole book at least. Therefore, I'll keep writing so I can include you in my up and coming projects. Thank you Momma for keeping me as strong as you through your prayers you kept my mind focused on God and the goals at hand by telling me; "I lived for you Tony and your brothers, you got to live and do what's best for your children. "Thanks for the blessings Ma! Thanks pops for giving me the space to say whatever it is I'd like to say with respect because if it wasn't for your help I wouldn't be here.

PROLOGUE

Life had dealt Gayle Foster another fatal blow. She had survived the first one, but might not be so lucky the second time around.

Staring at her reflection in the bathroom mirror, she couldn't help but notice the darks circles, bloodshot eyes and tear-stained face which were a drastic change from her normally polished appearance. Wiping away the last of her tears with the back of a trembling hand, Gayle then gripped the edge of the sink because her knees were buckling and felt as though they would give out on her at any moment.

On the surface, Gayle could say that the tears were the result of the disturbing news she had received from her doctor; but reality was that her pain was deeper than that. The root of her tears stemmed from worrying about her son Tre. Karma had come back to bite her in the ass – and it hadn't taken just a small bite either. Good thing she had some to spare.

Her cancer had been in remission for two years, but it was back with a vengeance. There was no way around it; she would have to have a second surgery; removal of her right breast this time. She had barely made it through the chemo and other treatments that helped prolong her life; now an added surgery on top of everything else. She had a sneaking suspicion that God had only kept her around so that she could right old wrongs. Unfortunately, she didn't tackle that aspect of her life right away; allowing one excuse after another to prolong the inevitable…and now this!

"Please Lord! I don't want to die. Not right now!" Gayle cried out, closing her eyes against the pain that washed over her soul and caused her breathing to slow down to almost nothing.

Mentally contemplating her options, Gayle knew she would have to turn over all of her real-estate investments to her only son Tre. That was probably not in her best interest, but it was the only choice she had. If she died, then things would happen as they should. The problem would come if she survived. She knew that if she made it through, Tre might feel that he was entitled to keep every dime and leave her with absolutely nothing; especially after what she had done.

Before going under the knife the last time, Gayle revealed the skeleton that she had kept in the closet all of his life. The dirty secret she exposed trumped the kind of little white lies that landed white collar criminals in Club Fed instead of the State Pen where they belonged. No, Gayle exposed the truth behind a lie that would force Tre, even as much as he once loved her, to hate her long after she was buried six feet under.

Worried that she might not make it through her first surgery, Gayle came clean to Tre about her past and the real reason why his father had left them. For years she had led him to be believe that Travis, her former husband and his father, had just up and left his family to fend for themselves on the crime-infested streets of Chicago. For years Tre believed that his father was just another dead beat dad who decided that the good life did not include a wife and child. Gayle had planted that seed and harvested it over the years.

But the truth was far from what she had led her son to believe In fact, she was the one that was shady. Not Travis. She was the one that started the ball rolling that caused Travis to leave. Gayle was the one who had been caught in the act of cheating. She was the one caught with her thighs wrapped around Travis's best friend, amongst passionate screams of ecstasy echoing through the family home.

She would never forget the look on Travis's face when she looked up and saw him standing in the doorway with a vein throbbing at his temple and a hard glare in his dark brown eyes. The look on his face removed every ounce of pleasure that was pulsating through her body at the time. It all vanished just as quickly as it had appeared.

That was years and years ago, but she still could see the look on his face. It was forever etched in her mind. Shame for what she had done forced her to lie to her son. She could not bear telling him the truth and seeing the same look that she saw in Travis's face on the face of her son. So she lied; over and over again until the day of her first surgery.

Nothing had prepared her for Tre's reaction to her confession. After all, she had deprived him of a vital part of his life. To make matters worse, she had the balls to flip the script and place the blame on the one man that Tre had loved more than life itself. A man who had done nothing more than love her, despite her flaws. A man who had treasured his son above all else.

When the first tear fell from Tre's eye, it was followed by another and yet another; Gayle felt a knife piercing the center of her heart. Anger she could handle, but the look on his face, which said that Tre's very soul had been shattered into a million little pieces, was more than she could emotionally bear. As she remorsefully poured out her confession to her only child and watched his reaction, she found it hard to determine which look of disappointment was worse. The one she saw in her husband's eyes due to her betrayal, or the one she saw in her son due to her lies.

From the moment she told Tre the truth about why his father left, he was never the same. She had lost both her husband and her son and life changed for all three of them. Most dramatically for Tre. It wasn't long after she poured her heart out to him of her sins when she began to hear whispers of rumors that her son was on the fast track to become a big-time drug dealer – spiraling into a life of crime in order to mask a pain that matched her own. They both felt the sting of being without Travis in their life; and they both blamed her for being the source of the pain.

Gayle knew that Tre wouldn't listen to anything she had to say about how he should run his life. That would be like the pot calling the kettle black. After all, she had ruined his life once, so why would he listen to anything she had to say. She knew she had no choice if she wanted to save her son from the streets, other than to call Travis. A son needs a father, and she knew that Tre needed his. Reuniting father and son was an answer to her prayers. Only then did some of

Tre's pain go away. Only then did the angry scowl and deadly attitude that seemed a permanent part of his existence disappear like a wisp of smoke on a dark, rainy night.

Travis's words of wisdom caused Tre to understand the reality of three things: jail, the grave, or living a legitimate life were his only choices. Tre had always said he was allergic to prison bars and barbwire; and he definitely wasn't ready for a dirt nap, so that left only one option in his book. He had to fly straight.

A week after those first valuable conversations with his father, Tre left the game and didn't give it a second thought or a backwards glance. Instead he embraced the idea of becoming a legitimate entrepreneur. He knew he liked money; might as well make it the legal way.

Travis managed Yehia's Beauty Salon in Hyde Park, and with Tre back in his life, there were plans to start a family business that would bring father and son together, as well as the younger brother Tre never knew he had.

The grand opening of their beauty salon six months ago was a huge success; bolstered by the fact that the media had learned that...

Tre had turned his life around and was a role model to other young men in the community who had embraced the game. Young men who had turned to selling drugs as their only way to make ends meets and build street cred in their neighborhoods.

The guests ranged from successful businesswomen, celebrities, politicians and even Oprah stopped by to show support. Balloons, banners, and the impressive clientele all served to prove the point that Travis had made to his son, which was, *Live your life in a way that doesn't have you looking over your shoulder, dodging a bullet, or leaving family members to mourn and cry over a silver casket because another young life had been taken too soon.*

Travis had even encouraged Tre to forgive Gayle. At his father's insistence, Gayle and Tre were slowly rebuilding a relationship she had always taken for granted until it was gone. It wasn't easy, but they had been making progress. Each day was a new challenge and she prayed daily for more time to see things through.

But evidently Fate had others plans.

Karma was such an absolute bitch!

CHAPTER 1

August 31, 1999
6:30 a.m.

Ignorance is bliss, and such was the case as Trevon "Tre" Foster steered his passion red painted Ferrari into the driveway of his lavish Tinley Park home; unaware of the detectives staking him in an unmarked police car from across the street. Chicago's finest watched as one of Chicago's biggest drug dealers navigated into the first of a three-car garage which also housed a Corvette, Lexus and a Lincoln Town Car. Green is their envy as the officers whose take home pay for a year did not equal Tre's for a month watched his actions; but their badges made them keep their feelings in check.

After stepping out of his car and closing the garage door with the remote, a woman with a golden complexion and curvy body that was straight out of a rap video ran out to embrace him. She stroked a hand over his bald fade; favoring the 6'3' man with brown skin and a slender build with a kiss so passionate that it made the detectives exchange a knowing glance.

"That must be his wife," Detective Odell grumbled, taking a sip of coffee that had become cold and bitter. "Damn, Timmy! Why can't we live like that?"

"We will soon enough. Don't stress yourself!" Detective

Kruger replied, reaching for the binoculars to get a closer look as the woman retrieved several shopping bags from the front seat. They had been assigned the case nine weeks ago, and had yet to see the young man slip up and give them a reason to step in.

While taking a better glimpse at their suspect, Kruger understood his partner's frustration. Mini mansions containing expensive jewelry, designer clothes, and all the luxurious trimmings that carried a price tag higher than what the two detectives would make in a lifetime; sat along a posh tree-lined street with well-manicured lawns; a picturesque view that spoke of people who lived the perfect life. The sun's rays beamed down as though to make the point that the two men in the blue Grand Marquis would always be on the other side of Tre's kind of life. That fact alone was enough to make stake-outs, like the one they were on, especially hard for men who lived in homes, with their wives and children, which barely measured 1500 square feet from door to door. Men who had to remain honest by turning over millions of dollars in cash and drugs; a constant reminder that slapped them upside the head daily that crime DID pay. And judging by Trevon Foster's flashy lifestyle, it paid well. But the money isn't what disturbed Michael Timothy Krueger the most. The fact that Tre was young and black was enough to make him split his gut.

They definitely had it out for the "slim nigger" who sported a red V-neck cashmere sweater and shirt from *Brooks Brothers*, matching jeans and loafers straight from *Louis Vuitton* as though he was a hard-working business man, instead of just another stiff peddling drugs on the south side of Chicago.

Tre was a flashy dresser to say the least. His attire always spoke fresh, upscale, classy, and debonair. The shelves of New York City were his master and he had no problem being a slave.

Minutes later, Detective Odell nudged his partner to look up as Tre peeled out of the driveway in the Town Car – the business car.

"Heads up. Time to go."

Krueger started the car and trailed behind Tre at a respectable distance so they wouldn't get made by their target.

*****

Tre turned off onto I-294 calculating a few things in his head so he'd have it straight before reaching the stash house. He had to give Doc thirty bricks so the man would stop sweating him. After that, he hit Brian and Brandon with their twenty, which left a hundred in his personal stash. A hundred was more than enough to rake in the kind of money that would put him ahead for a long while.

The sun made a mad dash from behind the clouds, beaming so brightly that Tre had to squint to see the road clearly. Normally, he would circle the block twice, but he was certain that no one could be trailing him on such a beautiful morning. Jay-Z's, "Dead Presidents" blared through the speakers; putting Tre in a business frame of mind. He punched a number on speed dial and moments later he was connect to his partner.

"Yo, Doc, what's the business?" Tre asked, switching the radio off so he could focus. "You ready for me or what?"

"Ain't no question." Doc responded with a raspy voice, the result of having just smoked a little chronic. "Where we at with it?"

"Up at our breakfast spot out west."

Tre glanced at the dashboard, noting the time. "Meet me in forty minutes."

"Bet! ."

Tre had been giving Doc his kilos on the upside of about five grand more than the original cost. He could afford to take it down to two, since he was about to retire from the game. His current run was going to be his last as he was going to turn his connection over to the brothers; Brian and Brandon. From there, Doc would have to make his own way.

*****

Doc coasted up Garfield in a sparkling aqua Range Rover with rims that could cause blindness upon sight. Smiling as he disconnected his call, Doc returned his focus to the unscheduled meeting with Spook.

Spook was "the man," plain and simple. No other introductions were needed. A well-known baller and shot-caller on the south side of

Chicago, somehow Doc found out from his network of informants that Spook was supplying Tre with kilos of cocaine for only ten thousand a pop. In turn, Tre was selling them to Doc, Brian, and Brandon for fifteen stacks each; pocketing a cool five grand from each of them in the process. A fact that did not sit well with Doc.

Tre was supposed to be his boy, so Doc felt he should've been getting those kilos for the same price Tre did. What the hell good was it to have friends if you can't get a hook up every now and then? When Doc ran into Spook at the Cotton Club, he was amazed at what he saw. Spook was acting in the exact manner that mutual associates and old classmates of theirs had described; laid back, to himself, and sitting in VIP like he owned the joint. Ice cold was his demeanor and he possessed not a care in the world. Calm, cool, collected, and being entertained by an entourage of women as well as close street friends, Spook had the presence of a celebrity, right down to guards who were up for busting a cap in the ass of anyone with intentions of causing who they would called their "Governor" harm.

Spook's glassy-white eyes stood out amongst everyone else's in the joint because of the dark rings around them which gave him a slight resemblance to a raccoon. And at the moment, they looked midnight black due to a lack of sleep.

Doc and Spook locked eyes on one another as if they both made it a practice never to forget a face. Then Spook smiled showing off his small, front buck teeth. Instantly Doc felt an advantage. He knew Spook was out of his league trying to pull one over on him. Even though they were friends it was clear that Spook had no idea who he was dealing with when it came to business.

Doc geared up and slowly walked towards him. Spook stood up; his frame, small in stature, much like that of Gary Coleman, further added to an appearance that Doc felt was beneath him.

Spook whispered in the ear of the tall man wearing dreadlocks who stood beside him. An action which prompted him to tap another man with a similar appearance on the shoulder who in turn gestured to the rest of the crew to let Doc through the crowd. Once they were closer to one another, Doc greeted Spook with some dap and a slight hug as they both sat down to converse.

Dom Perignon flowed freely from the glasses of both men,

followed by a couple of shots of hard liquor chasers. As the warm liquor took over, Doc felt confident that his associate would be off his square enough to answer a few questions. Spook's speech became a little slurred as the liquor buzz kicked in full force.

Doc leaned back on the leather sofa and peered at the man over the rim of his second glass of champagne.

"What would fifty of them thangs hit me for?"

Spook's head snapped in Doc's direction, blinking as though to clear his head.

"Damn...That's a lot of shit. I didn't know you was getting it like that," he said calmly.

Doc let out a long, slow breath, realizing Spook was drunk, but evidently not drunk enough for the underlying meaning of the conversation to go over his head.

Spook just stared at him for a long while and Doc could practically hear the gears in Spook's head shifting to, *why would this nigga even attempt to approach me like this and undercut Tre?*

Doc peeped the troubled expression that had been signaled in the mind of Spook and quickly added, "Naw, naw...This ain't all me. Brandon and Brian are goin' in wit' me; you know how it is." He shrugged as though it wasn't a major thing to ask. "We just tryin' to get a better deal." He lied and hoped Spook's drunken state was buying the shit he was shoveling.

Spook's eyes were focused on the chilled bottle inside the bucket in front of him and he couldn't seem to make eye contact with Doc for more than a hot minute.

Doc contained his urge to stare at his drunken acquaintance. He had found out before their meeting that Spook only dealt with three individuals – including Tre – who were buying one hundred or more kilos of cocaine. Plus, since Brandon and Brian had attended Lindbloom High School with Spook, they would have been the ones more likely to cut a new deal. Doc hoped that Spook wouldn't knock a man for trying to eat filet mignon instead of ground chuck. Maybe it wasn't the right move to be making, but hopefully it wouldn't come back to bite him in the ass. Evidently he needed to convince Tre to show them all some more love.

Tre was a legend in the game. Game recognized game and Doc

knew Tre was one of the all-stars. He had started with only $500,000 in assets – minus the sports car, brand new Benz, his wife's Lexus and only $50,000 left to close the deal on a $450,000 home. He had proven himself to be a major player, and Doc hoped that Tre would be lenient to the brothers along the way.

Ironically, Spook's connection had initially dumped a heavy supply of cocaine on him, more than he normally handled at the time. So when Tre came through to cop fifty kilos, Spook gave him fifty more on consignment and Tre took it and ran with the opportunity. Reality was that one transaction had allowed both of them to step their street game up tremendously.

Tre hadn't looked back since. Spook gave him an inch and Tre took a mile, and the rest was history.

After talking with Spook, Tre agreed to sell Brian, Brandon and Doc their kilos for $12,000 apiece.

Unbeknownst to Doc, the only reason Tre had been giving the stash to him for the price that he was giving it was because he was about to retire from the game. His current run was going to be his last run. He was done. It was time for him to move on. Besides, he was also going to turn his connection over to the brothers, Brian and Brandon, and let them rise up their game as he slowly backed out.

*****

As Tre rounded Congress Parkway closely approaching his destination, he made one more call.

"Whaddup, pops? We still meetin' up at the *Waffle House* in Hyde Park, right?"

"Why wouldn't we?" He asked in a raspy voice that signaled years of nicotine abuse. "I'm trying to spend as much time with you as possible, son."

Tre could only nod to his father's statement. The fact that they had been estranged since his mother had done everything in her power to keep them apart, still caused a barrier between them that was hard to remove. His mother had even gone as far as telling him that his father had died. Because of all that, it was hard for him to try and rebuild feelings for someone he had written off as dead in his mind. Since the moment his mother came clean with the truth, Tre had been building a solid relationship with Travis; but the once close bond he had with his mother had virtually went up in smoke after her confession. At one time he would have taken a bullet for his mother, but that changed to the point that he dodged her calls like straight shots aimed at an innocent bystander.

"By the way," his father said, snapping Tre back to the present. "I've been getting' plenty of stares driving' round in your SL-55. This black muthafucka ain't nothin' but a…uh… uh…pussy magnet for an old playa like myself." he chuckled, causing Tre to grin. "Shit! Last night after I closed the shop, there was this bad ass chick sittin' on the hood. And guess what? She didn't even have no panties on."

"For real?"

"Had the nerve to be wearing a short and tight, lime green miniskirt that barely covered her ass . I told her, 'Baby, after you finish buffin' my whip with all that ass you got back there, you can buff this dick.'"

Tre doubled over with laughter, making it hard to keep the Town Car in his lane.

"Pops, you crazy for real!"

The laughter died down when Tre thought of the upcoming meeting with the brother he never knew he had. "Yo, I've been seriously considerin' handin' over those car keys to lil' bro once you finally introduce us. You know, sort of like an ice breaker." Tre sighed, whipping into the complex parking lot. "I don't know why we've been keeping this shit on the low. You know the streets forever talkin'. Niggas are bound to find out eventually."

"Believe me I fully understand," Travis countered smoothly. "But the main reason it has to be done this way is because of your status. These vultures will love to snatch up anybody close to you and hold 'em for ransom. We need to get to him first and tell him that ya'll are related. This way he'll know what and who he's up against."

Tre gave his father's reasoning a bit of thought. Things had become a little more vicious since he kept his business a separate entity from his associates. It seemed that the moment he decided to go straight, everybody and their crew had been gunning for him. And he had his doubts about Doc too. The man was becoming more and more aggressive about things that didn't concern him. Business is business and bullshit was bullshit. Tre wasn't sure if Doc realized that.

"Besides, this little dude is so stubborn it's pathetic," Travis said. "His mother played the same games as yours when we broke up. At least she allowed me to visit him, but only when she felt like it. Shit was always on her schedule. So to him, I'm nothing more than a birthday and holiday father. Ain't that a bitch!" he spat, and Tre could picture his father's disgruntled face set into a scowl. "But, he wouldn't be in this situation if she would've let me get at him."

"Yeah. Or if we all would've had each other at one time or another," Tre replied, sighing again as he thought of how much time had been wasted because both females had a hard time just letting let go of the man and doing what was best for their children. "You know, sometimes I look at moms and feel like telling her she deserves being struck wit' cancer for lying to me all these years."

"Naw, man. Don't ever think or say no shit like that again!" Travis admonished. "Two wrongs don't make a right. Never disrespect the woman who gave birth to you. She could've easily aborted you, given you up for adoption, or just abandoned you. But instead she chose to give you life. She's done a great job raisin' you too. So, appreciate her while she's still here…you only get one mother in life."

"I feel you, pops," Tre replied, pondering his father's words of wisdom and feeling the weight of all he had been dealing with for the past nineteen years.

Between his mother's betrayal, establishing a new relationship with his father, and the brother he never knew he had; Tre felt like he was spending more time dealing with personal shit than finalizing his plans to get out of the game while he was still on top.

"Check it, I gotta go and handle some business real quick so I'll see you in about an hour."

"Alright Tre. I love you."

Tre disconnected the call and held back the tears that were threatening to make an appearance. He could feel a knot building in his throat. Tre wasn't big on showing emotion, but he was glad to be reunited with his father again. The words of advice that Travis had given him made him view life differently. The fact that his father had made his way in the world with a successful legitimate business was just the inspiration Tre needed to step away from the drug game and get into something that wouldn't land him in jail or six feet under.

When Tre finally arrived at the stash house near Madison and Kedzie he pulled up next to an all-white, late model Taurus. He recognized the slender brother with the Frankenstein scar that stretched from the middle of his dark brown forehead and stopped right above the bridge of his nose.

"Face Mob!" Tre yelled. "What's that deal, baby boy? Is everything taken care of?"

"Believe that," Face replied with a simple head nod. "In fact, here comes Munchy's fat ass right now wit' 'em." He jumped out of the car, yelling to the short, chubby man strolling up the block. "C'mon, nigga, hurry yo' big ass up."

Munchy put some pep in his step and waddled down the wooden steps with a black suitcase in each hand as he made his way to the Taurus. Face helped him put the cases inside the trunk as Munchy said, "Yo, Tre, I did like you said and pulled out the rest of those. They sittin' out ripe and ready for division and delivery; feel me?"

Tre grinned at Munchy's attempt to impress him. "Good lookin' out Munch," he said, with a chuckle that caused Face to frown.

"Nigga, that shit sounded dumb as a muthafucka," Face snapped, whining, "Division and delivery?" Then his voice returned to normal saying, "what the fuck that s'posed to mean?" He snatched the driver side door open and gestured for the big man to get in the passenger side. "Nigga, let's ride!"

"Yo, bro," Face said to Tre as he turned the key in the ignition. "I'll get back up wit' you after we shake this load. Now, you fo' sho' that when we meet up wit' Doc over by *MacArthur's* he's gonna take Brandon and Brian they shit too?"

Tre's stomach grumbled at the mention of the popular soul food joint. He hadn't eaten since he exited his flight from New York at 5:44 a.m. Business first, necessities later. "Yeah, he'll do it. And you can tell them cats that we getting together at *Club Clique* tomorrow night. Me and wifey going out to the *Signature Room*, we'll get with ya'll after that." Tre gave Face a sly grin. "As a matter of fact, why don't you and yo' girl join us?"

Face looked to his right, then grinned at Munch who didn't have a girl to speak of. "You talkin' 'bout that spot at the *John Hancock* building?"

Tre nodded, "That's the one."

"Hell, yeah. I'll be there," Face replied. "I mean 'we'll' be there. Shit, probably an hour before you."

"Ya'll niggas trippin," Munchy mumbled as beads of sweat dripped from his nose. That wasn't anything new; but the fact that Munchy seemed paranoid was a cause for concern. "Talk about that shit later. We got too much to lose right now."

"He ain't lying," Tre said, stepping away from his car. He leaned on the passenger window and held out his fist to them as he said, "Ya'll be safe," and dapped them both on the fist with his own before making his way up the stairs.

The moment the Taurus tried to back out of the driveway, a blue Grand Marquis appeared out of nowhere, sirens blaring as it blocked Face in. Two Caucasian plain-clothed officers jumped from the car with their guns drawn.

"Goddamn!" Face yelled, eyes widening to the size of saucers. "Where the fuck these bitches come from?"

"Shut the fucking car off right now!" Krueger shouted.

Odell rounded the car, running toward Tre who had scaled the stairs toward the house. "You on the porch! Lay the fuck down and put your hands where I can see 'em!"

Kruger inched toward Face, weapon aimed towards his head. "I said shut the fucking car off!"

Face turned to Munchy whose panic-stricken expression mirrored his own. "Man, fuck this. We outtie!" He checked his position through the rear view mirror, and stomped on the gas.

Smoke billowed around the car and the scent of burning rubber whipped through the air as the tires on the Taurus began spinning out of control; forcefully pushing the unmarked police car back into the street. Another unmarked vehicle came to a screeching halt on the other side of Taurus, closing off any possible chance of escape.

The two black officers, Simmons and Choice, who were behind the wheel of the silver Crown Victoria, were the first to initiate the investigation into Trevon Foster's criminal activities. Tre had been smart enough to have a stash house far out west; which was totally out of the jurisdiction of the 61st precinct where Krueger and Odell worked, so the collar wouldn't be theirs.

After all three suspects were cuffed; they were taken inside the house, away from the nosey prying eyes of the neighbors who had come out to see what all the noise was about. Krueger and Simmons followed, carrying the black suitcases.

"Wow, boys! Just look at what we got here," Krueger said, grinning as he gazed at a table covered with a hundred kilos of cocaine. "Gosh, this is a lotta shit," he said shaking his head slowly. "Too bad we got to turn it all in."

"Whoa, hold on for just a sec," Simmons countered, holding up the case in his hand. "Let's see what we're working with inside these first. Then maybe, just maybe, we'll call for back up." Simmons chuckled as though he was joking, but when his gaze swept across all of the drugs in the room, it was obvious that the "Maybe we'll call for back up line" was a serious one

"Odell, help Simmons keep count," Krueger said, passing the case to his partner. "Choice, you follow me upstairs so we can air out the dirty laundry." Then Krueger focused on Odell. "Oh yeah, I'm gonna need your gun too."

Odell's bushy eyebrows shot up as his gaze narrowed on the white man next to him. "My gun?"

"What? Did you think that my bullets were going to be the only ones sending these niggers to hell so we can all retire with some serious cash in our pockets?" His demeanor was firm as he looked Odell straight in the eyes.

The other three officers laughed as he added, "Now give me the damn gun!" Showing he was serious about his request, Krueger held out his hand, staring Odell down. Sensing that Kruger meant business, Odell cautiously slipped his Ruger 9MM from its holster and put it in Krueger's open palm.

"And Simmons, you can pass yours over to Choice."

Krueger walked up on Tre, who was posted up in a corner of the living room on his knees with his hands cuffed behind his back.

"Man, what? Ya'll want that bag? Its right here. Ya'll ain't gotta kill me to take it!" Tre said loudly, and Krueger could almost swear he smelled piss, but it wasn't coming from the master mind. One of his little minions had soiled himself. Fear could do that to a man when he was looking down the business end of a pistol.

Krueger pulled Tre to his feet, marched him over to an open closet directly across from where Odell was crouched on the ground, still counting the number of kilos in the suitcases.

"Hey partner…," he said, pausing until he had Odell's undivided attention. "You see this piece of shit right here? I want you to say goodbye to him because this is the last time this nigger's gon' be a problem for us."

Odell chuckled as Krueger chambered a round. "Sure thing, partner." Odell turned to Tre, snickering as he said, "Goodbye, you black son of a …"

The deafening blast from Krueger's gun overpowered the sound of Odell's last words. His body slumped over and froze as the blood in his throat gurgled while he grasped desperately for air. At that moment his body became still.

"Shots fired! Shots fired! Officer down!" Krueger yelled into his radio. He glanced over at his former partner and said, "Sorry man, it's just business; never personal. I know you can understand that, can't you?"

Simmons, who stood frozen in the living room area, parted his lips as though trying to take in more air, or at least come up with an explanation for what happened. Mostly, he was trying not to piss his pants as two of their suspects had done. Krueger watched the emotions play across Simmons' face before the shock gave way to suspicion. It was obvious that he was just as vulnerable as Odell had been.

Simmons' gaze slowly wandered to the drugs, then down to the lifeless body of Odell, before turning so that he was staring into the face of the grim reaper; awaiting his own fate.

"Hey, Simmons! Simmons! Snap out of it man!" Krueger inched forward, waving a hand in front of the man's face. "Look, fuck Odell. He was going to do all of us in if I hadn't got him first. Don't go falling apart on me now!" He gestured to the other suitcase under Odell's limp body and said, "I need you to count the kilos in that suitcase too. Then remove the ones with blood on 'em and dump the coke all around the house."

"Fuck, Krueger! What the hell's gotten into you, huh?" Simmons just looked at him, then at the dead man on the floor, but didn't move an inch to comply with Krueger's command. "Fuck! Fuck! Fuck! Fuck! Fuck," he yelled, pounding the palm of his hand against his forehead.

Kruger gave Simmons a cold stare. "Stop whining like a bitch-ass and count the kilos." He grabbed Tre by the back of his neck. "Come on, Choice. Let's get these knuckleheads out the way."

Tre swallowed hard, staring into the barrel of the gun pointed at him. "Bitch ass nigga!" Tre said as two bullets dropped him to the floor.

Kruger turned to check on Simmons. "Yo', what's the count on them kilos?" He asked, wiping down the .9 mm before placing it in the palm of Tre's hand and firing off four shots in Odell's direction. He unsnapped Odell's holster and stuck his gun back inside, making it look like his partner had tried going for his gun while Tre tried to gun him down.

Simmons' voice trembled as he replied, "Got forty-seven kilos here."

Krueger's gaze swept across the room, noting that Simmons had done the other thing he requested. There was enough powder lying around to make the story they would tell believable.

"Take 'em out to your car," Krueger ordered.

Simmons let out a sigh as his shoulders relaxed. Then as though his survival instincts had kicked in, he moved as quickly as he could, obeying Krueger's last order.

Choice stepped towards the other two hoodlums, aimed his partner's nine millimeter glock and pulled another one from the back of his waist band.

Face glared up at the officer standing over him and growled, "What? We s'posed to cry or somethin'?"

"Yeah," Munchy added. "Suck our dicks, you bitch ass po--"

Choice permanently silenced Munchy's insults as he fired a bullet into his left temple. He shot Face just before he could draw a single breath, sending fragments of the back of his skull splattering all over the carpet and wall.

"C'mon, everything's in place," Krueger said, gesturing for Choice to clear the area as the sirens of the second team signal their rapid approach.

CHAPTER 2

6:00 a.m.

While peering into his rearview mirror, Captain Theodore Bullock watched as the tan brick building that housed his luxurious Hyde Park condominium faded from sight and the view of the Lake Michigan's shoreline spread out before him. The breathtaking skyline coupled with the stunning view of the lake, always had a way of relaxing him. Bullock merged his way onto the Eisenhower expressway, the turbo engine of his ocean blue Porsche cutting through evening traffic like a knife.

As the beautiful melodies of R. Kelly's song, "Sadie" echoed through the speakers and caressed his ears like a warm massage; Bullock couldn't help but think of his late wife, Linda. Sometimes the jolting view of a new day dawning eased the pain and loneliness. He smiled as he reminiscenced about his twenty-two years of marriage. Then his smile soon faded as flashbacks of Linda replayed in his mind of her laying in a fetal position besides the bed as if she had fallen asleep; except that wasn't the case. She had stumbled and fell and hit her head. The trauma caused sudden cardiac arrest and she died in his arms. He remembered that moment as if it just happened.

Bullock pulled into his reserved spot at the 11th precinct, a place where he had served for the past eight years. He started as a Detective on Chicago's south side, and then worked his way up to Special Task Force Agent. It wasn't but a few years later that the department needed his undivided attention on the "Fly Swatter" operation which he played lead detective for the entire investigation. Shaun "Fly Guy" Bradley was the main target and a pretty big fish to catch. But due to Theodore Bullock's keen sense of weak human prey, it hadn't taken him all of three years to nail his suspect that gave him the notoriety that he once dreamed of.

Bullock made his way through the bustling activity in the hallways, carrying a cappuccino in one hand, and a copy of the *Chicago Tribune* in the other. As he passed by benches with street life handcuffed to each one, he scanned the front page of the paper and grinned at the photo of the city's Mayor shaking hands with Roderick Hayes a former police captain.

Roderick, who was also the husband of the city's treasurer, Kathy Hayes, had just been appointed the position of Police Commissioner. In turn, Rod pulled some strings that forced Bullock in his old position. The new captain of the Precinct on Harrison and Kedzie always knew that if he had the right man in play, the right plan would come into full effect.

Bullock slipped into the oversized executive chair behind his cherry wood desk. Several framed photos of him with other politicians hung on the walls. However, the special picture of him and his good friend, Sergeant Phillips, was proudly displayed on his desk. Within the next hour, the two of them would be meeting to discuss the business of the day which included proceeds, profits, and illegitimate hustlers.

A familiar tapping on his office door made him swivel in that direction. "Come in, please," Bullock said, knowing that the knock was specific to the evidence clerk.

Victoria Singleton strolled in wearing uniform blues that seductively hugged the curves of her hourglass frame. He took a moment to appreciate the delicate beauty of the petite caramel-skinned woman with long, jet black hair draped over her shoulders.

She stood on the other end of his desk, staring at him through a pair of wireless rim *Channel* specs. Her hair was pinned up in a bun and small pearl earrings hung from each ear. The perfect likeness of a sexy English teacher which was every man's fantasy.

"Sorry if I interrupted you Captain," Victoria said in a voice so husky, it made him sit up straight in his chair. "God, you're looking mighty handsome; *Mr. Eternity?*"

Bullock smiled, giving her a throaty chuckle. "Your nose deceives you. Guess again."

Her tongue trailed across her strawberry glossed lips. "And if I guess wrong again, what's going to happen?"

After checking the time on his watch, an *Elini* diamond bezel that was a gift from his late wife, he looked up at her. "Let's just say... explode and swallow."

"Hmmm explode and swallow." Victoria's lips pursed in her classic pout. "Does that go both ways?"

Bullock stepped around to the front of his desk, leaned against it, folding his arms across his broad chest. "And why wouldn't it?"

Victoria gave him a smile that matched the mischievous gleam in her dark brown eyes. As if undressing him with her eyes, her gaze scanned the length of his 6'2", 220 pound frame, and then stroked a hand across the blue *Armani* coat jacket and the white shirt underneath before straightening the red tie around his neck. She kneeled near the tip of his *Cole Han* shoes and inhaled as she looked up at him.

"*Issy Miyake*, right?"

"Wrong again," he said, letting his hands play in her silky hair. "*Dolce and Gabbana.*"

She snapped her fingers as though disappointed. "Aw, you got me."

"I guess you have to pay the penalty now Vicky my dear," Bullock teased, as she placed her hand on his trousers and forcefully tugged his zipper down.

"Damn, I was sure I knew the answer." She licked her lips between each word.

Bullock reached into the opening of his pants and pulling out his erection. Vickie's eyes widen as she stared at the mushroom head before slowly tracing the tip with her tongue.

She closed her eyes, parted her lips and took as much of him as she could handle in one smooth glide.

Bullock's head tilted back, and a moan of pleasure escaped his throat. His hand gripped her head and released the ponytail she had pinned up, allowing the silky strands to flow between his fingers. He could barely contain himself as she sucked away on his shaft with an expertise he had never felt from anyone else.

Moments later, he could feel his dick pulsating inside her mouth. He knew he was close to the point of erupting.

"Ohhhhh…Oohhhh…Shhhhh…Shit."

Victoria's jaws tightened around the full length of him as she went faster. Unrelenting was the grip of her cheeks around his dick as she pulled him to the brink of orgasm.

"Y- y-y young g-g-g-g…girls…gon' be…the death of me…yet." Bullock stammered, balancing on the edge of his desk. His body shook and contorted as his orgasm traveled through his shaft anxious to be released from his body. He erupted right into Victoria's lovely throat, gasping as he fought to catch a breath. She continued to suck him, swallowing every last drop of semen and licking her lips in satisfaction when she was done.

A minute later, she stood up, pinned her hair back up into a ponytail, adjusted her uniform and made her way to the door. She turned back to face him. "I supposed you still want me to have Ortiz get those boxes ready for the 7th District?"

"That would be a damn good idea," he replied, then smiled as he watched her plump rear jiggle out the door and march down the corridor.

*****

Ortiz disconnected the call with Victoria and turned to the two men who had been piling up bricks of coke along the aisle.

While hawking Turner and Canal's every move, Ortiz took special note of the weapons, DNA samples, tons of marijuana, cocaine and heroin that filled the 600 square foot room. He couldn't allow either one of them room to make any mistakes. Ortiz had been in charge of running the type of operations which was meant to be kept under the radar. Discovery would mean that his life; his freedom and everyone he loved would be placed in severe harm.

Ortiz felt this was his one and only opportunity to stand up for his Latino race. Whenever he visited his old hangouts in Chicago's Little Village neighborhood, his family and friends taunted him calling him, "fucking cerdos" and "puta" which meant fucking pig and bitch in English. Some had even gotten beaten with flashlights for spitting on him. But due to a few "Latin King" cousins telling the streets of their relations, the community showed leniency. Especially now that the same community was officially a part of what would now be the biggest housing development in Chicago which caused a connection straight to the Mexican Cartel pipeline.

Bullock trusted Ortiz's cocky attitude because he knew Ortiz was the key source in replacing the precinct's inventory. This made him a valuable asset and got him promoted to active Lieutenant throughout the precinct.

"Canal, after you seal that box, sit it here next to me," Ortiz said, gesturing to the officer and then jotting on his notepad. Canal's skin went from pale to pink as he clutched the roll of masking tape and rose to his feet towering over Ortiz like Goliath to David.

"Listen you little…" Canal began…

Turner interceded immediately rushing between them both before Canal could finish his sentence.

"Hey, calm down. You two are acting as if it isn't all our asses on the line right now"! He then turned to Ortiz, "I don't know if it's the short man syndrome that's making you abuse your authority; but at this moment everything means green to me." Turner finished doing a round-about face toward Canal hoping he understood.

Canal cracked a grim reaper smile showing off his coffee stained teeth then said, "Your right partner, it's all about the Benjamins."

Ortiz stood firm at his 5'4 inch stature with his hands on his waist still standing behind the two officers as they proceeded with their duty, "That's it. You listen to your partner's advice or you'll be eating the crumbs from my table"! He laughed loudly."

"I suspect you got everything taken care of Lieutenant because the Captain is on standby waiting." Ms. Singleton chimed in walking up the aisle with her log book in hand.

Ortiz turned to her. "Yes, it is Vicky. Yes, it most certainly is," Ortiz repeats. "Eight down two more to go!" He stated.

"No problem," she uttered following behind. "Let me go and give him the status." Placing her pen behind her ear, Victoria left the men to finish their job.

"Turner, did you hear what I said?"

"Sure thing boss." Turner quipped, while rearranging the kilos to make more room in the box. "Just let me place the guns on top of these."

Ortiz tugged at this necktie to loosen it a bit. He could feel the thin sheen of perspiration on his forehead. Camouflaging ten kilos of cocaine was no easy task.

"Alright, but hurry up! We've got nine more boxes to get to before 7D rolls in with our shipment."

Turner sighed for the fifth time in the last three minutes. "Be easy, Lieutenant. We got this," he said looking at his partner. "Trust me."

Canal smiled, but the way he rolled his eyes toward the ceiling spoke to the fact that he was becoming agitated with the constant urgings to hurry things along. "Fucking wetbacks shouldn't be overseeing the white man anyway," he mumbled. "Who the fuck do he think he is?"

"You got something to say to me, Canal?" Ortiz asked, coming to stand over Canal who was kneeling down.

"No, we've got it under control."

"That's, 'Sir we've got it under control, Sir!,'" he corrected, and didn't miss Canal's angry glare.

CHAPTER 3

Bullock gripped her hips and thrust inside her with as much power as he could summon.

"Is everything in order, baby?"

"Oooooooh, yes, daddy," Victoria, crooned as she heaved forward under the weight of his movements. "Oooooh, daddy…get it…get it," she moaned.

Victoria was bent over the desk, pants bunched around her ankles as Bullock fucked her from behind.

"Uuh…shhhiiitt," he growled the moment Victoria's muscles gripped his swollen cock. The heat, the wetness, the sound of her voice; all were working in unison to drive him absolutely crazy.

"Thissss isssss…your pussy," she hissed, as she heaved forward again and again. "Oh, all yours Captain."

The sound of his balls smacking along her ass echoed throughout his office, but he could swear he heard something else.

Bullock slowed his pace for a moment, tilted his ear in the door's direction. He quickly dismissed the thought that someone had been knocking the moment Ms. Singleton whispered, "I'm about to burst."

He picked up the pace again, driving deeper and harder into

her creamy walls, banging the tip of his penis against her cervix with his long strokes. She trembled so hard that her legs almost gave out on her; he caught her before she slumped to the desk, chuckling when she knocked his name plate to the floor.

"You want me to get that?" she asked, her body still bent over with his dick inside of her.

"No. Just hold your position." He grabbed her by the waist and held her steady. "I'm about to fill you up with a load of protein, if you know what I mean."

Ms. Singleton looked over her shoulder and smiled.

Bullock had found his rhythm, but before he could reach the grand finale, his office door swung wide open.

"Theo!" Sergeant Phillips stood at the threshold, gun drawn. "What the hell?"

"Oh my God," Victoria said, gathering her clothes and scampering to hide behind Bullock, burying her head into his shoulder as Phillips holstered his weapon.

Bullock pulled up his pants. "Shit, Duke! Don't just stand there. Close the goddamn door!"

Phillips slammed the door behind him and locked it. "Man! I can't believe you. You're slipping!" he said, focusing on Victoria who struggled to pull herself together. "I could hear all that noise from out there and you didn't answer when I called. I thought you were in danger!" He ran a trembling hand over his bald head, exhaling in the process. "You're putting us all in jeopardy! All we need is for one asshole to walk in and catch you like this. Next thing you know Internal Affairs gets word and they'll send in the Feds."

Phillips took a seat in the chair opposite of the desk and sighed. "We all know how the Feds get down. If those nosy bastards were to backtrack everything that's been going in and out of the evidence department, our asses are through."

"Calm down, Duke," Bullock said zipping his pants, and looking over his shoulder to find that Victoria was fully dressed. "Nothing's going to happen to us because nothing ever gets logged in. Now I--"

"Excuse me, gentlemen," Victoria interrupted, stepping out from behind her lover and giving them both a sheepish smile. "I'm going to get back to my station." She sashayed seductively for the distance from where she was standing to the door then turned back toward Duke. "And Sergeant..." she paused until he locked gazes with her. "I deeply apologize."

Bullock glared at Duke's slow scan of Victoria's body, before continuing with his train of thought. "Back to what I was saying, I look over everything we do myself. So fuck the Feds!" Bullock spat harshly. "They're nothing more than a bunch of sharp dressers obsessed with big-time dope dealers."

Duke's gaze swept over the files on Bullock's cluttered desk.

"They snatch them off the streets using that psychological bullshit and trick 'em into believing that they're facing a bunch of time in prison," Bullock said, shifting a few papers out of Duke's sight. "I've seen that tactic stretch many tight lips. That's how most of their work is done. They have snitches solving their cases while our men shed real blood, sweat and tears trying to make this a better and safer America. And by the way, these suit-wearing bitches will be here for that stuff in two weeks."

Bullock thought back to 1995, when the Mayor informed city council members that the Chicago Housing Authority had made inadequate progress in improving public housing, also known as "The Projects," and temporarily brought in HUD to bring about improvements. Chief Deputy Hayes was a part of the city council and learned that the true design behind the move was to sweep out all lower-class and poverty-stricken tenants to Englewood, South Shore, and the suburbs; and to usher in more desirable residents that were more in line with keeping the city's image as the new tourist hot spot. Hayes tipped Bullock and Phillips off to the "Plan for Transformation" which was all about replacing the public housing with scattered site housing that resembled expensive condominiums and townhouses that very few blacks were able to afford.

Three of them agreed to implement a plan to buy up foreclosed and condemned property in Bronzeville using cash and drugs from the 7th and 11th Districts. They wanted to generate revenue so blacks could have a solid foundation laid within the city limits for generations to come. But they never realized how many lives were at stake, nor how much would be involved in keeping an undercover operation going with so many eyes and ears focused on the force.

Bullock was brought back from his trip down memory lane by Phillips pushing the door to his office completely shut. "I hear what you're saying Theo, but we still have to be a lot sharper." Duke's gaze lowered to the ground. He leaned in, picked up the small square foil and lifted it so that Bullock could see. "So, do you think that you can keep your dick in your pants or maybe water the clerk's bush outside of this building? 'Cause believe me, your most trusted officers will break your ass if they're ever confronted with a life sentence."

Bullock picked up the waste can next to his desk and aimed it so Duke could toss the condom wrapper inside.

"Plus, we already have a major problem. One of your officers has gotten out of control with this shit. Killing fellow officers? What type of shit is that?" Phillips crossed one leg over the other. "We're not a fucking gang, Theo. We just want to buy up as much property in the Bronzeville area before the masses do." Sergeant Phillips preached, "We all know what happens if they monopolize. The rent will shoot up so high that it'll be hard for any black family to afford staying there. They'll be tricked into moving into the suburban areas, while the whites trickle on down into the inner city. Gentrification don't love nobody!"

"Like I said before Duke, You're going to give yourself a heart attack, take it easy. Bullock said, stepping from behind his desk to perch on the edge of it. "I'm going to make sure that none of my people pull anything like that again. You got my word on it." He tried to assure Phillips. "Anyways, look at the bright side, a least this time a white guy killed another white guy." Bullock chuckled, placing a hand on his shoulder. "But on the serious side, I know we don't need the heat, and who knows, maybe Krueger peeped a flaw in Odell that we don't know about."

Duke took out a cigar and lit it up despite Bullock's insistence that he hated the smell of his nasty habit.

"Right now the only thing that matters is the hundred keys I'm sending your way," Bullock smiled, crossing his arms on his broad chest. "So, what do you have for me?"

Phillips allowed a ring of smoke to dissipate as he kept a steady gaze on Bullock. "Six kilos of heroin. Do you think you can handle that?"

"*Can* I?" Bullock said, smirking at the fact that the man doubted his abilities. "I'm doing one in two to three days over at Be-Be's old spot."

"You mean Jack Be-Be's dope spots? How'd you pull that off?"

"My nephew has a connection with Jack's relatives, so whenever we do a raid in the area, I send the heroin in his direction and he distributes everything to his Black Sole and 4 Corner Hustler buddies. That's what he's into."

"Tell me about it," Phillips quipped. "Lil' Duke is on standby as we speak. Oh, and here…" He placed a briefcase on Bullock's desk. "That's for Krueger's service. I have Simmons and Choice on the same deal."

Bullock flipped open the locks and peered inside, doing a quick mental count he could tell that the total was $450,000 in rubber band stacks inside the case. "I'm impressed, but why so much?"

"I told Duke it'll look good on his resume if he got them off for as much as possible. That way Krueger, Choice, or Simmons wouldn't have a problem doing it over and over again." Duke stood, perched on the edge of the desk and scooped up the photo. "Keeping everybody happy is what we want to do; right?"

"I guess," Bullock said reluctantly.

"How much does he charge for those bricks?"

"In Rockford he gets them off for fifteen to twenty grand but a lot of things are about to change now that Trevon Foster's out the way. We have his coke, his connect and his clientele. So, my son is more than happy to give these officers all the proceeds off the odd 47 they stinged for."

"That's cool right there. What's up with your son, Jr.? How's he handling things as a rookie?" Bullock inquired, leaning back in his chair.

"He's learning. Just give him a few years he'll be ready to take the detective exam. At least that's what he told me his plans are." Phillips made his way to the door with Bullock coming up right behind him. "I'm going to get out of here so I can make sure Lil' Duke's shipment arrives on time." Phillips extended a beefy hand. "So take care and I'll see you at the ceremony."

Bullock shook his friend's hand and watched as he strolled down the hallway past the evidence clerk who gave him a smile and a two-finger salute before he made a fast exit out of the building.

CHAPTER 4

Robby stood on the sidewalk yelling up to Tone's apartment on the second floor. The sun was shining so brightly. He covered his eyes with black *Gucci* frames to mask the sun from distorting his vision. He barely dodged a group of kids playing 'It" on the curb. He quickly jumped to get out of their way before they practically knocked him down while running to their hiding spots.

"Tone. Tone! What's the demo Sir?"

He smiled when he saw the curtain being pulled back from the window. But instead of Tone staring back at him, she did instead.

"Robby! Why the hell are you yelling like that up at my window?"

"Oh, snap." Robby cringed, covering his mouth when he realized Tone's grandmother had answered him instead of his boy. "M-m- my fault, Ms. Wiley I was just trying to see if Tone was ready to go shopping. I didn't mean to disturb you."

She wanted to be made but how could she? Robby was light skinned; about six feet tall, with a low tapered haircut, dressed to perfection and boy did he have the prettiest white teeth she had ever seen. How could she stay mad at that? "Never mind me, Baby," she said softly. "You better be more concerned with Big Momma. She sits right down there in the front room and she's too old for all that racket.

So, keep the noise down."

"Alright, Ms. Wiley," he said, giving her a big smile. "It won't happen again...I promise."

"Okay, baby. Now, Tone is downstairs in the basement," she said, gesturing toward the right side of the building. "You can knock on the last window back there in the gangway."

Without waiting for a response, she slipped back into the apartment and closed the curtains. There was only one reason Tone wouldn't be outside waiting for Robby. He had to be otherwise occupied. Instead of walking towards the concrete pathway trailing between buildings, Robby hopped back into his '87 Chevy Caprice, thinking, *my nigga ain't had no pussy in a couple years. I know he probably knee deep in some right about now. I know I would be.*

He had a feeling who Tone was sticking it to and for a moment, Robby thought of ruining the party...

While Tone was locked away, Robby sent money, made sure to visit and when he couldn't make it up to Statesville, he sent letters; all to keep his best friend up on all the street news. Robby didn't hesitate to inform his buddy that Doc was trying to push up on Sheree, a teenage love that had been with Tone since they were eighth-grade graduates. Evidently, Tone was in a forgiving mood; or maybe Robby needed to remind him of a few things to keep him on point. Doc was making the kind of moves that could make him more of an enemy than an ally.

Robby cranked the engine and pulled off, then turned on his stereo CD system. DMX's song, 'Slippin' came booming through the speakers.

To live is to suffer, and to survive...well, that's the fine meaning into suffering.

Robby repeated the jewel that DMX dropped in the beginning of his song. A jewel which his homey, Tone had to witness first hand...

*****

The moment Tone walked out of Statesville Maximum Security Prison after serving time for attempt murder, Sheree Thomas awaited him on the other side of the fence.

Sheree's assets were in all the right places. Her 34D breasts had become more supple and perky than he remembered. Her buttocks were plump and perfectly shaped like a crescent moon. Chestnut brown hair now hung to her shoulders and her hazel eyes could brighten the darkness in any room. Her once golden complexion now resembled toasted honey, a few shades deeper than he remembered. Obviously, while he was locked down in Statesville Maximum prison among Chicago's most hardened criminals, she had taken the time to have some fun in the sun and it wasn't with him.

Tone drilled her several times about the things that Robby had told him, but she denied everything and maintained the position that she would never sleep around with any of his friends. She said it was something only skanks and whores did, and she was neither.

He didn't know what to believe, especially since he hadn't heard from her during the first six months of his incarceration. When he finally did reach her, their brief conversation on the phone ended with a cold statement of, "Things done changed Tony," before she hung up as quickly as when she answered.

Stepping outside of the concrete walls of the place where he had survived the crevices of perpetrating hard correctional officers, homosexuals, and men who would never get the chance to touch a woman with a ten foot pole for the rest of their entire life, Tone froze the moment he locked his eyes with hers. It was the first time he'd seen or heard from her and he wondered what her true agenda could be. He slipped into the passenger side of the car and dozed off the minute his head touched the smooth leather headrest.

As Sheree lay in Tone's basement apartment between his legs in his king sized bed with her head rested on his burly chest, the faint glow from the 60" television music channel played Babyface's, "Whip Appeal" in the background. The music video beamed over her body which glistened with oil. The room was dark, but it was in the same condition it had been before he left. Candles were on both of the night stands flanking the bed. A large painting of a naked man and woman embracing each other in a kiss hang over the bed. Black silk sheets lined the bed and the ambiance of the room set the stage for good sex. But if Sheree was banking on the insanely passionate lovemaking session, which had lasted from the moment he had reached the bed until well into the next day, to be the tool to get Tone emotionally attached to her again, she would soon learn that it would take a lot more than just her spreading her legs to accomplish that goal.

Sheree rubbed her hands down Tone's long braids, then slid her upper body down his chiseled, caramel toned frame until her face was in line with his balls. She licked them, slowly – using circular motions – then blew a cool wisp of air on them.

"Whoa! Babe, whatcha doin?" Tone jerked up, but she pressed him back on to the bed.

"Baby," Sheree whispered between licks. "Am I doing it right?"

He smiled and closed his eyes again, relishing the sensations that were damn near unbearable. His toes began to curl and he could feel heat pulsating down his entire spine.

"Hell, yeah," Tone growled, then grabbed her thick mane of hair with both of his hands, pressing her closer to his dick. "Just keep it up... damn that feels good!"

Sheree sat up and held his erection in the palm of her hands, rubbing slowly, yet firmly along his shaft. Then she sensuously leaned in, taking his dick so far into her mouth that she gagged.

Tone laughed and said, "Girl, you on a suicide mission or somethin'? You know you can't swallow this long motherfucker. But that was still a good try." He closed his eyes and sighed, forcing her back into position. "Now suck on it 'til I bust off."

She flinched backwards out of his reach and looked up at him. "Hold up, baby. I'mma do whateva you want me to do; but just don't cum in my mouth, alright?"

"Yeah, a'ight."

Tone opened his eyes, watching as his first love continued her efforts. As her head bobbed up and down he wondered to himself, *how many other niggas you did this to since I've been gone?* He couldn't help shake the fact that her ass wasn't into sucking dick before he went to prison, so there was no telling who had taught her the skills of her new little trick.

The moment Tone tensed up, she bobbed faster; sucking like her entire life depended on pleasing him. The moment she tried to come up for air, he applied more pressure to keep her in place. His balls pulsed with a need to release and his grip tightened as he convulsed and the warm, creamy fluid burst all over her tongue, filling up her jaws.

Sheree trembled with what could have been anger, but she swallowed the mouthful and only then did he release her.

She jumped up, both hands covering her mouth as she ran straight into the bathroom to vomit. Minutes later, she returned to find Tone sitting on the edge of the bed slipping into a pair of jeans.

"Are you going somewhere?" she asked, her hands on her hips as she sashayed toward him in what she probably thought was a seductive manner.

Tone stood, pulled up the zipper and reached for his shirt. "Yeah, I'm going' somewhere… why?"

Sheree detected the bitterness in his voice and smacked her lips. "Damn…I was just going to tell you that I'll stay here another night if you want me to."

"Nah, I'm straight." Tone replied, giving her a sly smile. "As a matter of fact, you can get the fuck outta here right now!"

Sheree stepped back, one penciled eyebrow shot up. "What? Where is that coming from? Why you trippin?"

Sheree knew the answer to that question better than anyone. She had abandoned Tone at a point in his life when he really needed her the most.

Tone had stated in several of his letters to her from prison that he didn't care if she was faithful or not because he was physically gone. All he wanted was for her to write him once a week to show that she still at least thought about him. She was his first love and had found a way to break his heart. First, by not doing the one simple thing that mattered the most to him; and second by committing another major mistake – sleeping with someone in his inner circle. As far as he was concerned, she no longer mattered to him the way she once had. At one time in his life, he would have died for her. But that was a lifetime of heartbreaks ago.

Tears formed in her eyes, but they weren't enough to move him in the least. "Why shit gotta be like this, Tony?" she asked, sniffling as she stared into his eyes.

"Things done changed Sheree," Tone spat, zipping his jacket

"Do you remember that?"

Sheree wiped her tears and threw on a white, *Bill Wall* leather rider jacket. After picking up a white, Louis Vuitton overnight bag containing her clothes, she faced him again, slipped the shirt over her head and whispered, "I'm sorry baby. I really am sorry."

Tone looked down at her, taking in the baffled and pain-stricken expression, he could see that she was broken up, but he could care less. The words on the front of her t-shirt read, 'The Future Mrs. Wiley.'

He couldn't help but laugh. "For real?"

Sheree reached inside the bag and pulled out a wad of perfectly stacked cash and tossed it his way. "I've been saving this up for you."

Tone was surprised by the move, but kept his expression neutral as he leaned in so close their noses almost touched. "What? You think this bullshit's gonna make up for the letters and pictures you ain't never sent? Huh?"

Sheree rolled her eyes, but inched back from him a little. "That money right there ain't got shit to do with my fuckups, Tony. And I ain't expectin' shit in return." She peeled her hair back and slipped on a ponytail holder. "Other than that, I guess you'll just have to forgive me whenever you feel like you're ready."

On that note, she turned and stormed out the door and slammed it behind her. Tone was right on her heels. He wondered where the money had come from. However, his curiosity turned to astonishment when he saw her hopping into a black and white, Mercedes Benz convertible *CLK 320 – the* next generation of Benz up from the one he had given her before he left to do his time. He hadn't clocked that when she had picked him up. As he stood outside the car, he watched as she dropped the top down and sped off leaving more questions than answers swirling in his mind.

He had to wonder if Sheree had anything to do with what happened a few years ago…

*****

Two years earlier

The block of 55th and Winchester was lined up with crazy clientele. Dope fiends were hustling for their next fix and dope dealers were more than ready to supply the habits that some of them possessed for more years than they could count. Flye had parked on the block in a black BMW 740II, listening in while Tone schooled Click on the game.

"Yo, Click. Did you get the money from ol' girl sittin in that blue car over there?" Tone asked, holding a clear zip-lock baggy filled with little red vials.

"Yeah, Moe," He gestured "I got everybody's scratch that ain't drove off."

When they reached the blue Saab, a dark-skinned woman was sitting behind the steering wheel with a paranoid look on her face. "Gimme my five so I can get the fuck out of here."

"Here you go baby girl," Tone said, passing her five dime bags of rocks. "But, you might as well grab that eleven for the hundred right now to save yo' self a trip from comin' back."

"Nah sweetie," she said, scanning the area before giving him a wide smile. "This'll do for now." She put the gear in drive and burned rubber.

"Damn Joe," Tone complained "Now I'm stuck wit' these last six." Then his gaze slid to the porch as Click rolled another blunt. "Here," he said handing the six to his young student. "You might as well pop these boys off. I practically done sold the whole pack for ya ass already. If I keep doin' it like this, you ain't gone learn shit… Have you ever heard of the fisherman story?"

"Naw," Click replied, passing the blunt to Tone in hopes it would relax him enough to shut the fuck up. "I ain't never heard of no damn fisherman story."

"Flye hipped me up to it," he said, nodding toward the BMW a few feet away. Flye gave them an almost unnoticeable head nod, and the two men gave him one back.

"There was this fisherman who wound up sick on his deathbed," Tone explained while arranging his money, making sure all the faces were upright and matching each bill together. "The fisherman's oldest son came into the room one day and was like, 'Daddy, you gotta get up 'cause we starving.' The fisherman asked his son, 'Why don't you go fishing for the family and...'"

"So to make a long story short," Click interrupted, twisting the dreads in his hair, "The family starved to death because Pops never showed them how to fish; right?"

Tone nodded, patting his student on the back. "Exactly. See, that's another reason why we should call you Click instead of Kyle. Besides them bogus ass *Penny Loafers* you used to wear...you be catchin' on quick as a muthafucka. Click, click."

They both roared with laughter and even Flye joined in.

*****

The sound of a racing car engine quickly caught Tone's attention. "Ain't that a bitch?" He whirled on his heels just in time to lock eyes with the one driving the grey Cutlass.

"Click! Grab the sword, and hurry up!"

Click dashed into the gangway, reappearing with an M-4 Carbine seconds later. "Wh...who you 'bout to air out?" he asked scanning up the block as though he could see who the target was.

"That GD nigga, Shane. He just rode through here," he said, gesturing the spot that was still filled with smoke left behind from the screeching tires. "Motherfucker use to be with us until folks offered his greedy ass two keys and a governor's spot over the guys on 51st and Woods." Tone snarled "Playboy's up to somethin'. I can feel it. That nigga know it's on between us and them."

Then suddenly a barrage of bullets blasted into the left side panel of Flye's car, shattering the window. Shane ran toward the car, letting off four more shots. Chunks of Flye's face went flying along with the rest of the debris.

"You bitches is dead!!" Tone yelled, running at top speed, an assault rifle hoisted and aimed at his intended victim. He squeezed the trigger. Angry shots blasted more holes into Flye's already bullet-ridden ride, similar to how the car Tupac was in looked the night he was assassinated.

Three shots exploded from the four door Cutlass as Rocko

covered Shane long enough for him to make it back to the car.

Tone's weapon propelled miniature missiles directly into the vehicle as it sped right in his direction.

Shane struggled to maintain control, jerking the steering wheel to stay upright. The car rocked from side to side.

"Rocko!" Shane yelled, choking the steering wheel. "Shoot that nigga! Shoot that nig…"

Rocko cringed as two bullets silenced Shane's voice. His blood painted the inside of the automobile.

"Shane! Shane!" He screamed, but his friend fell forward crashing his head against the steering wheel. The car horn blared in protest of the weight lodged against it.

The car began to veer toward a concrete light pole.

Tone yelled, "Click, go grab another clip! Hurry up!"

Tone pressed his back to a tree, keeping an eye on the Oldsmobile as Rocko scrambled to snatch Shane to the side and climbed over him. Once Rocko was in the driver's seat, he slammed his foot on the gas pedal.

"Fuck-Fuck-Fuck-Fuck-Fuck-Fuck!" Tone yelled, stomping around in the middle of the street, regretting that the Cutlass sped away before he could even the score.

Tone ran to the beamer and froze at the driver's side door. Flye's head had a cavity in it the size of a grapefruit. Another hole had blasted through his jaw, exposing the inside of his mouth.

Tone stared helpless at his motionless friend. Before he knew it, the gun slipped from his hand. The man who had taught him how to survive the game, hadn't lived to survive it himself.

*****

Later that night, Tone blasted Tupac Shakur's, "Life Goes On" from the speakers of his Chevy Tahoe truck. Sheree, Robby, Shawn, and Click all sat on Tone's front porch; reliving the times they had with their fallen comrade.

"That nigga, Flye, was always ridin' me 'bout my *Penny Loafers*." Click chuckled as he tossed back a fifth of Hennessey. "I'mma miss him callin' me Click."

Robby took another pull of the black jack cigar filled with hydro. "Yeah. Remember when we tried to creep up on Mike G and his boys. Those damn clickity-clackity ass shoes blew our cover fast as hell. Shit, them niggas turned around instantly."

"On the real," Click said with a grin. "We had to burn them cats right then and there."

Everyone busted up laughing.

Tone's smile faded as he looked toward the street. "Wait. Hold up," he said, noticing the two unmarked police cars pull up.

Click zoomed in on both officers as they exited the vehicle, dressed in Cashmere jackets and suits. "What the fuck do these bitches want?" he asked under his breath.

"You already know," Shawn replied, exhaling weed smoke through his nostrils. "Information."

Robby rocked back in the chair and didn't bother putting out his weed. "What seems to be the problem, officers?"

"There isn't one," said the officers who were suited up as if they were limo chauffeurs as they pinpointed their stares in Tone's direction. "I believe we got this under control."

One officer, tall and slender compared to the round one standing next to him said, "He fits the description the victim gave us earlier; light skin, long corn rows, triangular face."

"Yeah, he does. Let's cuff him." Both officers advanced forward, standing over Tone as he sat in the space between Sheree's legs. "Sir, you're under arrest. You have the right to remain silent. Anything you say--"

"What the fuck's goin' on?" Sheree snapped, as they slapped the cuffs on her boyfriend. "Ya'll can't lock him up. He ain't did nothin'!" Her pleas fell on death ears and they yanked Tone forward.

"Robby, take the keys out my truck and put 'em upstairs," Tone said just as they sat him in the back seat of their vehicle.

He was taken down to the station and booked on attempted murder.

"Attempted murder?" Tone was uneasy.

"That's right buddy. Attempted murder," the pudgy one said. "You fucked up. Shane's still alive. Officer Burns turned to take in the expression on Tone's face and grinned. "At least in the midst of all that gunfire no innocent bystanders were hit."

Doc was Tone's first visitor and he brought a lawyer with him. As the sheriff buzzed the steel door, Tone as well as the other inmates, burst into the visiting room like horses at a raceway park. The eggshell colored bricks were graffitied all over with multiple gang symbols – five and six point stars carved into the paint. All Tone could think about was, *how could I shoot that stud and not kill him. Now I'mma be sitting in Cook County's hell hole for God knows how long.* In hopes that his visitor was Sheree, he had brushed his shabby braided plaques with his hands trying somewhat to look like his usual self, which would be impossible because he hadn't had his hair braided in weeks.

He scanned each five-inch glass booth that separated the inmates from their visitors until he spotted one that wasn't occupied with one of his peers. All of the inmates were dressed in a Cook County Department of Corrections Khaki shirt and pants which had the C.C.D.O.C. letters engraved in black. Just as he spotted an empty booth at the end of the room his feelings were partially let down as Doc threw his hands in the air grinning from ear to ear. Being that Sheree wasn't with him kind of disappointed Tone, but seeing the Jewish man with Doc put him back at ease.

"My big homey brought that mouth piece, this what I'm talking about!" Tone grinned while picking up the receiver. "What's the deal G, pardon the doo, you know I can't get used to letting no nigga's braid my hair"

Doc smiled, "Its ok pretty Tony. That don't stop you from bringing the message you bring cuz you in the belly of the beast. You gonna have to cut it all off before you go in front of the judge anyways. No question." Doc nodded. "And this situation you in don't make it no better that's why I brought Tom Ellis today."

Doc wound up getting the complete rundown on who had killed his cousin, Flye. The big picture was that law enforcement had bagged Flye's corpse a few hours before Rocko drove Shane to the hospital. So when Shane said that someone opened fire on him and his friend – around the same vicinity – the police who were present at the hospital simply put the two together. They perceived that whoever had tried taking Shane's life was retaliating for Flye's death. When they showed Shane the mug shot, Tone was immediately identified as the shooter.

Doc told Tone, "Flye mentioned that he was preparing to move you to the next level of the game." He spoke into the phone as Tone listened behind the glass. "I'm from the old school and I believe in loyalty. So here's the plan…I'm going to offer Shane five grand to disappear so he won't be able to testify against you."

That was the plan and Tone thought that his nightmare would go away. Doc left the jail, found Shane and made the proposition to him. Shane's greedy ass gladly took the money and left Chicago on the next train smoking. Unfortunately for Tone, based on Shane's initial statements, the State's Attorney didn't terminate the case and had enough evidence to convict without Shane's testimony. Tone was up the creek without a paddle.

He knew that if he took his chances by going to trial he could end up getting anywhere between six to thirty years. His lawyer advised him that he should plead guilty to a lesser charge of aggravated battery and would receive four years with the possibility of parole after serving half. With no other option, Tone took the deal and served the time.

Doc had spared Shane's life to save the future of his cousin's protégé, but Tone had made no such promise to let the man draw breath. Being out on the street after a two-year bid, he had a score to settle with Shane Stevens. Tone would be slipping if he didn't live up to the code and put that nigga six feet under.

CHAPTER 5

Tone and Robby pulled into the parking lot of *Matteson's Steakhouse* and finished the last of the blunt.

"Tone, you're really testing my street cred here." Robby said, half-jokingly.

When they stepped through the door they were greeted by Robby's cousin, Chookey. Chookey was a dark chocolate honey dip with a banging short hair style; what was known on the streets as a, "thickem'" meaning she had it going on in all the right places. But her waitress uniform, which consisted of a mid-calf dress and a long apron, didn't do her body any justice at all, but she was still poetry in motion each time she moved.

"What's up big ballers, shot callas?" Chookey said smiling as she walked over to the reservation list and added their names alongside the other reservations.

"Cuz, I know yo' ass better leave a tip this time," she teased. "Family or not, you ain't eatin' for free."

Tone laughed, causing Robby to narrow his stare on her. "Damn, Chookey. So that's how you gon' do your favorite cousin; huh?" Robby shook his head. "Well, what about Tone? You ain't mentioned nothin' about him getting' taxed for his food."

Chookey stared Tone up and down. The way she undressed

him with her eyes was not lost on anyone in the room.

"Nah, he gets a pass since he's only been home for three days. But next time, have some spare change Tone." She giggled, running her fingertips over his smooth dark brown leather jacket. "Or better yet, you can come up off that fly ass jacket. *Sean John,* no less."

Chookey's gaze lowered, admiring the denim *Ryan Kenny* jeans he was wearing; and his leather *Timberlands.*

Tone might have been away for a minute, but thanks to the trip they had made to Ford City Mall, he was definitely dressed like he never missed a beat on the latest styles.

"Let me get ya'll a table real quick."

"It's about time," Robby mumbled as she ushered them past the no smoking section. "I was wondering when you was gone stop running off at the chops."

"Shut up boy," Chookey said, popping him in the head with her pen. "Now," she said, gesturing to table next to the salad bar, "is over there cool?"

Robby brushed past her. "Yeah, we straight. Now, get back on the job before I tell boss man to come get ya'."

This time Chookey slapped him in the back of his head with her hand causing Tone to double over with laughter as Robby whined, "Ouch, girl! That shit hurts."

"Good," she said, passing the menus, which they both put to the side. "Now, what do ya'll want to eat?

"Two roundhouse steaks, well done, with some baked potatoes."

Chookey jotted on her pad. "No dessert?" she asked.

"Yeah," Tone said, "You can put me down for a strawberry cheesecake."

"Alright, ya'll order gon' be up after a while. I got other customers, so I'll see you all later." Chookey moved to another booth.

"So," said Robby, "are you hittin' Tre's funeral with us Monday?"

"No question." Tone replied, settling into the booth. "Tre was a real nigga before he became a millionaire. Remember how he used to sponsor those *Great America* trips with Phil? He always looked out for the shorties that couldn't pay." Tone sighed, shaking his head at the loss of such a great man. "Man, I hate he went out like that. I still don't believe it went down the way the police said. Sounds like some straight up bullshit to me."

The restaurant was filled with patrons and the line to dine in was outside the door. The walls were filled with moose heads, old swords, and big pictures of cowboys. It had an old western movie feel to it; but nevertheless, the steaks were good and they cooked them fast.

Robby nodded. "Yeah, it's definitely a lot bigger than what *WGN News* had to say. You know, like I know, Tre wasn't cut from that type of cloth."

"True that, true that," Tone agreed from the opposite side of the salad bar as he covered his salad with ranch dressing and they both headed toward their seats again. "By the way, what's up wit' Doc's fat ass? I heard him, Brandon, and Brian lost behind that demo."

"Yep, big time," Robby replied, his lips over the rim of his water glass. "Them niggas lost fifty bricks on that shit."

"Man, that's messed up. Now I see why Sheree tryin' ta get back wit' a nigga. Doc must be fucked up right about now."

"Yeah, picture that; niggas like him got A-1 credit in these streets. He wouldn't sweat it if he didn't want to," Robby said gnawing on his salad as though he was the one who hadn't had a good meal in years. "Anyway…I thought I told you that ol' girl wasn't fuckin' with him? I mean, you must don't think my word is concrete?"

"Nah, it ain't that, my nigga," Tone countered smoothly. "It's just the bitch drop me five stacks earlier today like it was nothin'. Then she zoomed off ridin' a Benz that wasn't nothin' like the one I bought her before I did that bid." Tone pushed his salad. "I know how big of a trick that nigga Doc can be. Plus, I ain't heard of her fuckin' around wit' nobody else."

Robby's fork froze on the way to his mouth. "So, you don't know what she's been doin' for a living?"

"Nigga, I been gone for two fuckin' years," Tone snapped. "So hell naw I don't know!"

Robby looked out at the television above the bar, then locked his eyes on Tone. "You mean to tell me that you *really* don't know what shorty been doin' out here?"

"Would you stop asking me the same shit? If I knew, we wouldn't be talking about it, now would we?"

Robby shrugged and for some reason, couldn't seem to make eye contact with Tone again. "Well, do you *wanna* know?"

"Know what?" Tone replied, and finally reached across the table and grabbed his friend up. "Quit procrastinating, and drop it on me man or I'mma kick that ass!"

Robby let out a long sigh as though he had been carrying a heavy load. "A'ight then… Sheree been workin' at *Club Extreme*, for the last year-and-a-half."

Tone released Robby at the same moment Chookey walked up to the table asking, "Everything alright?"

No, everything was far from alright.

*****

When Sheree arrived to work, she sighed, noticing that nothing much had changed. Not the shabby, rundown building and certainly not the generic hand-painted words scribbled across the wood grain panel posted right above the entrance. *Club Extreme* didn't look like much from the outside looking in. A clever disguise created so it wouldn't attract too much attention. It was a hideout for *CTA* bus drivers, police officers, and retired men who wanted to spend their pensions on something they could feel, even if they couldn't take it home with them.

"Damn!" Sheree snapped, pulling into the crowded parking lot. "A bitch ain't been gone two weeks and they done already gave somebody else my spot."

She sighed, whipping her car to the other side of Pleasure's silver Mercedes. She squeezed a few drops of *Visine* into her eyes, hoping to erase all signs of the tears that hadn't stopped flowing since she walked out on Tone earlier in the day. *Why was he so fucking mean? Didn't he realize how much she loved him?*

As Sheree stepped through the smoked glass door, the smell of sweat and Juvenile's joint, 'Back That Ass Up' met her at the door. She looked around the club and thought, *tonight's going to be a good night; tricks are everywhere.*

The stage was surrounded by the hood-rich niggas makin' it rain on Jazz who was doing her famous booty clap. There was a crowd in each VIP section, and even the small stage in the back of the club was crowded. Dead presidents were flowing free and G-strings were getting fatter and fatter.

Sheree hurried to transform into her alter ego; she was all about that paper, everything else was secondary and she wasn't about to miss out on getting hers.

A bouncer, resembling a giant linebacker, spotted her standing near the entrance.

"Hey, Sasha baby! Long time no see," he yelled, grinning ear to ear.

Sheree stepped over to him. "Hey, Goob. I see ya'll got my parking space occupied."

"Hey," he replied holding his hands up to ward off her wrath. "I ain't had nothing to do with it."

"Yeah, whatever!" Sheree said, rolling her eyes as she leaned against the bar. "Who's that," she asked the moment her eyes landed on the fresh face on stage, bouncing her naked ass seductively to the music.

"Oh, that's the new girl," Goob said, pointing at the mixed Puerto Rican and black hottie with crinkled mahogany hair, grey eyes, caramel skin and high cheekbones that gave her the face of an angel.

Sheree was unable to move as she became mesmerized by breasts the size of perfectly rounded grapefruits, an ass that could stop rush-hour traffic, and thick thighs that Shree would love to see wrapped around her own body. As Sheree observed the girl's body twirl down and around the pole she found herself hypnotized by the body in motion in front of her. A rhinestone top, silver crochet bikini bottoms and *Jill Stuart* lace boots hugged the honey in front of her. Sheree was so caught up in a sexual fantasy involving taking the hottie for a ride on her face that she didn't even realize Goob was still talking to her.

"Her name is Candace, but Pleasure calls her Pain, and I haven't the slightest idea why. Maybe it's because when she --" Goob tensed up. "Awe shit! Hold up, Sasha."

Goob ran towards the stage as some rugged, three-hundred and fifty pound maniac jumped up on the stage and became wedged between one of the stripper's legs. His pants were bunched up around his knees, and his erection was in plain view. Apparently the sight of the stripper masturbating spread-eagle with a policeman's flash light was too much for him to handle. He couldn't contain himself and wanted in on the action.

Goob yanked the man from the stage and ushered him toward the door.

Sheree didn't mind the interruption. Goob was probably about to say some lame, perverted shit anyway. If it wasn't for his bodybuilding physique, he'd be totally lonely night after night. He wasn't the most attractive guy in the world and his game was whack. Those two things alone equaled lonely nights and blue balls.

Shree sat at the bar and swiveled the stool to the side so that she faced the action on the stage. She wanted to watch Pleasure in action. She knew it would be a good show.

Pleasure's *Dolce and Gabbana* bikini top was laid across the top of a police officer's head. Two other officers, enjoying the view, had turned their caps backward so they wouldn't miss a thing. They packed bills into Pleasure's garter belt as she remained in split position shaking her ass cheeks one at a time.

"Yeah! That's what I'm talkin' about baby!" One of the officers shouted, gawking at her 38DD breasts as they swept across the floor. "Shake what yo' momma gave ya!" The officer yelled gyrating along with her movements as if there were no one else in the room but the two of them.

Pleasure stepped from the stage with bills in every denomination peeking out from her bikini bottom. Her skin glistened with perspiration. Sheree wondered what it would be like to drape her tongue across that creamy skin.

Sheree hurried from the bar and went into the dressing room. Upon entering, a ton of fresh, exclusive fragrances smacked her right in the face! Each vanity mirror along the wall reflected attributes of sexiness such as hers. She figured Sasha's saga must be continued since her ex-boo didn't want her anymore.

"Hey, bitch!" Sheree yelled, pushing her way through a crowd of girls who were dressing for their turn on the stage. "I know yo' ass saw me sittin' over here."

Pleasure giggled, putting an arm around Sheree's shoulder. "Anyway! I thought you quit. Wait...hold up," she said. "Let me guess. Tone found out you were stripping while he was locked up and thinks you're damaged goods. Now you want your job back."

Sheree rolled her eyes. "Nope, you're wrong ho. He doesn't even know about me working here. But he *is* mad at me," she sighed, "talking 'bout I left him for dead. Then his punk ass had the nerve to put me out after I sucked his lil' dick and let him nut in my mouth." She shuddered at the memory. "That shit was nasty!"

"Bitch, you funny as hell." Pleasure said, with a laugh. "When you all happy, his dick is big as fuck; but when you mad...his shit's little. So quit lying to yourself."

Sheree cracked a smiled. "Alright, bitch, you got me," she said and they both laughed. "And it seems like he grew a few mo' inches. Mm hmm...girl," she crooned, body trembling as though trying to hold back an orgasm. "That nigga had me climbing up the walls and grabbing at shit that wasn't even there! I couldn't even take it from the back. I was biting the pillows and screaming and shit. Neighbors probably thought he was fuckin' me up."

"Shit, the way you talkin' girl...he was!" Pleasure joked.

As the two women started walking back to Sheree's dressing area, still laughing at the details of Sheree's porn act, they ran into Pain. She was fully dressed, slipping her feet into a pair of *Prada* sandals.

"Pain, I want you to meet my girl Sheree. She used to work here." Pleasure stepped over to her locker and gave Pain a sly smile. "And she was kinda nervous, just like you, the first time she danced too."

"Hey, Sheree." Candace said shaking the hand that Sheree extended her way. "It's nice to meet you, but I gotta run. I gotta pick up my son from my mother's place."

Those grey eyes locked on Pleasure, who watched as Candace zipped her bag. "Pleasure, thanks for everything."

"It's cool. I'll see you tomorrow; right?"

"Yep, tomorrow." Candace said, heading for the door. "Again, it was nice meeting you Sheree. Bye."

Sheree watched the curvy woman walk out the door. The woman was beautiful beyond words, but what Sheree saw in those grey eyes was enough to chill her soul. "I can see why they call her

Pain. She seems….numb. You know, like she's been dealt too many of the wrong cards."

"Well, that woman's intuition is working for you. She's been through hell." Pleasure replied, "She lost her man on the very night he proposed to her. The Feds seized all their assets: the house, jewelry, furs, cars, everything. The only reason she's still driving her Lexus is because it was in her mother's name."

"For real?"

"Yeah, you should've seen her yesterday, Sheree. She was sitting, all teary-eyed, at a table in that rock-n-roll *McDonalds* up north. I could tell right away that she was hurting real bad, so I stopped to help her out. I helped clean the smeared makeup from her pretty face. Then she went on telling me what happened and how she'd been job hunting downtown. No one would hire her because she doesn't have many skills or work experience. And the ones who did want to hire her, wanted her for something other than the job they had posted. She's way too pretty for her own good. Looks like hers can be a curse sometimes."

Sheree nodded, remembering the beauty of the woman's red lips and how much she wanted to taste them herself. "Damn. So basically, her story is a lot like ours; she's been walking around with no idea that the higher you climb, the harder the fall's gon' be. Is that when you invited her to the club?"

Pleasure nodded as she raised her hand to Sheree's head to help tame the piece of hair that was sticking up. "I told her to come have a few drinks with me. The next thing you know, she got drunk, and jumped her ass up on stage. She was a natural. You know the same cops you seen me dancing for tonight; Simmons and Choice?"

Sheree frowned, picturing the dirty ass cops in her head, and then nodded yes.

"They gave her ass $500 and the bitch barely pulled off any clothes! All she did was throw her hair back and open her blouse as though she was about to let them fuck her. She had a way of seducing them with her eyes. With very little effort and still fully clothed, she had them digging deep in their pockets forking over cash. I guess she woke up this morning like, 'Fuck it! That was easy. I'm gon' dance,' and she showed up here again."

Pleasure switched off the lights in the dressing room. All the girls were already headed to the door and lined up to pay the house before they left for the night.

"Pain doesn't realize that money isn't gonna change her problems. Only time can do that." Pleasure blurted, "That's why I named her Pain. That girl's got issues!" Pleasure sighed while shaking her head, "I believe we could help her out right now since we can definitely relate to the situation. What you think? We've been there and done that! Might as well use what we know to help her out."

"I'm with you, girl," Sheree replied, "Now I see why you were always telling me to count my blessings. Compared to other women, especially single mothers, my problems practically don't exist."

Pleasure embraced her friend as they made it to the parking lot. "Thank you for understanding Sheree. Girl, when am I gon' see you again?"

"It don't matter. Just call me." Sheree hopped inside her car, cranked the engine, and pulled from the parking space. But before she could make it to 147th Street, Pleasure pulled up on the left, gesturing for Sheree to roll down the window.

"What now bitch," Sheree asked, lowering the driver's window part of the way down.

"See, that's why Tony put yo' ass out in the first place, you snobby ass hoe!" they laughed.

"Naw, that ain't it. He just want me to kiss his ass, and that's not somthin' I'm about to do. I said I was sorry, and I meant it. Bottom line."

"Yeah, right!" Pleasure shot back. "You know dudes of his caliber are a hot commodity. That penitentiary glow make them niggas look powerful and potent…just like women like; you hear me?"

Sheree bit her tongue to keep from saying something smart.

"So whether you get back wit' him or meet another man, realize it's the strongest supporter who gets the trophy." Pleasure said. "Ugly or beautiful don't matter. As long as she holds it down, a man with standards is gon' appreciate her."

Pleasure slammed on the gas pedal and sped away, leaving Sheree to chew on the mouthful that had been spit her way.

CHAPTER 6

The vehicles parked outside *Gatlings Funeral Home* caused a major traffic jam down the long stretch of Halsted Street. A transparent casket encasing Tre's body was inside a cherry oak wood carriage, pulled ceremonially by two white Clydesdale horses trotting down the street as though royalty was inside. Grieving relatives and friends lined the sidewalk outside the funeral home; reminiscing and consoling one another as they waited to enter.

Spook, Brandon, Brian, and Gayle's brothers were all honorary pallbearers. As they maneuvered the casket through the door, Robby and Tone made it up to the front entrance and waited for the procession to finish.

"That's how you know Tre was a 'made' nigga out here. He's got a well-known millionaire toting his body." Robby boasted nodding toward Spook G.

"You ain't bull shittin'." Tone said evenly. "He's a real nigga for showin' love like that. I know its gon' be fucked up for him tryin' to find somebody else he can trust to move as much weight as Tre did. That nigga could push that shit like it was an art form."

"Brandon and Brian told me after shit die down a little bit, Spook was gon' compensate them for their loss. Then they was gon' get me and Stevey set. Robby added, reminding Tone that Stevey was

Robby's little brother and that he was familiar with the streets and the drug game. It just came with the territory, so it was second nature to him.

"So I figured if we move the work at a fast pace we can get them in the same position Tre had with Spook."

"I'm feelin that whole demonstration." Tone agreed as they moved closer down the aisle to view Tre's body. As they approached the first rows of seats, his gaze swept over to Sheree who sat next to two gorgeous females. Each of them was crying, but even with their makeup running they were all sexy as hell.

"What's this bitch doin' here?" Tone whispered to Robby.

Robby scanned the area before looking back at him. "Who you talkin' bout?"

"I'm talking 'bout Sheree's stank ass. She sittin' right there in the front row with Tre's people.

Robby spotted her and the other two girls, and grinned. "I see she got that ho' Pleasure on the side of her. She must be some kin to Tre or somethin'."

"Who, Sheree?" Tone's eyes darted back to the three women. "She would've told me a long time ago if she was related to him."

"Naw, nigga. I mean Pleasure. She must be related to Tre." Robby said as the line inched closer to the casket. "Can't just be anybody sitting in the first row if they ain't family. Sheree's probably here to console her friend on her loss."

"How you know the other chick?"

"From the strip club. Me, Shawn, and Stevey stretched shorty out for a nominal fee when she did a private party for Stevey's birthday last year. I'll say this about her, she definitely got skills!" Robby gave Pleasure a once-over and smiled when she looked his way. "I sent you some flicks of that night. I don't know how you could forget baby girl."

"Oh, yeah she looks different without the weave. But that's the same shorty you said Shawn's crazy ass didn't want pussy from 'cause ya'll ran through it already; right? The one he fucked in the ass; right?"

Tone covered his mouth to hold in his laugh, trying not to show any disrespect at the funeral.

"Be cool, nigga." Robby shot back as the two of them peered over Tre's body. "You gon' have people thinking we laughin' at Tre."

At first glance the two men quickly became silent showing respect to their homeboy. Tre laid in the see-through casket looking like the Last Don of the South Side dressed in a platinum *Armani* suit and black *Prada* shoes. He was still young and handsome despite the discoloration within his eyelids. A haunting reminder that signaled Trevon Foster was no longer in the land of the living.

A sinking feeling stirred restlessly in the pit of Tone's gut, making him wonder if he would be stretched out the same way someday.

*****

Sheree nudged Pleasure's arm when she saw Tone. "Look at my baby; bitch. He's looking fine as hell!"

"Mm hmm. He damn sure is!" Pleasure said, looking at Tone as she undressed him with her eyes. "I see Robby's cute ass is here too. Tre sure knew a lot of people; didn't he?"

Sheree shrugged, and looked around at all the people filing into the chapel.

"All of them part of the same circle. If they don't know each other personally, they know somebody who knows Tre."

"Yeah, I know." Pleasure shifted in the hard seat, trying to get comfortable.

"Girl, what's wrong with you," Sheree asked curiously. "You lookin' like you gotta fart or somethin'."

"Hell naw. It's just that this silk *Prada* skirt ends up sticking to my ass if I sit still for too long. It'll have me all sweaty and stuff." Pleasure's tone was suspect. Sheree puckered her lips and stared at her with her eyebrow raised. She could tell everything coming out of Pleasure's mouth was a lie. She grinned, knowing that Pleasure was really hoping that Robby's presence didn't mean that Shawn was there too. Just thinking about Shawn probably sent a shocking pain up her ass. Pleasure made it a point of saying that the incident with Shawn was her first and last time ever taking it that way. Shawn's ten inches had taught her to leave that stunt for the white girls who were experts and loved receiving a man in that way.

Sheree curled her lips in a sly smile. "Yeah, whateva! Yo' stank ass probably got wet in the panties after seeing my beau."

"Puh-leeze!"

The little boy sitting on his mother's lap next to Pleasure looked over at her.

"Momma," he asked, "how can daddy sleep with all these people in here?"

"I don't know, Tre-Tre," she whispered, trying to choke back the tears that had been non-stop since she had heard what happened to her husband. "I just don't know, honey."

Pleasure embraced Sheree, and Candace laid her head on her mentor's shoulder.

"You know…I always called him my 'Sunshine,'" Candace said, dabbing the tissue along her eyes. "Now my world is dark again."

It had only been four years since Tre had reentered her life and changed it for the better. Candace remembered, through her tears, how she and Tre rekindled a relationship that started as childhood sweethearts; but had come to a halt when Tre moved to Chicago with his mother. They came back into contact with each other after Tre went to visit his Grandmother in a suburb outside of Vegas. He spotted Candace's picture while thumbing through an escort pamphlet, trying to trick off during his visit. Old feelings rekindled themselves and Tre had brought her back to Chicago with him, and from that point on, Candace had called him her, "Sunshine," because he had been the light at the end of her tunnel of darkness that had kept her trapped for most of her life. His return to her life brightened her days. But that was four years ago; today was a different story.

Tre's death made Candace see nothing but darkness again.

Pleasure definitely identified and connected with Candace's hardships. Pain knows pain and Pleasure felt Candace's sorrow down to her own core. Witnessing her tears compelled Pleasure to make it her business to be a friend to her and stand by her side from the moment she met her. Her dedication Candace made Pleasure phone Sheree and suggest that they attend Tre's funeral in support of the grieving woman.

*****

Brandon, Brian, Spook, Stevey, Robby, Shawn, Tone, and Fred walked towards the rest of the men standing near the exit of the room. They had a way of dominating the room, especially when they were in the same place at the same time.

"Cuzzo, what's the business?" Tone asked as he greeted his cousin Fred with dap on the fist and a shoulder to shoulder hug. He hadn't seen Fred since he left town to earn a degree at Southern Illinois University. Now the man was a big time real estate agent and looked every bit as successful on the legit tip as Tre had been on the other side of the coin.

"Nothing much. I'm coming through to pay my respects; then I'mma break it back out. What's up with you brothers? This is a crazy situation." Fred asked shaking each guy's hand as he passed by them.

Everyone in the group was dressed in suits and linens to impress; but for Fred, this was his everyday attire now; a drastic change from his days of sportin' jerseys and jeans. Fred now rocked *Gianfranco Ferre* lenses, a *Kenneth Cole* button-down long sleeve shirt, black slacks, and a pair of black *Paul Smith* loafers worn with no socks.

"Man, Fred, I'm feelin' the playa's card. It's a nice piece." Spook complimented Fred's pinky ring as he shook his hand.

"Yeah, man, my fiancé bought this for me at *Michael Beaudry Jewelers* three weeks after we got engaged."

Fred paused for a moment, and then shoved his hands into his pockets as though realizing that his statement could be seen as boasting.

"She say if somebody steal this bitch and try to trade it off, it'll be impossible. It's laser inscribed with a six-digit ID number."

"So that boy's irreplaceable huh?" Robby inquired with a knowing look in Tone's direction.

The viewing line for Tre's body was finally coming to an end and the room quickly filled to capacity with no empty seats and barely any room in the aisles. Sniffles and short outbursts of loud cries could be heard over the organ music that was playing. The family was being greeted and given words of condolences, and the ushers were working their way to the front to close the casket.

"Hell yeah, you heard him!" Shawn exclaimed as though he had purchased some of those special diamonds for himself. Shawn barely had two nickels to rub together, let alone a woman that would consider him special enough to buy him anything.

"Man Cuz, I thought yo' ass was just talkin'!" Tone said with a chuckle. "You about to tie the knot for real?"

"Yeah, once me and Nicole graduate and get our stability in order. We haven't decided on a particular date yet."

"Ay Fred, did you ever close the deal on that Greystone building in the Bronzeville area?" Stevey asked, running a hand over his waves.

"I remembered the last time we kicked it you was talkin' about it."

"Shit, I just closed on it day before yesterday, that's another reason I'm up here. Me and my architect got to look over the blueprint for it. I plan to have it under construction six months before I graduate next year." He glanced over at Tone. "I hope this lil' nigga have his shit ready by that time."

As he spoke, Fred caught a glimpse of the *David Yurman* watch on Tone's wrist. At first glance he knew that Tone's watch was much more expensive than his own. He kept his thoughts to himself and leaned in and whispered, "Tony, don't let ignorance overtake you, it'll only bring trouble your way. Quitting while you ahead isn't the same as quittin' on time."

When he pulled away, Fred made a sweeping motion with his dark brown eyes across the group of men.

"It's time for me to head out," he announced, "I'll get at ya'll later on." He gave Stevey a nod. "Whenever you're ready to invest in real estate, I'm your agent. That goes for any one of you all." Fred said as he made his way to the exit door.

Everyone said their goodbyes in unison as he parted.

Brian watched Fred as he slipped behind the wheel of a silver Range Rover. "I wish I would've stayed my dumb ass in school. Look at that nigga. He came from where we came from; the same block and everything." Brian turned and locked a gaze on his brother Brandon. "But he still managed to make the right choices 'cause he focused on his goals and was determined to make it out. That's how we gotta be,

I'm telling you."

Brandon bristled under his brother's hard glare. "I'm wit' you on that issue all the way. But first we have to get a head start all over again. Speaking of which, why the hell Doc leave here so early? His thirsty ass is the reason Tre got caught up. We weren't in a rush, so he shouldn't be."

"Doc said he couldn't stand seeing Tre like that." Brian said in a voice just above a whisper. "We ain't make it no better either. Just 'cause we wasn't complaining about the prices, we didn't decline the deal when Doc talked Spook into persuading Tre to charge a lesser price so we as guilty as he is."

Spook flicked his cigarette into the grass. "Brian is right; B, but Tre has to take some of the blame too. I told him once; you're on another level from the rest of these niggas. Tre started slippin' because he was hanging with Doc a lil' bit too much. Instead of dropping off the work to ya'll at the normal time, he let Doc rush him into doin' it on *his* time when he would normally dictate the pace." Spook looked back in the direction of the chapel, shaking his head. "He let Doc, who's not on his mental level, think for him. Now my nigga's dead because of that one mistake. And aside from the fact that his son gotta be raised without his father, who else can I trust to feed the streets?"

"That's real talk, Spook. I never looked at it like that before, but you still got us out here." Robby said before his lips set in a thin line, and he began reading the obituary.

Tone's mind began to wander and he instantly thought that Robby was probably picturing his father who was serving a life term sentence in a Federal prison. Robby and his brother were now selling dope because the hustlers on the streets had become their father, instead of the man who had biologically made them.

Tone swept stared intently at Brandon, Brian, Robby, and Stevey. Suddenly he realized that all of the men had more in common than they thought – people will find their own mentors when there are none prominently available.

"Now that I think about it, my cousin probably made it to college because every night he went to the crib, his moms and pops was there. They both worked good jobs and kept their foot in his ass.

If they even sensed he was making the wrong turn…" Tone's words faded as the reality of his meaning set in. "None of us had that type of stable household. And if we don't get our shit together, we're going to end up just like Tre."

"Tony! Is that you man?" Hearing the familiar strong, baritone voice; Tone and his boys looked down the hall to see an individual standing six-foot-three inches tall with a neatly groomed goatee. He had a low haircut and smooth butterscotch skin. The three-piece grey suit that he wore looked as though it came directly from Michael Jordan's closet.

Tone broke away from his guys' circle to meet the man halfway who was calling his name.

As he walked away, he vaguely heard Brandon, Brian and Spook speak the individual's name.

"What you want?" Tone asked harshly after recognizing the man.

"Nah, better yet what you doin' here? Didn't my momma tell you yesterday when you called that I'd call you back when I got a chance? Now here it is you following me, callin' me out in front of my peoples! What is up with all this shit man?"

"Tone, calm down man," the man interjected. "I called to tell you…"

"Tell me what?" Tone interrupted. "A bunch of bullshit excuses about why you ain't support me for any part of my life?" Tone snapped again. "I didn't talk to you or even receive one letter from you. Momma said you'd just drop off some money for me and kept it moving, like you've been doing for years. But guess what? I'm my own man now, and I'm able to make my own money. I'll get at you when it's convenient for me." Tone turned on the heels of his *Havanna Joe* boots prepared to walk away.

"Tony…," he stammered, "Tre was your brother, man! He was your brother!" Travis revealed. "That's all I wanted to tell you." Travis began to advance towards the double doors. Tone stood in place, his mouth wide open upon hearing such an astonishing revelation. Travis was almost at the entrance of the sanctuary when Tone called out to him.

"How pops?" Tone managed to say in a much calmer tone.

Travis' heart melted upon hearing his baby boy call him by that name.

He hadn't heard a fatherly acknowledgement from Tone in years. He immediately came back towards Tone's direction.

"W-w-why you just now telling me this?" A lump was forming in the back of Tone's throat even though he tried to hide it.

"It's a long story, Tone. I'd rather wait 'til we're alone…by ourselves. All I ask right now is that you keep this on the low until we get together; alright," he asked Tone as they stood face to face.

Tone was confused as to why his pops chose to keep that bit of information from him for so long. That secret was his opportunity to raise his status through the roof. Every major playa in the game was there at Tre's funeral. He knew if they found out he was Tre's brother, the torch would be passed down to him immediately. On the other hand, he had to know who blew the whistle on Tre. Unbeknownst to him, his childhood desire for a sibling had already been fulfilled years ago. Tony had always wanted at least one brother or sister he could share his innermost feelings with. Little had he known, he had a brother all along. As Tone thought about it all, he was still shocked by the news he had just received.

Travis' hand on his shoulder snapped him from deep contemplation. "I know what you're thinking man, and believe me, when that time comes…the city will be eating out the palm of your hands. Just lay back until we get to the bottom of this. In the meantime, look for any suspicious acts from those two cats; Brandon and Brian.

I done heard fucked up rumors about their old man pulling some snake stuff on your boy Robby's daddy. Almost like the same situation with Tre, only your brother's life was ended out here on the streets." he explained to Tone with his undivided attention.

"Now don't quote me on that 'cause I might have my info misconstrued, but you can never be too careful. If there is any truth to the matter, then the apple don't fall too far from the tree. So look out for them and Doc 'cause that's who he was hanging out with his last few months on this side of the dirt. I told him, in so many words, not to associate with his customers 'cause them same dudes would try to learn his every move. You gotta keep these cats off balance Tone. They just like crabs in a barrel; every time one makes it to the top, another tries to pull him right back down to the bottom."

Travis was attempting to impart his pearls of wisdom on Tone. He knew it was far too late for him to play daddy by talking him into leaving the streets alone. All he could do now was make sure Tone didn't make the same mistakes Tre made in the game.

"I got you, pops. I think I'm gon' find me a job until I get things in order. Or at least till this parole shit is over." Tone paused as he spotted Sheree approaching.

He sighed with disgust. "What this broad want?" He knew a part of him was still in love with her; but the thought of another man spotting them together and using the opportunity to converse about how he fucked her, or how she gave a superior 'private rendezvous' made him not care to see her again ever in life. His ego just couldn't handle it, and he did not need the drama that would come with such a confrontation.

"Excuse me. Tony, can we talk for a minute," she asked with an air of sophistication about her.

She wore a cream-colored *Berbonese* skirt and jacket, parading her *Cartier* diamond navel piercing.

"Make sure you call me sometime this evening, aight? I'll let you all talk." Travis said as he walked away.

""Yea, pops. It'll be this evening for sure." Tone answered, not realizing what he had just done by addressing Travis as he had.

Sheree quickly caught on.

"Why you call him pops? Is *that* your father?" She asked with curiosity dripping from each word.

"Naw, why you say that?"

"'Cause you just called him pops… and ya'll favor each other…a lot."

"I call all the old heads pops," he lied, "you know I haven't seen my old man in almost five years. What is it you wanted to talk to me about?" he asked, changing the subject.

Sheree could tell he was keeping something from her. She knew Tone too well. He didn't know how to lie without looking away. His eyes always showed signs of stress and deception when he was lying, but she left the issue alone.

"I wanted you to be the first to know I'm thinking about going to Atlanta for school," she announced awaiting his response. But Tone showed no concern at all. Still, she felt the need to further explain. "You know my mother's been down there two months now. She said Clark University is the best school down there. Only way I'll leave is if you don't want to work out our differences…'cause financial aid will pay for me to go anywhere I'd…"

"Have a nice life Sheree, I'm good baby." Tone coldly remarked, not allowing her to speak another word.

He simply walked off, leaving her words stuck in her throat, feeling like someone kicked her in her windpipe. Sheree tried to hold back the tears that were welling up in her eyes. The first one dropped from her right eye as she turned around. She wiped it away with her index finger and exited the funeral home.

Remorse sank in as she remembered how things used to be between them. Sheree knew that at one time Tone loved her dearly. He used to wait on her hand and foot; he never cheated or lied.

Although every female in the hood tried to take his woman's position, Tone remained faithful because she was his first love, just as he was hers. But she had to face the fact that she had violated his trust by abandoning him at the lowest point in his life. The situation hurt him deeply. His eyes told her that much. He had resolved to never settle down with one woman again in life. He figured they were all one in the same; down for you when you're up, and up and running when you're down. She felt a sense of shame that she had been the tool that made him feel that way.

When Tone made it back to where the guys were standing, Robby was the only person still there.

Tone was well aware that Robby knew his old man personally. He just hoped he didn't blurt out his business to the rest of their people.

Robby could see the baffled look on his friend's face. "I done told you once before, don't nobody control your feelings but you. Don't let dude steal your joy, my nigga," he said in an attempt to cheer him up.

"Nah, he hadn't been able to do that in years," Tone replied nonchalantly. "Didn't I hear Brian or one of them say Travis' name as I walked towards him?" Tone inquired.

"Yeah, they mentioned that Travis runs the beauty shop for Tre."

"That's all?" he questioned while rubbing the peach fuzz on his chin in deep thought.

"To my knowledge…why what's up?"

"Nothing, man. Nothing."

"Yes it is nigga. Spit it out," Robby urged.

"Did you tell them Travis was my father?"

"Hell naw! I wouldn't even put your business in the streets like that. It's your business to tell them; not mine. And from his absence in your life, you say he's a mere stranger to you. So I look at him the same way. Please don't assassinate my character again," he replied offended. "First, it was the rumor about Sheree and Doc I assured you of, now you doubt my discernment skills." He continued confidently, "C'mon Tone, you know I'm a lot sharper than that. I wouldn't embarrass you in front of the guys; if that's what you were worried about."

Robby continued to pledge his loyalty upon seeing the troubled looked on Tone's face as he returned towards him. He assumed Tone's look was dictated by a curiosity as to whether or not he had disclosed the identity of Tone's father to the boys.

CHAPTER 7

Detective Ron Canal – the five-foot-eight, 193 pound, clean-shaven, blonde detective with the crew cut style – had cold and beady blue eyes that projected evil and hatred toward people of color. "If it ain't white, it ain't right" was the motto he lived by. His prejudice beliefs ran deep enough for him to even wish that the Canal street sign was white and green instead of green and white. However, this common illiberal attitude didn't just begin with him. Such a diseased mind frame of thinking was the norm for him; passed on to him through the bloodline; bred through generations of ignorance.

Even still, as a young man Ron Canal had to learn the hard way that his lily white skin would never be able to withstand basking under the rays of the most powerfully radiant star, the one responsible for sustaining every life form on planet Earth.

After repeated sunburn and receiving skin grafts, lotions and ointments to help treat the fiery red patches on his back and other mole-like blotches covering his arms, neck, and face; his doctor informed Ron of an important scientific fact.

"Caucasian people possess very little pigments of melanin to help protect us from the sun. Unlike people of color who contain more natural melanin than any other race, Caucasians are better off developing tans by using tanning machines. Another option is to vacation in certain parts of the world where the climate gives off some sort of shield, and receives low heated sun rays which don't demolish the skin during its transfiguring process."

Canal was infuriated; but he was also enlightened. The doctor's words had a way of making it crystal clear why his forefathers had worked the black slaves under the scorching sun. Part of their reasoning was definitely forced labor to build America, but the other part was geared towards mock punishment.

The plantation owners were secretly jealous and envious to the fact that they would have never been able to absorb such an enormous amount of heat. And so today, Ron Canal lurked Chicago's ghettos tormenting people of color for the natural hell he'd been cursed with.

"Listen Ron, and listen to me carefully," Detective Kruger said, schooling his new partner on the dangers of the inner city streets as the two drove northward up Kedzie. "I like you, but you're a little too feisty. I would hate to see you end up like…like…uh…like…Odell. I gave him specific instructions not to enter that house before backup arrived," Krueger sighed. "But, he just had to play hero," he said forcing a counterfeit tear from his eye.

Detective Canal felt sympathetic. He patted his hand against Krueger's leg.

"It's gonna be alright Mike. Trust me. I know my position, and I'm aware that working here in the field is a totally different world from being one of, Ortiz's flunky ass deputies," he said in an agitated tone.

Canal sighed. "Then to think, the cut that I was getting off the brake was crumbs compared to what you, the Captain, and Ortiz's wetback ass were making."

Kruger smiled, "Well, now you're in the big league. All you gotta do is follow my lead. And please, please promise me one thing…"

Canal looked puzzled. He slowed the car to a halt at the traffic light on Jackson and Kedzie. "What?"

Kruger gestured, nodding his head toward the car sitting to their right. "Don't go spending your money on a Cadillac the same color as his."

As Canal glanced through the passenger window he had no

idea that the flamboyant character in his view was the one and only, Bishop Don Magic Juan.

"Now, what type of man would paint his automobile green and gold, and dress himself in multicolored suits?" Kruger asked.

"A fucking clown ass nigger; that's who!" Canal replied.

They both found the Bishop to be comical. Inwardly, however, they both envied his spell over the Caucasian girl sitting in his passenger seat. She was beautiful and sexy enough to pass for Carmen Electra's twin sister.

Canal hissed like the snake his was. "Ssssss…This country is seventy percent white, and that bitch rides around parading with a nigger!"

As the detectives cruised through traffic, Kruger's cell phone rang. He pulled it from the inside of his suit jacket and read the caller ID screen. He answered.

"Yes, sir, Captain."

"Where are you right now?" Bullock asked.

Kruger looked out the passenger window. "Uh, just passing *Edna's* Restaurant."

"Good. I need you to ride on over to Homan and Monroe right away. They're giving us problems if you know what I mean."

"Sure thing, Captain. Right away, sir." Krueger hung up and turned to his partner. "Make a left and go back down Kedzie, then make a right on Jackson and another on Christiana."

Once Canal hit the last turn, Krueger instructed him to park on Monroe. They grabbed the binoculars and began bird watching a fair-skinned young male yelling at the top of his lungs.

"Blows…Weed…Park!!!" The youngster announced waving for customers in cars to pull over, while remaining conscious of the other customers approaching on foot.

"Gimme ya'll money. And no singles!" he warned. He then pointed to a building next door from where he was standing. "My man's back there in the gangway," he said, directing them.

A petite woman quickly stepped up to him and asked, "Damn baby. You gon' make me walk all the way back to the store for a solid ten dollar bill?"

The young hustler paid close attention to the way she scratched her arms and fidgeting her boney legs like a cricket. She twitched like she had to pee badly. But he knew she was just desperate for a fix.

"Listen baby. I'mma do it this one time. But next time come correct; aight?"

She smiled. "Thank you so much sugar!" She stepped off to retrieve her daily dosage. Several other customers swarmed around him with their bills in hand.

They shouted, "Gimme five...ten over here... Seventeen, Cutie Pie! Gimme twenty-six of 'em Chucky! You know how I get down."

Chucky immediately recognized the bald man. "Come to the front, Ray Cool. And yo!" he said, addressing everyone else, "All ya'll move the fuck out the way and let my favorite customer get through. He came to shop big with a nigga."

When Ray Cool made it up front he said, "Good lookin out; youngsta. Them boys out there on Kedzie living off of Be-Be's name serving that bullshit. I told 'em, 'Chuck got the good stuff on the next block'," he chuckled. "I'll be back later; aight?" He turned and vanished through the gangway to get what he paid for.

Kruger had seen enough. After his estimation of how many houses up he needed to move, he pinpointed the exact location of where the one known as Chucky, had been directing traffic.

"Pull around through the alley," he told Canal. They headed toward the back of the gangway.

Several seconds later, after the crowd had dispersed, Chucky began counting the cash.

He smiled, thinking about what he was going to do with his cut of the earnings. While arranging the bills in order, and making sure that the faces of the dead presidents were all flipped upward, he totally forgot about his man.

June was still inside the garage at the end of the gangway. He grabbed another hundred pack of blows from the trunk of an old black Park Avenue for Chucky to sell. After he had what they needed, he slammed the trunk closed but its rusty hinges caused it to fly open again. He sighed, and tried slamming it shut again with a little more force.

It made a loud bang but did not close. June smirked, "Ain't this about a bitch!!!" he said, feeling frustration rise in his bones. He took a deep breath before trying it again. This time he used his own weight. The trunk's latch finally caught with another loud bang.

"Shit man! I gotta find another spot. I can't keep goin' thru all this," June said, stepping toward the entrance of the garage. But before he could get one foot out the door, something cold and hard whacked him upside his head. June fell to the ground with a grunt. "Aghh, shit."

"Don't move, piece of shit, or I'll blow your fuckin' wig back!" Kruger said through clenched teeth. As he held his rifle to the back of the startled kid's head, he patted around June's waistline; checking for a weapon.

Canal soon swooped in, frightening June even more. He placed the barrel of his standard issue Berretta firmly on the boy's forehead.

"Grab the keys Ron." Kruger turned and headed through the gangway.

"Hey, June," Chuck yelled, making his move through the gangway, wondering what was taking him so long. Just as he was about to call out to him again, he quickly spun around on his heels and took off running.

"Freeze little pussy! Krueger shouted, sprinting up the gangway, clutching the rifle. "Stop or I'mma shoot!"

Chucky could definitely hear him, but he was scared to death. He shot out the gangway, hit the block, and continued racing up the street. He wasn't going to allow them to catch him that easily; especially since he knew he had a Ginseng 380 handgun cuffed inside his waistband. He already had two gun charges on his record. A third one would certainly get the book thrown at him, and he didn't want the Feds picking up the case. He knew it'd be at least an automatic eighty-five percent of a ten-year sentence if they did.

"Ain't no way!" Chucky mumbled between breaths, huffing and puffing as his legs kicked harder. Just as he was about to bend through another gangway, he lifted the front of his *Coogi* shirt.

Kruger, still on the chase, caught sight of the sudden motion. There was no time to think. He squeezed the trigger. Pop! Pop! Pop!

Chucky's body jerked and jolted as the slugs struck him from behind. The first one went into his back, the second went completely through his abdomen and the last bullet pierced his chest permanently ending his heartbeat. He fell; face forward to the ground seemingly in slow motion.

Detective Canal pulled the car around the block, searching for his partner. June was handcuffed, sitting in the backseat, looking from the window when the car stopped next to Kruger. He couldn't believe his eyes.

"Man! Why ya'll do my guy like that," he asked hysterically. "We ain't no major niggas. Ya'll bogus as hell, man, for real. Ya'll didn't have to kill him. Ya'll didn't have to do that shit, man!!!" June's eyes filled with tears of anger.

Chucky and June had been saving up their money while working someone else's block. They were hoping to make enough to cop twenty-four grams of diesel and two pounds of weed to disguise the dope line. They knew the police would sweat the hell out of them if they found out that they had been selling heroin.

A week before, the two of them had gotten authorization from their gang chief to open up shop for themselves. All they had to do was get off all three, one hundred packs. They would've yielded ten thousand as their cut to save.

But June was right. He and Chucky were no big wigs. They were only small fries on the up and coming.

Canal was awestruck by the gruesome sight of the young man's body sprawled out lying in his own pool of blood. He could just barely see the nickel plated steel protruding underneath the pelvis area. Kruger immediately spoke up.

"I told his dumb ass to stop!" he spat. "We'll leave it just like this until Homicide and Internal Affairs arrive. After they see what type of threat that these young bastards are to the CPD, maybe they'll stop blowing smoke up my ass about how I could have taken more 'precautionary measures' that day Odell was murdered."

As the detectives stood over the dead body, they noticed an audience forming. Canal posted himself and took a stance to block off the angry-looking mob.

"Partner," he said, "I sure hope Homicide and Internal Affairs get here quick 'cause it seems that we're gonna need the backup."

Someone from the crowd shouted, "Ya'll the real fuckin gangsters! Ya'll the real gang!" Several other spectators joined in bellowing their frustrations as well. Others rang in with "yeahs" and "Amens" in agreement.

*****

Captain Bullock was in deep thought when his cell phone began vibrating on top of his desk. He leaned forward in his seat and casually answered, "Bullock speaking."

"Unc, whassup with the shit that just went down out here?" Bullock's nephew asked aggressively.

"First off, lower your voice. And never use that tone with me again. Now what happened is my men took care of that business. So, what's the problem?"

"My boy, Chuck, is dead because of Kruger's hot ass. That's what the problem is," his nephew snapped. He sighed, "Unc, when I told you it was slow 'cause of the guys on Monroe, I didn't mean for you to send your people on them. I was just giving you a daily report as usual."

Bullock leaned back in his recliner and sighed. "Well, Josh, now you know what will happen every time I receive an update like that. This is *our* cookie jar you dipped your hand into. Therefore, you're going to move on *our* time. Anyone and I mean anyone, interfering with that time will witness the same results as your boy Chuck—including you!"

Josh frowned, pulled the phone away from his ear and looked at it in disgust. He was bewildered. For a second, he could've sworn it was just another street cat he was chattin' with. He had never heard his uncle's gangsta dialect. He placed the phone back to his ear.

"Know what, Unc? You're right. I apologize for even bothering you about that shit. I'll holla at you when my time's up." Josh sarcastically replied.

"That'll be a good idea. Tell your mother I send my love."

"Yea, aight." Josh hung up. He smirked. "On *ya'll* time, huh? Picture that!" He steering his royal blue, XK8 Jaguar through the blocks of K-Town and turned up his stereo to the Speednop Mobsters' "Warm Embrace."

Captain Bullock drifted back into what he had been meditating on prior to his nephew's call. Internal Affairs wanted him to place Detective Kruger on suspension. Chucky was Kruger's second murder in a single month. The community and its leaders demanded justice.

The entire CPD already had a bad reputation and Bullock hated the fact that Kruger left him with no other choice. Still, there were six more keys of heroin that had to be moved. Kruger was the one he initially chose to patrol the area and oversee the distribution of the product. But now, he was going to have to entrust full responsibility to Ron Canal.

"But would Canal be able to score the winning touchdown without fumbling the ball?" Bullock wondered. As the thoughts raced through his mind, he lit up one of his favorite cigars and puffed while contemplating his next move.

CHAPTER 8

As she stepped into the revolving doors of the Dirksen Federal Building in the city's downtown area, she drew a noticeable amount of head turns. A navy blue and white pinstriped *DKNY* skirt suit cuddled her body. A pair of *Dior Homme* sunglasses concealed half of her beautiful face and a *Christian Dior* headscarf fashionably spoke of her determined character. She was no stranger to the Federal Headquarters. She moved gracefully across the hall towards the security station, flashed her FBI badge and passed through the metal detector.

The time on her watch read 8:00 a.m. as she waited for the elevator in the busy lobby. She silently observed the familiar faces of several lawyers, prosecutors and judges who were all headed to their destinations. To them, she remained unnoticed.

When the elevator reached the lobby floor she boarded with others and pressed for the thirteenth floor. She switched her *Coach* briefcase from hand to hand as she wiped her sweaty palms on the sides of her skirt. When she replayed the messages on her answering machine last night, Prosecutor Shawn Tussman's voice came off pretty harsh. She could tell that he was beyond pissed.

She had already accepted the fact that she screwed up her mission. Her tasks were simple, but her emotions got in the way.

Instead of striking her target, it was he who made his bull's eye – to her heart.

Once she exited the elevator, she stepped straight ahead and pushed through the double glass doors which read 'U.S. District Attorney's Office.' She made a right turn, walked down the hall and landed herself in front of a thick wooden door. She took a deep breath and knocked. She stood there waiting, hoping Mr. Tussman wouldn't answer. She sought any excuse to leave.

Send me my walking papers through the mail or you could tell me over the phone, she thought. *How could I have been so stupid*, she asked herself, reflecting on the sexual act she was caught participating in a little over three weeks earlier. She felt her career was definitely terminated. She prepared to walk away, and just when she thought she had gotten off easy, the door cracked open.

"Please, do come in." Mr. Tussman told her.

She walked into the office.

Mr. Tussman stood in front of his desk bearing a striking resemblance to a young Maury Povich. He stepped over, pulling open the door a little wider for her to pass through. "Have a seat," he said, motioning to a chair in front of his desk.

She took her seat, unraveled the scarf around her head and removed her shades. She straightened her sitting posture and crossed her legs.

Mr. Tussman cleared his throat. "Ms. Singleton, do you have any idea as to why I called you in here today?"

She raised her chin high and replied, "No, sir. But I'm sure whatever it may be, I have a reasonable explanation for…" she stopped midsentence at the beckoning of his hand raised in the air.

"Save it. I have your entire explanation right here."

Tussman pulled out a hand-held tape recorder and sat it on top of his desk. He pressed play. Her voice clearly played through the small speaker.

"How can I serve you, my Captain?"

Tussman quickly pressed the fast forward button. "Ooh yes. Yes, baby, right there… right there. Mmm. Oh. I'm about to cu…"

Tussman pressed stop. Ms. Singleton was stunned to hear her passionate affair with Captain Bullock captured on audio.

"Listen, sir," she pleaded, "when you gave me this assignment two years ago, your exact words were for me to do whatever it took to nail Bullock. And well, sir, I was just fulfilling my duties."

"Michelle," Tussman sighed. He stood from his seat and began pacing the floor. "I felt this was going to be a risky job. And I came to you because I wanted a young woman who was intelligent and wise in knowing how to use what she has to get the job done. I saw you as the fresh face who sought recognition in this bureau."

"A-a-and I am sir. Just give me a little more time, maybe six more months to do what I..."

"I'm sorry, Michelle," Tussman declined, "but from the sound of this tape recording, it pretty much seems to me that you've been enjoying your job a little too much."

Ms. Singleton frowned. "Enjoying it? All of that moaning and going on was acting to boost his ego."

Tussman stopped pacing and gave her a stare, long and hard. He was no fool. "Michelle, this wasn't the first, or the last time I've witnessed what you call acting. I've seen women before you fuck up entire assignments because they couldn't control their feelings for these suave, smooth-talking criminals. And every one of them went running off at the mouth about everything. And what happens next? Witnesses are dead and female agents abandon their livelihood by moving out of the country with the assholes they were supposed to be investigating!"

Ms. Singleton became agitated. "But I'm none of those women!" Michelle firmly defended her position. At this point she could care less about what he was going to do, but she wasn't going to allow him to diminish her dignity.

Tussman sighed, shaking his head. "I'm sorry that I have to make a call like this, but..."

"Before you speak upon my termination...I resign!" Ms. Singleton interrupted.

"Tussman gave a surprised look. "Resign?...terminate?" He chuckled, "How could a woman like you think she'd be fired?" he sarcastically asked. Ms. Singleton looked at him like he was a crazed lunatic.

"Tussman sat and reclined in his chair. "Michelle, I could tell from the credentials on your records from Harvard that you're a very strong criminal justice woman. That's why I've decided to pull you off this assignment. I refuse to stand by and watch you allow your emotions to destroy everything you've worked so hard to get in life."

"I'm not going to hold one lousy, dreadful mistake against you. Besides, you and I are the only ones on the force who know about your secret rendezvous, and I plan to keep it as such. But what I do need for you to do now is relocate to Cleveland."

"Ohio?!" Ms. Singleton was stunned.

Tussman nodded, "There's no other Cleveland I'm referring to. I need you to be there within the next ninety days during which I also need for you to turn over everything you have on Bullock and his cronies. Hopefully, my new assistant will be able to pull someone from the agency, to get close to Ortiz. The other audio feeds we've gathered tell me that he's a pretty uptight guy. But if we grab him and shake him up a bit, he just might provide us with enough info to bring down the whole operation."

"Sounds like a plan to me sir. But I have two questions: why Cleveland and not New York, California or Florida?"

"The fact is the agencies in those areas run their ship with an iron fist. Our main focus is the number of convictions we can raise throughout the Midwestern region. Now, what's your second question?"

She sighed. "Well, when are you going to introduce me to your new assistant so we can go over things?"

Tussman picked up the phone and said, "Right now." Then he pressed four buttons and placed his mouth to the receiver. "Hey, Ms. Sternbergh, I need you in my office pronto. It's only going to take a sec."

Tussman hung up the phone. He pulled a brown folder from his desk drawer. "Does the name 'Sternbergh' ring a bell," he asked, glancing through the contents.

"Sternbergh...I've heard that name somewhere before." Michelle replied searching her mind in an attempt to put a face with the name.

"I'm sure you have. Her father is Defense Attorney, Michael Sternbergh. He's the one who represented one of Don Juan's girls,

Annie Boo. She was the one who robbed the famous singer and pianist, Libarachi."

Ms. Singleton's eyes lit up. "Yeah, I remember! I first heard about that tale when I was a little girl. So, all this time, it's been a true story?"

"Yes. It's all documented here in her file. She got off with a slap on the wrist even after Liberachi himself testified to the courts that while she was performing a sex act on him, she managed to slip *Visine* into his drink. He passed out for a few hours, during which a seventy-thousand-dollar mink coat and two hundred thousand dollars in jewels went missing."

Tussman laughed. "Yeah, I gotta hand it to Sternbergh. He went up against the toughest prosecutors in these times and ended up creating a name for himself as a Defense Lawyer."

Ms. Singleton was puzzled. "So why did she join the enemy?"

"It's simple. She doesn't want to become successful by lingering in her father's shadow. Her drive is just like his; but she'd rather gain her own notoriety."

"No offense, but if it were me, I'd keep the family name going."

"You see, that's why the two of you are different in more ways than one," Tussman sarcastically replied, leaving her pondering on his statement.

Knock. Knock. Knock.

Tussman turned to the door and said, "Come in, please."

A young, blonde, white female stepped into the office wearing an elegant violet, red and white *BCBG Max Azria* cotton tie dye dress. Her *Park Voge* cashmere cardigan sweater was comfortable for the September weather. Her feet were dressed in *O' Oscar* suede high heels. She stood with her *Carrera* sunglasses sitting above her forehead, clutching her white *Rebecca Minkoff* leather satchel. She smiled.

"Hi. You must be Michelle. It's a pleasure to meet you," she said motioning for a handshake. "I'm Melissa Sternbergh."

Ms. Singleton accepted her warm greeting. "I know who you are. It's a pleasure to meet you, too." She smiled, thinking about the remark Tussman made. *Different in many ways, huh,* she thought, *I knew this bastard was racist. Hmm. That statement is gonna cost him.*

"Michelle, would you care to do lunch with me so we can go over some things?" Melissa asked.

Ms. Singleton knew that her invitation was genuinely friendly. "Of course," she agreed. She turned to Tussman and said, "Have a good day."

"Mr. Tussman, I'll see you in an hour," Melissa said as she and Ms. Singleton headed for the door.

Tussman nodded and nonchalantly watched as the two beautiful women exited his office.

CHAPTER 9

Doc pushed through his part of the land in his mint green Riviera. When he began making his rounds of delivering heavy product to his clientele, he had ten bricks of cocaine. He dumped three, and then headed to the corner of 53rd and Wood to dump off three more. When he got there, he didn't see the one he was supposed to meet, so he picked up his cell phone.

"Man, Joe. Where you at?" He asked, scanning the area.

"I'm right here in front of the corner store," the slim dark-skinned male responded just as he stepped outside with his pants sagging halfway from his buttocks. He turned his head looking side to side. "Why? Where the hell you at?"

"I'm sittin' here in front of the school's parking lot."

"Bet. Here I come."

From his bird's eye view, Doc watched every move the man made from the time he dashed back inside the store to when he came out carrying a brown paper bag. He was one of Doc's rivals. Even though they agreed to set differences aside to do some business together, he still didn't trust him. Doc popped the lock on the passenger's side to allow the man to hop in.

He smiled. "Rocko, what's the thought of the day playboy?"

Rocko tossed a bag of money into Doc's lap. "Cha Ching,

nigga. Cha Ching," he smiled.

Doc opened the bag and took a quick peek. "My man, my brand. Reach down under your seat for that tre-piece." He rolled the bag close.

Once Rocko got his hands on what he came for, he examined it closely. He was impressed. "You see, this what I'm talkin' 'bout right here! This that Peruvian flake, huh?"

Doc nodded. "Ain't no question."

"Bet. Make sho' you keep five more on standby for me," Rocko exclaimed, locking his bid early.

Doc thought to himself, "Five mo'? What this nigga on?" He smiled. "Yeah. I can do that. I see you tippin' hard over here too. Last time it was one and a quarter. Now you gettin' three of these thangs?"

"Shit. That's 'cause I've been making moves down there in Lovington, Kentucky. Me and Shane…" he paused momentarily, checking Doc's reaction, "…been knockin' them niggas upside their heads for fifteen hundred an ounce."

Doc wanted to jump out of his skin, but he played it cool. "Yeah, I'm feelin' that," he replied nodding his head. "Listen, I gotta ride out and make a few more moves." He held the bag up. "So this is everything; right?"

"Hell, yeah. The only way I know how to come, is correct." Rocko stepped out of the car.

"Aight. Just hit me on the horn when you ready for that five piece." Doc cranked the motor and headed out to his final destination.

*****

Robby was sitting on his front porch with Tone when Doc called. He followed the instructions he was given on the phone and gave Tone Doc's number. After they spoke over the phone he had almost forgotten how thorough Doc was. Doc tried everything in his power to get Tone off the case of shooting Shane.

Even though Tone was salty as hell when he found out that Doc had been trying to holler at Sheree, he had to respect the game. He knew if she chose to fuck with another dude at *any* time, then she wasn't really his to begin with.

Robby had just looked up when he spotted Doc, making a left turn at the Damen light. "Here comes your boy now. Remember to start high; and if he asks how you gonna move it all, tell him that I'mma help. He knows that between the Moes, Lil' B, and the Vice Lords from 54th, I'll run through at least twelve to thirteen zones a day."

"Oh, yeah?" Tone gave Robby a doubtful look. "Well, why you steady coppin' a quarter bird at a time? You should've been came up," he stressed.

"Don't even trip." Robby said as he stepped from the porch. "I'm on my way to pick up the last piece of what I've been savin' up for."

When they got to Doc's car Tone asked, "And what's that?"

"You'll see when you get back. I should have everything up and runnin' by then."

Robby pushed the passenger door closed after Tone hopped in. "Doc, what's the demo,you well ?"

"Most definitely," Doc answered smiling with confidence. "What other way is there to be?"

Robby chuckled. "Ain't no question. I'mma let ya'll gone and ride out. We'll get together later on or somethin'."

"Believe that." Doc pulled away.

Tone was checking out the interior of the state-of-the-art Sedan. "Man, Joe. When you cop this boy?"

"I bought it from the twins off of 54th and Laflin St."

"Who? Goodie and Patches?"

Doc nodded. "Yeah. Them lil' niggas always buying somethin' fly. Then they hook it up and sell it."

"I already know how them brothas get down. Majority of the brothas over there eating good. That's all I'm on from here on out. If it don't make dollars, it don't make sense. Im tryna eat big homie." Tone tooted in a cocky manner.

Doc chuckled, "Say that then. Listen, Lil' Tone, I never got the chance to thank you for punishing Shane's punk ass for killin' my cousin. So, thanks my nigga. You know what's really crazy about the whole situation is Flye was on the phone with me when them niggas snuck up on him. His last words were 'I think it's time to take Tone to the next level.'" Doc shook his head and sighed. "Next thing you know, I hear shots goin' off."

"I feel you, my nigga. I miss the shit outta Flye myself. He taught me everything I know about these streets," Tone admitted as they sat at the light on 55th and Ashland both thinking about Flye. "Aye, pull up to the gas station real quick. I got some of that lime green off 66th and Marshfield."

Doc snickered. "I see you on point." He pulled a clear bottle from his arm rest and showed Tone the frost-colored buds inside. "I got some of that Dro off Sangamon, too," he boasted.

When Tone stepped inside the station, he immediately made eye contact with the cashier. He noticed right away that she favored a honey blonde version of Nia Long.

The cashier kept her watch over Tone long after he broke eye contact. She almost bit a hole in her bottom lip admiring his slim physique and light complexion.

"Mm mmm damn" she said, trying to keep her voice down. "Deandra, look at this cute ass muthafucka right here!" She told her coworker. "I ain't never seen dude here before. He can't be from around here 'cause I would've recognized that sexy ass walk a mile away."

Deandra stood up after she finished stocking the candy shelf. "Girl, you crazy. Let me see who this is," she said, standing on her tippy toes. She was stunned. "Damn. He is fine as hell! And with them waves sittin' on top of his bald fade, he could easily be a model for *Duke's Hair Texturizers*. Let's see if he talks as sexy as he looks."

"Give me two *Black Jacks* and a box of *Cigarillos*," Tone requested. His mild, deep voice sent chills down the cashier's spine.

She passed him his order. "You sure that's all you want?" Her smile showed off her brilliant white teeth and deep dimples.

Tone assumed by the smooth looking texture of her vanilla skin tone that she used nothing but the best beauty cosmetics. His reply was as smooth as her question. "Are you sure that's all you wanna give me?"

Beautiful almond shaped eyes sparkled and she blushed before answering. "No, but I'd like to give you my name if you give me yours…with a number where I can reach you."

"Hmm...Is that right?" Tone teased her with a seductive smile of his own and began mentally undressing her.

The cashier stepped back and allowed him to get a clear view of all of her goodies. She placed her hands on her hips revealing her small waist and showed him her plump derriere. As she posed, her mind flooded with thoughts of him. "This nigga got self-esteem higher than the *Sears Tower*. Ooo, and he's so mysterious with it too!"

She cleared her throat. "That's enough sightseeing for now. So are you gonna give me yo' number or what? I got customers behind you."

Tone quickly regained his composure. "Well, one thing I ain't tryna do is stop you from doin' your job." He retrieved his merchandise from the counter. "The name is Tony, and my number... Well, I'll bring that to you later." He spun off nonchalantly, without showing any interest.

The cashier was puzzled. Other guys who frequented the station had always tried their best to get at her, but she always saw through the bullshit. Tone, on the other hand, stirred her curiosity.

Who does he think he is? She mumbled to herself, with an air of curiosity surround her thought. Lucky for her he forgot his receipt. She quickly grabbed the microphone next to the register. "Sir, you left your receipt."

When Tone stepped back up to the window she said, "Always get yo' receipt sweetheart. I could've overcharged you."

Tone reached for it as she slid it through the window. He immediately noticed she had her number and name scribbled on it. "Nah, shorty," he rejected, "you don't even look like the type."

The cashier smiled flirtatiously, "Ain't the type? Oh yeah? Umm, could you elaborate on exactly what you mean by that?"

Tone read the name she jotted down. "Alicia, maybe later; aight?" He turned away again, leaving her mesmerized.

As he headed to the car he thought, *The less you say, the more you stand out. Works every time.* He smiled as he stuck the number inside his pocket.

"Mmm." Alicia said out loud as she bit her bottom lip.

"Girl, what are you 'mmming' about?" Deandra asked.

"Nothin' girl. It ain't nothin'." Alicia lied, still lusting over her newfound potential beau.

Tone watched the rear end of Doc's ride flow down with ease after stomping the brakes twice and pressing the cigarette lighter two times. The hydraulic stash spot magically opened. Doc reached inside and pulled out two kilos; tossed them in a duffle bag and sat it on Tone's lap.

"So shorty gave you her number; huh," Doc asked as he closed his secret compartment and pulled off.

Tone was baffled. "Yeah, how'd you know?"

"Cause I saw Flye do the same shit millions of times. I didn't believe it worked at first. I thought he was trickin', telling broads he was gone buy 'em somethin' in order to get the digits. Then one day we blew through Nike Town and I tried that shit on this chick Joyce."

"Yeah? Whatever happened to ole' girl?"

"She's sitting at home pregnant with my second shorty." Doc pulled up in front of Tone's house. "Look, them thangs goin' for eighteen G's a piece, but I want you to keep flipping em' until you coppin' at least five at a time. That's as long as you getting them from me."

Tone sighed in disbelief. "C'mon, Moe. Don't even assassinate my character like that. You know it's about loyalty and respect with me."

"I'm feelin' that," Doc said. He smiled. No wonder my cousin cuffed the youngster he thought to himself. "Man, Lil' Tone. I like the way you think. As long as you keep thinking that way, you'll never have to worry about what happens for you in the future. Just focus on gettin' through the day."

Gon' head and put them two demos up. I'm gone run these other two on Hermitage to my man's Dink & Gunz. You should be ready to roll by the time I get back; right?"

"Hell, yeah. It shouldn't take me no more than five minutes to stash these." Tone grabbed the bag preparing to leave the car. "So, you want me to give you thirty-six stacks altogether then?"

"Naw," Doc shook his head in disagreement. "Family prices are $15,500 apiece. I'll call your phone when I'm back out front."

"Bet!" Tone clamored. He turned and ran up his stairs. *Fifteen Gs,* he thought to himself. *Shit, I'mma stack me a couple hundred thousand, and then leave this shit to the next man. I ain't tryin' to make no career out the dope game and end up in the belly of the beast again...or worse, wind up like Tre. He had enough dough to quit a long time ago.*

The sight of a dead body – a body that once belonged to his brother – had been enough to make Tone realize that he indeed wanted a better way for his life.

Later that night Tone was getting irritated knocking on Robby's basement window trying to get his attention. But how could Robby hear him? He had the music blasting and from what Tone could hear it sounded like he had company as well. They were even tryin' to talk to one another over the loud playing tunes.

Damn, Tone thought. He definitely didn't want to disrespect Ms. Bradley by ringing her doorbell, especially knowing he reeked of marijuana. Suddenly the music stopped. Tone knocked again. Robby appeared a few seconds later.

"Damn, nigga. Why you bangin' so hard?"

Tone blew him off. "Man, Joe. Save that shit. I've been knockin' for hours," he exaggerated.

Robby smirked, "Would you beat it with the jokes man. I know you ain't about to stand nowhere for an hour, so you can get outta here with that one." They both chuckled.

Tone followed Robby into the basement. He was surprised to see that it had been fully remodeled with black and crème colored wall-to wall-carpet and a crème colored leather couch and matching love seat. Robby also had a wooden lamp table with crème colored marble tops and a giant sixty inch plasma television.

Tone smiled. "I see what you been spending yo' money on. This boy off the chain!" he praised.

"You ain't seen nothin' yet. Come in here." Robby opened his bedroom door. "What you think, my nigga? You feelin' it?" Robby asked boastfully with his arms stretched wide in presentation.

Tone was speechless as he hypnotically gawked at a state-of-the-art recording studio.

Growing up together, he and Robby always talked about being in the music industry. They admired the careers of LL Cool J, Run DMC, Tupac, Notorious Biggie Smalls, Naz, Jay-Z, and others in the game.

"Tone!" Robby yelled, snapping him out of his trance. He pointed to a dark-skinned guy with long wavy hair pulled into a ponytail.

"This is my man Ville. He's from out west on Central and Augusta. That's Lil' B up in there laying down his verse." Robby pointed toward the sound booth. "I met Ville at Olive Harvey. Once we get our GEDs, we're gonna apply to Columbia College for sound recording and musical management classes."

Tone was all smiles. "That'll be a damn good idea. We need more music artists comin' out the city," he exclaimed.

"Ain't no question," Ville agreed. "You seem like you got skills too, Tone. Why don't you flow somethin' for us," he joked.

Tone chuckled, "Naw, Ville. I don't do the rap thing. I'll leave that up to ya'll."

Robby sharply snapped his fingers. "Ay, Tone, speakin' of skills, what happened to the book you said you were writing in the joint?"

"You wrote a book?" Lil' B asked.

"Well, I never got a chance to finish it, but I will one day. It's just a story about the typical shit that goes on right here in the city."

Ville smiled. "Yeah. That's the move right there 'cause I ain't read nothin' as real as the shit that go on out here."

"Did playboy ever bless you," Robby asked regarding Doc.

"*Did* he? Nigga, he hit me with two whole thangs," Tone replied.

"Cool. That should be gone in the next few days 'cause Brandon and 'em still don't got nothin'. Stevey's been getting little shit here and there from the BDs off 67th and the MCs from Princeton. So, what's the price on yours?" Robby questioned.

"Hard or soft?"

"Nigga, you betta not serve nobody no hard shit. Pops told me that one gram of hard is equivalent to a hundred grams of soft. So if you was to get caught with eleven grams hard and if I was to get popped with a key of soft, we're gonna do the same amount of time."

"You talkin' about the Feds though. We ain't Fed material like yo' old man and his folks," Tone stressed.

Robby shook his head. "The hell we ain't," he declared. "As

long as Bush stay in office, our black asses are prime candidates for Feds."

Tone frowned. "Yeah, you might have a point right there. And while we're on the subject, how much did Shawn get caught with anyway?" he asked in an attempt to find out about Brandon and Brian's father.

"I believe it was fifty to a hundred birds. I'm not sho' but it was somthin' like that."

"Damn! That's a lot of stuff. And he just let Boss off the case, huh?"

"Yep. He told them peoples that everything was his. Uncle Boss didn't have nothing to do with it."

"Your pops is a made man for real." Tone had a bewildered look on his face. "Well, Travis did say he heard a rumor about Boss being on the case. Now I see what really happened."

"So, what are you tryna cop?" he asked Robby.

"I'll take a nine first to see how it is."

"Aight. But I'mma have to charge you fifty-six right now. That's just so I can pay him back ASAP. You know I don't like owing nobody shit. The minute you owe someone that's when they feel like they own you."

"Now that's real talk," Ville agreed. "Robby you told me dude was sharp; but I ain't know he was that deep."

"Oh, hell yeah! My nigga is official. Him and my brothas are the ones who groomed me."

"So, Moe, you only want twenty eight hundred for a four and a split?" Lil' B asked.

Tone nodded, "Yeah. That's all. Next time around I'mma give ya'll a major playa's deal."

"Fuck it," Ville said. "Even though I already got some work, I'mma support the hustle Tone. What would you give me for a half?"

"A half of what? A zone?"

Ville chuckled. "Naw, man. I'm talkin' half a bird."

"Damn. Let me see," Tone thought towards a price to keep Ville coming back. "How much your people been charging you?"

"Around ten five to eleven."

"Aight. I'll give it to you for ten dollars today and if you like the work any time after this, you can get it at nine five a pop."

Ville smiled. "Say no mo'." He quickly picked up his cell phone and dialed his girl, Veronica. He hung up after instructing her to meet him out south with the money.

Flye's words loudly resonated in Tone's ears; "Stay true to the game and it'll stay true to you. The more you look out for your peeps and maintain a healthy relationships, they'll remain faithful to the end..."

CHAPTER 10

Detective Kruger's face turned as red as cayenne pepper when Captain Bullock told him he was going to suspend him for two months. For the first week he was heated. But when the Captain doubled back and secretly explained what was actually going down, Kruger knew that he was still the same old Bullock.

"Your suspension is sketched in black and white to make it look good. As far as I'm concerned – you're the best officer I have on this force. That's why I need you to fall back and become the eyes in the back of Canal's head.

The five percent tint on the windows of the wide track Pontiac Grand Prix camouflaged Krueger's presence as he oversaw the last kilo of heroin being distributed. He also kept close watch on Canal and his temporary new partner, Turner, who was patrolling the area.

Kruger missed the adrenaline rush he got from bringing the thugs to their knees, forcing their faces into the hood of his squad car, and hearing them cry about the burning sensation from the engine's heat. Just the thought of slapping a street punk upside his head and telling him, "To shut the fuck up" made his dick hard. He was naturally sadistic that way.

Kruger sighed. *This deep cover shit is for the birds. This is definitely going to be a long two months*, he thought to himself. *Yeah.*

Boring as hell, but I'm still clearing two hundred big ones just to sit on my ass; so fuck it.

Kruger could foresee that the growing line of customers, waiting on their turn to enter the building to get their early morning fix, would yield a nice return by late evening. He needed to call Josh to find out if he got in touch with the Connect so they could replace the six kilos in the evidence room of the 7th District Precinct. They also needed three more kilos for themselves; just to keep the ball rolling.

After scrolling through the numbers in his phone, Josh's number appeared. Kruger pressed speed dial. "Hey, JB, is everything in place?"

"Naw, man. Thangs ain't looking too good for the home team." Josh replied dryly.

Kruger frowned, "Wait a minute. What do you mean not looking good? With us behind you, it shouldn't be going any other way but good."

"So you would think," Josh answered sarcastically.

"I'm not following you. What is it you're trying to tell me?"

Josh sighed, "What I'm saying is you act like I make the shit or somethin'. I gotta wait until my peoples ready. I need mines too."

Kruger's blood boiled. "Listen Josh, and listen carefully. Fuck yours right now! What you need to be worried about is…" Kruger stopped talking when he realized he was talking to a dial tone.

"Motherfucker!" Kruger yelled in distraught. Things weren't going as planned. To top it off, Josh had the nerve to hang up on him.

Every attempt he made to call back was directed to voicemail.

"Fuckin' street punk!"

"I'mma give that cracka' somethin' to worry about," Josh said to his man Solo who was sitting next to him in the passenger's seat.

Solo was the cocky type; a slim, dark fellow from the old school who sported an afro with a grey streak on the left side. His tattoos covered both his arms and the picture of the sword of justice was tatted in the palm of his right hand. His look definitely made a statement to all who saw him.

Josh told Solo to look inside the glove compartment. When he did, his eyes damn near popped out of their sockets.

"Why you still staring at it?" Josh asked him, referring to the large stack of money. "You said you got bills to pay, and four kids to feed; right?"

Solo was flicking through the bills. "This is damn near ten Gs; ain't it?"

Josh smiled, "Yep. That's exactly what it is."

"Yeah, I can tell. You know, once you've been handling money so long, you can almost distinguish how much it is. You can feel if it's short or if it's all there." Solo set the stack in his lap and asked, "Now…who I gotta kill?"

"Why you say somethin' like that?"

"'Cause, Christmas is two months from now and you don't owe me a damn thang. I've been living forty-two years so I got sense enough to know that ain't shit in life free."

"It's cool man." Josh smiled, shaking his head side to side.

"But here it is. You a young dope dealer who runs a portion of the west side and you just gonna give me ten Gs like money grows on trees? Hmm. If I'mma fool, you a damn fool." Solo added still staring at the stack in front of him.

Josh chuckled. "We both know better than that. Although it may not be until Christmas when I need you." He sighed, "This is a big fish I'm tryna fry, but I gotta let it marinate first. You know, make sure he cooks out the right way. 'Cause if I don't, it'll leave a bad taste in every one's mouth; feel me?"

"Ain't no doubt. But…" Solo said as he stuck his hand in a begging gesture, "fill my palm with five more. I need fifteen up front and the other half when it's done."

"Huh? But I thought you go twenty large for hits?"

"I do. But it's bigger pay for bigger fish. Plus, you want me to wait before I take it down. That's time and labor. If you know what I mean."

Josh hastily reached into the inside pocket of his soft, burnt orange leather and mink Presidential jacket. He pulled out another wad of bills and tossed it over to Solo.

"There's ten mo'. I'll pay you the other twenty when it's done. And I'll hit you up with that five in a couple of days." Josh pulled up in front of the pool hall on 16th and Millard.

*****

Kruger stormed into the station to update Captain Bullock on the phone discussion he had with Josh.

"I swear, if that little fuck wasn't your sister's son, he'd be a wet blanket party." Kruger was still in a rage, frantically pacing back and forth inside Bullock's office.

The Captain retrieved a bottle of Remy Martin XO and two small shot glasses and filled them to the rim. "Here…have a drink."

Kruger sighed and took the glass. He downed the liquor in one gulp. "Ahh," he grunted feeling the alcohol scorch his tonsils. "Whew! That's some good shit! Gimme another one."

"Alright, but don't wear out your welcome," Bullock joked. "Now, have a seat. I know you've been through a lot over these past few days. But you need to be cool."

Kruger took his second shot and sat down. "Tell me about it."

Bullock sipped on his drink. "With regards to my nephew, you gotta ask yourself something; if you're making two mill a month from your enterprise and all you have to do is push out three or four keys of heroin every other month for us to keep the CPD off your back, would you give that up?"

Krueger nodded his head. "No sir," he replied.

Bullock smiled and placed his hands behind his head. "Precisely. So don't stress yourself about Josh. He'll have our order ready by tonight. Trust me on this."

Bullock looked toward the door upon hearing someone knocking. "Come in," he yelled.

Ortiz stepped in looking like he had been scratching through his hair all day. It wasn't slicked back as usual. He appeared to be in bad condition.

Bullock sat straight up, "Reymundo, are you alright?"

"I'm afraid not, sir. I've received a call from the 7D evidence clerk. She told me that the bricks we sent over weren't back yet."

"Son of a bitch!" Kruger jumped to his feet, looking at Bullock. "What the fuck! Are we all waiting on the same guy?"

"Wait a minute. Are you telling me Jackie, received a call?"

Bullock pondered.

"No sir," Ortiz replied with a nod. "I got the call. Jackie called in sick this morning and you've assigned Turner to temporarily tag along with Canal; so it was no one but me downstairs."

"Okay. Let's keep in mind that the day isn't over." He checked the time on his *Hora Mundi* wristwatch. "It's four o'clock. We've got until seven tomorrow morning to have everything back in place."

Bullock turned to Kruger. "Mike, send Canal and Turner inside that building after I make the call to Josh. It's time to make him sweat so he can put the pressure on his connect. But in the meantime, I'mma give Duke a holler and see what's up on their end. Ortiz, you just remain calm and do something with that camel lick on you head."

Ortiz sighed, "I know, Cap. I know." He turned and left the office.

"So what time should I expect your call and order?" asked Kruger.

"In no less than an hour." Bullock picked up the phone after Kruger left his office.

*****

Josh had just finished beating Big C out of two stacks for the fourth time in a game of one pocket. The loser wasn't trying to give up until he won at least half his money back. But the winner was not easing up.

Josh chuckled. "Man, Charlie. I knocked that nine ball in. You better break up yo' crowd," he warned staring at Big C's five solid colored balls that were still bunched in the middle of the table.

Josh announced to the spectators, "Watch this ya'll. Off the left rail, with ease." He struck the cue. The nine ball rolled and fell exactly where he called.

"I told yo' mark ass. Now you got problems." Josh chuckled just as his cell phone began vibrating on his hip. "Hold up. Let me answer this call. Ya'll watch playboy," he told everyone, pointing to Big C with the pool stick. "He might try pullin' a move on me."

"This J-Billa. What's the bizness?"

"That's what I'm trying to figure out."

Josh recognized his uncle's voice right away. "I'm still waiting. Ain't nothin' changed since I last talked to yo' gopher…" he smiled. "I heard his thirsty ass gotta hibernate for the winter. Hell, they should've forced him to hand in his star."

"It sounds good but I didn't call to discuss him. When will our boys be heading into the last quarter?"

"Well, my man just hit me from the stadium saying we two minutes away from halftime. That was like twenty minutes ago."

Bullock snapped. "What the fuck you mean two minutes from halftime? That game was supposed to have been over a long time ago. Another should've already been underway!"

"I'm sorry Unc. But things just ain't been right lately; ever since shorty got killed things been different. But I promise I'll have that package to you by tonight."

Josh hung up the phone. He was already regretting the idea of going into some of his own money to help make things right, especially for the likes of Bullock and Kruger.

It was only an hour later that Kruger's impatience had gotten the best of him. He parked outside of *Billy Goat's* Restaurant on Madison just as Canal and Turner pulled into the *Kentucky Fried Chicken* parking lot directly across the street. Kruger threw his car into drive and crept up alongside the brown Chevy bubble. He let down his window.

"Hey Comrades. The Captain just informed me that we've got a server crisis on our hands."

"What is it, Mike?" Canal was a bit apprehensive. He had a strange feeling he was about to be snatched out the field and thrown back inside that cage listening to Ortiz's shit talking.

"Is everything alright?" Turner asked feeling the same way as Canal.

Kruger sighed, "I'm afraid not boys. You're gonna have to do a routine search inside the building. It seems like our guy doesn't want to cooperate with the terms of our agreement."

Canal was instantly relieved that it wasn't what he thought it was. "So we gotta show 'em; huh?" he asked, pleased to have the chance to do some real police work for a change. "What's the apartment number?"

"Uh, I believe they're working out of 4B," Kruger guessed. "But, be sure to call backup before entering that building."

Canal sped off and hit the siren and lights. "Remember, Bob, all you find – all we keep," he reminded Turner.

*****

Ms. Singleton had been on the phone with Bullock for a little over thirty minutes trying to prevent him from coming to her Bellwood apartment to check on her. She was supposed to be home sick in bed, but she wasn't. She was still down at Federal headquarters going over the files with Melissa.

"Theodore sweetie, I'd love to see you but I need my rest," she whispered.

"C'mon, Vicky. If you wanted a day off, all you had to do was request it. You know I would've approved it. It's bad luck to play sick. You can wind up catching something for real."

Ms. Singleton was beginning to become aggravated. "And what's that s'posed to mean?"

"It means that you're not fooling anyone but yourself. A sick Ms. Singleton would've hung up long ago." Bullock stated sharply. "Why can't you just be honest? We're both adults. If you're with your little boyfriend just say it."

At first Ms. Singleton felt that Bullock was on to her being a spy, but as soon as he spit out his real reason for not believing that she could possibly be under the weather, it took everything in her might not to laugh in his jealous ear.

"You know what, Theo? If you feel I would lie about such a thing, be over here in the next ten minutes."

Bullock sighed. "I'm sorry baby. I'm trippin'. I know you would never lie to me about something so minuet," he said feeling like an asshole. "I really wish that I could swing by and play doctor, but you know what today is. So, I'm going to let you go. Make sure you rest up and if you feel better, call me later. Love ya."

"Mmm hmm. Same to you," she quipped sarcastically and hung up. She smiled, knowing that her bluff had worked, at least for the time being. There was no way he was going to leave the department. He always personally made sure that all monies and drugs were returned to their possession.

Melissa was up in Ms. Singleton's face, timing her as she placed her phone on the charger. "I don't mean to fret Michelle, but it seems like someone can't get enough of you." She cracked a smile.

Ms. Singleton sighed. "Tell me about it." She returned to her seat, "Now, where were we?"

"Uh, before we get back to the business at hand, would it be out of place for me to ask you a personal question?"

Ms. Singleton was guarded before answering, but she maintained a straight face. "That all depends on whether your question is answerable," she replied remembering that she was in the company of Mr. Tussman's assistant.

"Well, I don't really know how to ask this, but, umm…I've always wondered what is it like to make love to a black guy?"

Now why would this bitch ask me something like this? Michelle thought as a lump instantly formed in her throat. "Did Tussman let Melissa hear the tape? Is she trying to trick me?"

"I'll tell you this much, Melissa, you'll never know until you try it for yourself," Michelle bluntly stated, leaving Melissa's curiosity lingering.

*****

"Open up! Police!!!" Canal shouted, banging on apartment 4B with Turner and five other officers right behind him. When he didn't receive a response he tried kicking in the door.

"Ron, are you sure this is the right apartment?" Turner asked.

"I'm positive. Mike said 4B." Canal turned and shouted again. "It's the Police!!! Open up!!!" He used more force to kick the door again, causing it to fly from its hinges.

*****

Butch and Lotti Go were directly across the hall when they heard the banging. They quickly grabbed their pistols and ran up to the window.

"What the fuck's goin' on?" Lotti Go asked, whispering into his walkie-talkie.

"Police just hit the building," one from their security crew answered. "Ya'll better get outta there fast," he warned. He clicked off his walkie talkie and quickly left his post out front.

Butch crept up to the door and peeked through the peephole. He was surprised. "Man, they next door!" Lotti Go crept next to him. Both of them silently stood by the door with their guns cocked ready for a showdown.

*****

Once inside the apartment, Canal instructed two of the officers to stay on alert in the hallway. He told one to take the first bedroom, bathroom and hallway closets; and for Turner to take the living room and kitchen. He took the other bedroom.

When Canal entered the bedroom, he immediately whipped out his *Daniel Boon* knife, slashing the mattress into shreds. After finding nothing there, he headed to the closet and began rambling through shoe boxes, coats, and whatever else resembled a good cover for a stash spot.

Nothing's here, he mumbled to himself. He scanned over the room trying to make sure he hadn't overlooked anything. An angry grunt escaped his lips. "These niggers got something in this house; I know it."

He called out to his partner. "Turner! You guys got anything?"

"Just some guns and jewelry."

"Good. Keep looking," Canal said staring at a mahogany dresser against the wall. He flung open every drawer, but found nothing. Out of rage, he flipped the dresser over to the floor. Something suddenly caught his eye.

"What the fuck?" He gawked at the wooden board. Without hesitating, he pried it from the wall. "Jackpot! I knew it!" he exclaimed catching an eye full of the neatly stacked money and narcotics lying on top. He snatched a couple of pillow cases of the bed and began stuffing the merchandise inside.

Canal stepped out of the bedroom and called a team huddle. He passed out two stacks of bills to Turner and the other officers. "It looks like at least thirty k altogether. As far as I'm concerned, it doesn't exist and neither do the drugs. But, we're turning the guns in for exchange of days off."

*****

Butch and Lotti Go were still clutching their pistols when they saw the police leaving the building. A couple of minutes later, they hit the walkie-talkie.

"Lance, all's well?" Butch asked.

"Yeah. Those vicks just left. They took everything and just let ya'll go?"

"Naw!" Butch replied.

Lance sighed. "Well, whoever they hit, them muthafuckas was holdin'."

Butch wasn't taking any chances. He turned to Lotti Go told him to pack everything up. We switchin' up spots 'til JB explains what's goin' on."

*****

Ever since Bullock hung up with Ms. Singleton, he'd been tempted to drop all business ventures just to get a piece of her. But his phone rang, breaking his train of thought.

"Hello."

"I'm ready," says the voice on the other end.

"Meet me at the spot." Bullock said nothing more before hanging up.

Thirty minutes later, Captain Bullock pulled inside an abandoned factory where Josh was already waiting.

"I knew you wouldn't let me down!" He said, stepping from the car giving his nephew a firm hand shake.

Josh pointed to the trunk and popped it open with his alarm switch. Bullock smiled when he saw the contents inside.

"That's my boy! Always on business!" He set the scale on top of the trunk and weighed the drugs.

Josh felt his phone buzzing inside his pocket. He pulled it out and looked at the screen. The number code told him it was trouble. He placed the phone up to his ear. "Yo!"

"Man, the peeps just tried to hit us," said Butch.

Josh frowned. "What you mean tried to?"

"They came through, about five strong, and ran up in the crib right across the hall."

"What?!"

"Man, Joe. They missed us and went across the hall. And whoever crib that was, they were definitely holdin' heavy. Security say they walked out of there with at least four bags of D, C, W, and guns mixed."

"Yeah?"

"Straight up, J."

"Ya'll good though; right?"

"Yeah. We on our way to location B until you let us know the next move."

Josh sighed. "Aight, chill. I'll holla back later." He turned to his uncle. "Man, what the fuck were you thinking by sending your punk ass wanna be goons over to the spot to take all my money and merch? I told you I was gon' take care of everything!"

"Wait a muthafuckin' minute boy! Who hit the crib?"

"I just got a call from my crew sayin' about five of your goons hit the spot and took half the load and the money for the other half. I pulled out my own money and bought this shit just so things could go straight and be alright between us. But I see no matter how hard I try, it ain't good enough, Unc. I just want my cash. You and yo' pussy ass goons can keep the package. I'm through with all this shit. You hear me? I'm out!"

Bullock snapped, "You ain't through with shit! It's over when I say it's over. You got that?" He sighed. "Now, I didn't authorize nothin', but I'm gonna find out who did and make it all right; understand?"

Josh nodded. "Yeah…I hear you."

"Now, did you get the extra merch so we can keep workin'?"

"Yeah. It's in there too," Josh replied nodding toward the trunk.

Bullock smiled, "Good. That's the JB I know. I want you to chill until tomorrow while I see who made that hit over at your spot, 'cause if it's the DEA we're gonna have to retire; alright?"

Josh agreed. Bullock took the bags out of the Lexus GS300 and tossed them into the trunk of his police issued Crown Vic.

"Tomorrow," he assured. He hopped into his car and pulled off.

As Bullock drove down Kilpatrick he was trying to figure out who could've hit the joint. After he arrived back to the precinct, he dropped everything off to Ortiz so he can have the inventory for the FBI's evidence crematory. Then he went straight to his office to wait on Kruger's report.

Kruger was right on his heels. He stepped in with a smirk on his face. "You won't believe who that was earlier."

Bullock asked, "Who? And don't give me no shit!"

"Canal finally got some balls and took punk ass Turner with him. I can't believe it Cap! When he told me he had a side lick, I thought he was playing; especially since I wasn't invited. Probably 'cause he thought I would've tried to stop him."

"I know he's your nephew and all, but fuck him! He's checking two mill a month, dragging us along with a few bricks at a time like he's having such a hard time. JB's playing us Cap. It's time we play him a little for some extra cash. It shouldn't be no problem as long as nobody gets hurt and as long as you okay it, Cap. We'll be straight." He suggested. "Oh. I apologize for the move that happened today without your permission and knowledge; but hell, I didn't even know myself."

Bullock blew out a puff of hot air. "Listen to me Kruger, and listen to me good. I don't give a fuck about people getting' hurt or not nor do I care about you all hittin' licks. But the next time anyone of you pull another stunt like that without me okaying it, I'm coming for your badge. You got that?"

Kruger wanted to cuss Bullock out, but instead, he gracefully bowed out. "Yes, sir."

"Good," Bullock replied, standing to his feet. "Because no one shows me up. If heat comes down, or an officer gets hurt, I'mma have to answer for it. Personally, I don't like looking like a jackass in front of people by being blind to what's going on in my own house!"

"Now get Canal and the rest of those dummy's in here so we can see exactly what they retrieved because I want my cut!!! And of course, I suppose you want yours too?"

Krueger smiled. "Yes, sir. Right away," he answered with a wicked grin on his face. Then he disappeared from the office, and reappeared with Canal.

Bullock ordered Kruger to frisk him. "Make sure he's not wired or anything before we go any further. He might have the IA or

DEA down our backs."

"Stand up and kick off your shoes." Kruger told Canal.

"What?! What type of shit is this Cap?"

Bullock gestured with a wave of his hand. "Just do as he says."

Humiliated, Canal reluctantly complied. He felt like he was on the butt end of his job description.

"He's straight Captain."

"Cool. Now, first of all I'mma tell you like I told Kruger, you ever do anything without my consent again and that's your ass and your job! Secondly, I'm glad to see you finally contributing to the team instead of sitting on the receiving end. Thirdly, I want to know what the fuck you kept and what you turned in."

"Well, we turned in eleven guns and kept a Patriot 223, a Glock 40 and a 357 Python. We also got what looks like six or seven kilos of powder cocaine and maybe a couple of kilos of heroin."

"I'm not sure 'cause I don't have a scale nor do I have a way of detecting which substance is which. That's just what the other guys normally tell me," he paused, wondering if he covered everything. "Oh, yeah, I already took the liberty of giving the other guys ten k each."

"You did what!?" Bullock's eyes popped. "You dumb fuck. How much do you usually get after a sting?"

"Five grand or less Cap."

"Exactly. So, why in the world did you give them ten a piece?"

"Because I knew it would assure them keeping their mouths shut. It's not like they get paid a whole lot as it is."

Bullock cut his eyes over to Kruger. "Ain't this a bitch?" He looked back at Canal. "So, you don't know if you can trust them; huh?"

Canal felt stupid. "Well, I..."

"Just forget about it!" Bullock spat cutting him off. "How much money do you have?"

"Two hundred seventy-five thousand minus the fifty grand I passed out."

"Hmm. That's a good number. We're gonna go out to eat later. But for now, you take the odd seventy five, and give the rest to Kruger.

"Kruger, you take fifty out of it and bring me the rest. I gotta take care of Josh so he can stop whining. Then we'll have him serve the package, and split it between the three of us once we figure out what we have in total. Now, get to it!" Bullock demanded.

He watched as Kruger and Canal quickly left his office. Then he smiled. *This is going perfectly,* he mumbled to himself. He picked up the phone. "Let's see if my baby is well enough to go out for dinner."

CHAPTER 11

Business had been going extremely well for Tone over the past month-and-a-half. During his incarceration he had often wondered if it was possible to make his mark in the dope game, stack a nice piece of change, and retire alive. Thus far, he had learned nothing was impossible. The lonely nights he spent tossing and turning in that tiny cell thinking about grinding from the bottom to the top, had finally transformed his nightmares into sweet dreams.

Tone never fathomed the thought of seeing $100,000 running through his hands every week. Ever since Robby had been out of his own work, he had been assisting his man with getting rid of two to three kilos per week. Tone was moving fast for someone who'd only been out of prison for two months. The main things keeping him grounded were being reunited with his pops, and the newly discovered information surrounding his brother's death. Both of those events humbled him. Tone had decided that after he did another six months in the game, it would be officially over for him. Besides, he'd fallen for his new flame, and she didn't like drug dealers. He wasn't going to fuck that up.

Most of Alicia's boyfriends–including both her sons' fathers–were in the game distributing illegal narcotics. When her first son's father wound up in prison, she stood by him faithfully during his two-year bid. The difficulties of raising two children alone opened her eyes. She warned her second son's father, prior to his release, that she would never put herself out there again if he, too, didn't wise up. But her words fell on deaf ears. Not even days after he was home, he was right back into the mix messing with the same old crowd. The worse part of it all was that the Feds had that same old crowd under investigation. He unknowingly walked right into a conspiracy, and ended up with a fresh ten-year sentence. Alicia was a single mother all over again for the second time.

None of her boyfriends had ever revealed any solid plans that would carry them past the dope game. That was why she felt that Tone was different. He was intelligent, ambitious and smart enough to know that there was no future in living a fast lifestyle.

When Alicia learned of his goals, she was astonished. Here was a thug from the streets who had done time in the joint, yet knew exactly where he wanted to go and where he wanted to be in life. He told her that he was only in the game temporarily.

"All I wanna do is make enough money to establish myself as a real-estate investor. I'm also goin' to help my partner Robby pursue forming the hottest record label in the city."

Although Alicia didn't really approve of how Tone was going about his business, she had to respect his sincerity, his honesty, and his determination. She could tell that he had the full potential to reach the level of legal success that he desired. All he had to do was put his mind to it and it would materialize. So this time around, she was able to make a conscious decision. She had lived long enough to know that every strong man needs a strong woman standing by his side. Just to let Tone know that she was a hundred percent willing to work with him, she introduced him to her diehard hustling cousin, Dre.

Tone had just pulled up to the stoplight in his black on black Lincoln Mark 8. He picked up his cell phone and quickly dialed Alicia's number.

She answered the phone sweet and sexy as usual. "Hello."

Tone smiled, "Hey, baby. I'll be there in a couple of minutes."

"Mmm, I can hardly wait. I miss you."

"And I miss you too." Tone made a kissing sound through the phone which made her laugh. "By the way babe, is yo' cousin over there?"

"Dre? Yeah. He's out front. Why? What's up?"

"Put him on the phone real quick."

"Okay."

"I love you." Tone added.

"I love you too sweetheart. Wait, hold up..." Alicia paused. She cleared her throat. "Uh, how the hell you figure you love me already? We haven't even known each other long enough to be talking 'bout 'love' and shit."

"Oh, yeah?" Tone was a little insulted. "Well, what's long enough for you...'cause I could've sworn that your response was mutual. But then again, life is full of contradictions."

Alicia smiled. "Boy. You always trying to use that reverse psychology stuff. You ain't slick. I asked you the question first. You just tryin' to see where I'm at." She smacked her lips in repugnance. "You somethin' else."

Tone chuckled, "Yeah, my mom told me that all my life. Anyway, the best answer I can give you is, it doesn't matter how long we've known each other. Past experiences have taught me that love isn't something you're unsure of."

Alicia's heart skipped a beat. *This nigga is too real. He better not hurt me or I'll kill him,* she thought, staring into the mirror as she styled her hair.

"I agree. But, know this then. I'mma go get Dre."

"What's that?"

"There's no hurt in love either. So keep that in mind after those six months are up," she concluded, "Now, let me call my cousin to the phone like you asked." Alicia raced downstairs.

Tone mumbled to himself, "She's right. Love is love, and hurt is hurt." He knew better than anybody that taking penitentiary chances in the streets was a definite contradiction. How can you live a lifestyle that would cause the people you claim to love to worry themselves sick about you?"

"Tone, what's the deal?" Dre yelled through the phone.

"D-Boy! What up?"

"Nothin', man. Just waitin' on you."

"Aight. Let Alicia know I'll be over in about two," Tone said in code.

"Aight." Dre hung up knowing exactly what to do.

When Tone pulled in front of Alicia's flat on 64th and Normal, Dre hopped in.

"Damn," he said after shutting the passenger door. "Fool, this joint is sweet!" He comfortably sank into the interior of the luxury vehicle.

"This ain't nuttin', just a clean look for a work car. Give me a minute. I'mma bust somethin' real serious." Tone boasted as he pointed to an *Aldi* bag. "Grab that from under the seat."

Dre peeked inside. He was impressed with the product. "One love, my nigga. I'mma send Alicia out with the eighteen stacks."

"Bet. I'll rotate with you later."

Alicia stepped outside of her home wearing a fire engine red, *Escada* mini dress. Her clean shaven, honey golden legs protruded from the bottom of the dress. Her arms were wrapped in a knitted *Kimono* cardigan which was perfect for the crisp weather. She grinned as she stepped into Tone's car.

"Hey, daddy. So this is the car you said your father got for you? I like it. It's nice; but not too flashy."

"Yeah, it is nice, but this not it." Tone started the engine and pulled off. "You lookin good in that dress baby."

"Thanks, babe," she blushed. "Here..." she reached inside her *Balenciaga* red tote bag, handing over a stack of money, "It's all there. I counted it myself," she joked.

"Oh, yeah? I just might need to count it over then." Tone smiled.

"Boy!" she exclaimed, playfully punching him in his side. "I ain't gotta steal. I'll ask for whatever I want."

"I know babe."

A few minutes later, Tone pulled into the parking garage of Newport Towers located on Lake Shore Drive.

"Listen, you see that dark red car parked between those two cars," he asked her pointing towards a Mercedes.

"Yes. Is *that* the one your father gave you?" she asked, astonished. She had never seen a vehicle so pretty in her entire life.

"Yeah, that's it. Now here." He tossed her the keys. "Pull it out so I can park this one right there."

"Uh-uh," Alicia shook her head. "Tony, I'm not about to take no chances on tearing that car up. Hell, that's a Mercedes," she whispered. "I'll be working at the window for life if something happened to it." She tried giving the keys back, but Tone pushed her hand away.

"What did I tell you about love?" he asked. "It's somthin you're not unsure of; right?"

"I understand that, but…"

Tone gently placed his finger up to her lips. "Ain't no buts. Love isn't materialistic either. It's a deep affection and warm feeling for another human being. Now go and pull the car out. Love is gon' let you drive us downtown too," he smiled.

"Alright, daddy." Alicia reluctantly stepped out the car and approached the Benz. She carefully stepped in, stuck the key into the ignition, and turned it. The computerized voice startled her.

"Welcome to Benz Link; Mr. Wiley. What can I do for you today?"

A chain of fluorescent lights shot across the dash board gear shift and door panels.

Alicia thought to herself, *Damn, his daddy must be rich or something to be able to just give him a car like this. I've always dreamed of having one of these. The cran-apple paintjob matches my dress perfectly. I could get used to this!* She smiled. "He thinks he's slick," she mumbled, looking over at Tone, just as he sat down in the passenger's seat.

"Baby, I'm feeling this bad boy," she cheered. "But, I don't understand something. Why are you dealing if your father is…"

"Shh!" Tone gestured with his hands for her to be quiet. He knew that modern day cars were built with navigation systems that were tied into Network Global Satellites. "I don't do that at all."

Alicia was puzzled. "I was just saying…"

"Don't say at all." Tone kissed her on the cheek. "We'll talk about it some other time. Tonight, it's strictly me and you."

Alicia could feel her panties starting to moisten. "Babe, will you do me on the way?" she asked, smiling mischievously.

Tone chuckled, "Nah."

"Come on Boo," she begged. "I'll do you for the rest of the

night. I know you'll love every bit of that."

"Nah. Not in here. My tongue game already has you crawlin' up the headboard. You might tear some shit up fo' real in a car."

Alicia pouted, "Okay, Mr. Love-Ain't-Materialistic!"

Tone stared intently at her and thought, *What could a little foreplay hurt?* He reached over her thigh and began rubbing her clit through her panties, simultaneously nibbling her ear.

"Mmm, baby..." she managed to mumble right before climaxing.

Tone quickly stopped. "I got some more for you later," he whispered. "Now, let's bounce."

"Boy, you play too much." Alicia threw the gear in drive and pulled off.

*****

Doc sat on his pearl white, leather sofa contemplating the right way to persuade Spook into selling him a hundred bricks without suspicion attached to it. After playing out various scenarios in his head, he dialed Spook's number.

"Who this?" Spook answered casually.

"Man, it's Doc, big homie! Can I holla at you tonight?"

"Yeah. I was just on my way to get a bite to eat. Meet me at the *Beef-n-Brandy.*"

"Aight," Doc hung up and dashed from the house. Then he jumped inside his BMW X5 which was a bluish purple color, and dialed his connect to let him know everything was going as planned.

"7th District," a stern voice answered.

"Yo', I'm parking at my girl's house, so I'll hit you back later." Doc responded, speaking in code.

"Good. Call me when you're leaving," the voice replied.

Doc hopped out of his jeep, grabbed his purple *Pelle Pelle* jacket from the backseat and headed toward the entrance of the restaurant. He spotted Spook deep in the smokers' section with a *Newport* hanging freely from his lips. He motioned with his hand for Doc to come over.

"I hope this isn't going to be a waste of my time," he said as

Doc sat down. "Because you already know how I move."

Doc remained humble. "Man, big homie. I want that one."

Spook smirked. "When did you start making moves like that? Whose house did you rob?" he chuckled. "I never thought of you as a stickup kid."

"It's not like that, Homie. I got my new protégé, Tone, in rotation. He's doin' forty every month over there where Tre used to be at. And I'm doin' sixty. I figured it's about time for me to upgrade, you know?" Doc emphasized.

Spook visually read Doc. He pulled out a wire detector which looked like a two-way pager. He was satisfied with both readings. He smiled.

"You know the figures. It just so happens, I got just what you need right now."

"Well, we can roll out," Doc assumed. As he began to lift himself up from his seat, Spook stopped him.

"Nah. You can," he handed him an alarm keypad. "There's a crème colored Lexus on the corner. Go in the trunk, get yours and leave me mine, along with the alarm."

"Aight." Doc headed out relieved that everything had worked out so far.

*****

Tone and Alicia entered the John Hancock building and headed for the elevator hand in hand. The location was a place where hustlers and ballers came to unwind from the daily stress of grinding. It was a place Tre never got the chance to frequent.

"In all my years, I've never been here; or even knew they *had* a revolving restaurant baby." Alicia admitted as they made their way up to the elegant Signature Room.

"Yeah. I just found out too." Tone leaned over, kissing her softly on the lips. "I hope you enjoy it." They stepped off the elevator, waltzed straight to the concierge's desk, and asked to be seated.

"Smoking or non-smoking sir?" he asked in his French accent.

"Smoking." Tone replied. They were escorted to their table.

As Tone took at the exquisite view of the restaurant's setting he unintentionally locked eyes with the most beautiful white girl he had ever seen in his life. He didn't even realize he was gawking at her until Alicia broke him from his trance.

"Daddy! We're at our table."

"I know babe. Here, let me get your chair," he said, pulling out her seat. But in his mind, he was contemplating a way to bag the snow bunny that was still in eyesight. He wasn't going to let her get away.

As the waitress passed their table, Tone stopped her and asked, "Where's the restroom?"

"Down the hall to the right of the elevator sir," she politely answered, "I'll also be back in a moment to take your order."

"That'll be fine." Tone turned to Alicia. "Give me a second baby. I gotta go relieve myself right quick." He lied as he got up and pecked his date on her forehead.

Alicia smiled, rocking her head to the slow grooving rhythm of Anita Baker's "I Apologize."

Tone spotted the attractive Caucasian female dressed in an all-white, two-piece satin *Channel* suit. Ironically, she was on her way to the restroom herself. They both locked eyes in lust. Before she could walk through the door, he grabbed her hand.

"Excuse me," she said, with a flirtatious gaze. "Is this how you approach strangers?"

Tone grinned, "Nah. Not all the time. I just wish that I wasn't occupied at the moment, 'cause I would definitely take you with me tonight."

She grinned back, "There's always tomorrow."

Tone reached into his *Armani* shirt pocket and pulled out a card holding his contact information. "What time?"

"Whenever you're not busy. But out of respect, I'll be sure to call you in advance."

"That'll be a good idea." Tone casually stepped into the men's room. But before the door could swing shut, the woman called out to him. He gracefully spun around in his *Cole Han Edwin Captoe* crocodile shoes. His head was straight and his chest was out. She definitely had his undivided attention.

"My name. You didn't even ask me my name. How are you

going to know it's me calling?"

"Oh, yeah," he replied as if he totally forgot. But in reality, he totally didn't care. Her name was not important. He only wanted to fuck her, and he could see in her eyes that she definitely wanted to fuck him too.

"What *is* your name?"

"It's Jennifer," she answered. Tone nodded and disappeared into the bathroom.

*****

Doc sat on 71st and Western in the parking lot of the *Prestige Liquor* store for twenty minutes; paranoid as hell. There were a hundred kilos of cocaine packed neatly inside his SUV; and there were too many thirsty potential robbers lurking nearby. He finally pulled out this phone and dialed.

"7th Precinct, Sergeant Phillips speaking."

"Pops, whatcha still doin' there? I've been on point for an hour already," Doc exaggerated.

Phillips could tell his son was agitated. "Jr., I'm sorry, but my shift manger hasn't come in yet, so I told the Captain I'll work the front desk."

"Hell naw!!" Doc couldn't believe his ears. "So you just got me out here on a blank mission huh?!"

"Calm down Jr., I'm…"

Click.

Doc hung up before his father could get another word out. "Fuck this shit. I'm out!" He drove away in frustration.

As he rolled up 71st street approaching the stoplight on Damen, the spontaneous blaring of sirens startled him. He peered into his rearview mirror and pulled over hoping the police were just trying to pass. But instead, they pulled up right alongside of him.

"Damn! What these Vicks on?" he mumbled, attempting to exit the vehicle.

"Get back in the car," one of the officers yelled over the loud speaker. Moments later, two black male officers stood at opposite sides of his jeep.

"License and registration please," said the officer on the driver's side.

Doc reached in his inside jacket pocket, but sadly realized he forgot his wallet. "Uh, sir, if you would just…"

"Shut up, young man and step out of the vehicle."

"But I…"

"Shut up before we shut you up! Now, step out of the vehicle with your hands up."

Doc finally managed to exhale. Then he stepped from his jeep. He was told to face the car and place his hands behind his back. And yet, he continued his attempts at reasoning.

"If you run my name, you'll see I got a license."

"No need. I'll see once we get you down to the station."

"Holy shit!" The other officer exclaimed, staring into the trunk. "He's got about two hundred pounds of coke back here partner. We've hit a big one."

"Awe, naw. That's not mine." Doc was talking fast. "If you just let me use my phone this could be straightened out."

"Shut up." One of the officers walked Doc to the squad car and sat him in the back. He jumped into the driver's seat as his partner followed them to the station in Doc's jeep. Doc wondered how his dad would react.

"Mr. Duke Phillips Jr., it's a pleasure to meet you." The officer smiled.

Doc was baffled. *This punk ass cop must know my old man,* he thought to himself, *but he's still locking me up. Yeah, it's a damn pleasure alright. Especially when my pops snatch your badge for this bullshit.*

The officer laughed. "I could tell what your old man meant when he mentioned that you were shrewd dude."

Doc didn't see anything funny. The handcuffs felt like they were cutting off his blood circulation.

The officer continued, "Look man, I know you mad as hell right now; but since you wasn't at the liquor store when we got there, we had to apprehend you with a traffic stop. Anyone driving as dirty as you, wouldn't stop the car for nobody. Then again, there's no telling if one of your goons was following you for security purposes. Me and my man, Simmons, wasn't taking any chances exposing ourselves for you."

Everything was beginning to make sense to Doc. "So if playboy driving my shit is Simmons, then you must be…"

"Choice," he finished. "Officer Choice in the flesh."

Doc chuckled. "Ya'll the two cats who been taxing me like Uncle Sam; huh?"

"Business is business. Ain't nothin personal. Even the dudes associated with you in the Englewood area are covered as well. Now, when we get to the station we're gonna pull in right next to Simmons. He's gonna exchange the coke from your trunk to ours, then you can push back out; alright?"

Doc smiled. "Yeah. I got you. And you can tell my pop's old ass we gon' have a talk about this later on."

*****

After enjoying a nice dinner, Tone and Alicia went downstairs to the *Cheesecake Factory* for dessert. Afterwards, they headed home for the evening. Tone walked her to the car, opened the door and closed it behind her.

"I have another surprise for you," he said as he climbed into the driver's side. He couldn't help thinking about the white girl he'd bagged earlier.

Alicia smiled, "Really? What's the surprise baby?"

"You'll see." Tone left her in total suspense as they cruised Lake Shore Drive listening to Jaheim's, "Could it be."

Fifteen minutes later they arrived in the same parking lot they had switched cars in earlier.

"Sweety," Alicia whined, "I don't feel like driving."

"Who said anything about you driving?" He continued to roll straight through the lot and came to a halt in front of a garage. He rolled down the window, took a card from his visor and slid it inside a machine. The garage door opened.

"This is where we at tonight," he said, as he pulled in to park.

Alicia stepped out of the car. "What's this, one of your daddy's places?"

Tone stepped to her and kissed her lips. "No," he replied. They exited the garage and entered the condo.

"Damn, this is nice." She had never seen such an exquisite place in all her life. The dining room floors were pure marble. There was a butler's pantry. The family room was equipped with a bar and wine cooler adjacent to the granite kitchen island. The personal tour ended inside the master suite. The private balcony took her breath away.

"Look at how pretty Lake Michigan is at night," she said pointing towards the beach.

Tone crept up on her from behind and began kissing her along the nape of her neck. He slowly ran his tongue down to her shoulder and whispered, "You like it?"

"Mmm hmm...yes," she moaned, taken aback by the delight of his warm tongue against her skin.

"I'm glad, 'cause it's yours. This'll be the ideal spot for you and the kids. They don't need to be around Dre and his people serving out on the block."

Alicia turned, facing him with tears of joy in her eyes. "I - I can't," she uttered.

Tone shook his head. "Don't say another word sweetheart. I got this." He started running his tongue down her spine again as he unzipped the back of her strapless dress. It fell to the floor revealing her tender, round breasts.

Tone didn't care if they were still outside on the balcony. He began circling her dark brown nipples with his tongue, causing her breasts to stand erect like tiny, brown mountains. Alicia stood before him in nothing but red *Franco Sarto* patent-leather pumps, and red laced thong. She trembled when he dropped to his knees, moving her underwear to the side, and running his tongue from her navel all the way to her treasure chest.

"Awh shit," she mumbled, feeling her juices forming as he teased her clitoris; licking and pausing, licking and pausing. She rolled her head back in ecstasy, moaning and biting her bottom lip.

Alicia was no longer able to control herself. Her juices flowed down her inner thighs. "Oh, yeah, baby. That's it, right there. That's... it... right...there... Ohhhhh!" She quickly grabbed him by his ears and pulled him back up so that he was standing again.

Alicia slowly turned around and perched her ass in the air while holding on to the railing. "Come get it babe," she said, looking back at him with a dirty expression.

Tone loosened his belt, allowing his pants to fall to the floor. His member was already standing at attention. He gradually slid himself into her wet prize, and began his strokes of pleasure – slowly and deeply.

"I can take it daddy," Alicia moaned as he entered her warm and moist womanhood. "Awh…yessss. It's all yours Tone. Take this pussy. Ohhhh, it's all yours."

Just as the words floated from her tongue, he went deeper inside her until she surrounded all of his nine inches. "Oooh, shit. Tooooooone!"

Ms. Singleton strolled into Bullock's office wearing her civilian clothes. She had a disturbed look on her face. "Hey there Captain."

Bullock felt a weird vibration when she addressed him by his professional title. "What's up baby?"

"That's Officer Singleton," she corrected.

Strangely, he was somewhat aroused by her raunchy attitude. "Well, excuse me Officer Singleton," he smiled. "How can I help you today, and why are you dressed in plain clothes?" he asked her.

Ms. Singleton reached for the envelope in her navy blue *Nine West* leather pea coat and handed it to him. "I'm here to submit my resignation sir."

Bullock chuckled. "You've got to be kidding me, Vicky – I mean – Officer Singleton," he replied, assuming she was joking.

As she removed her jacket, he began licking his lips in a seductive manner. Her soft, medium breasts could clearly be seen through her golden sheer *First Lady* Halter top and matching *First Lady* Denim jeans. The jeans hugged her tightly in all the right places. Dictated by the mind in his pants, Bullock only had one thing on his mind…banging her back out.

Ms. Singleton sat right in front of his desk. "I'm not kidding at all Captain." She looked intently into his eyes with a straight face. She nodded her head towards her letter of resignation.

Bullock caught on. He glanced at the tiny note which was attached. It read:

Don't say anything Theo because the office might be wired. I need you to meet me at the Breakfast Corner in ten minutes.

Bullock continued to act appalled. "This is a game right; Officer?"

"No, it's not Captain," Ms. Singleton stoop up, "It's truly been an honor serving you." She left his office.

Bullock was dumbfounded. Whatever had Ms. Singleton acting so strange made his stomach turn. Still, he took her advice. He allowed her a fifteen minute head start before he threw on his black *Benny Blueitt* cashmere trench coat. He placed the letter in his pocket, hit the light switch, and headed towards Ms. Singleton's destination.

Moments later, Bullock stepped into the diner. He spotted Ms. Singleton sitting in the last booth near a window; he sat down across from her.

"What the hell was that all about Vicky," he earnestly asked. Although he was genuinely convinced that her actions were more in line with one of the games she liked to play before she slept with him.

"Listen Theo. I'm not playing about my resignation." She held up her right hand. "Honestly, as God as my witness, there are some things going on that you're not fully aware of."

Bullock could tell that she was beating around the bush. "Listen baby, tell me what the fuck is going on."

Ms. Singleton swallowed hard before she spoke. Just as the first tear fell from her eye, she replied, "There's going to be a big bust soon and the Feds and Internal Affairs want you baby."

"What?!" Bullock couldn't believe his ears. "Who the fuck told you that?" he was enraged. "Are you serious?"

"Shhh!!! Keep your voice down," Ms. Singleton whispered, looking around the diner for eavesdroppers. "Theo," she took a deep breath. "Yesterday IA and the FBI grabbed me and told me they knew about us and that you're a dirty cop. They threatened me and said if I didn't want to take the fall, I'd better give you up. But I defended you. I let them know that all you do is fight crime baby."

"Wait a minute!" Bullock grabbed a few napkins form the holder and passed them her. "Listen, slow down. Stop crying and tell me everything sweetheart. I'm sure we can work this out together."

Once Ms. Singleton knew that Bullock had taken her bait; she made her move. "The Feds are coming, and they told me I better get out the way if I didn't wanna go to jail Theo."

"Go to jail for what? You haven't done anything?"

She blew her nose with the napkins and continued. "They told me I would be indicted with you and the rest of the people in your operation if I didn't get out of the way Theo. So, I'm leaving for Ohio."

"Ohio? What the fuck is in Ohio?"

"I have a sister in Columbus. I'm gonna get a job with the authorities out there until things cool down."

Bullock sighed, "Look Vicky. There's nothing going on and you know it. So just sit tight and stop overreacting baby. Trust me."

"I wish I could Theo. I really do, but…I don't know. I don't want to end up an officer in prison, you know," she stressed.

"You're not going to prison for nobody. Trust me. I got everything under control."

She dried her tears and inhaled deeply and exhaled slowly. "Are you sure Theo? 'Cause they said…"

"I don't give a fuck what 'they' said," he ferociously exclaimed through his teeth. "This is my house! I got this! Ya hear me?" He stopped and put his hands over his face to calm down. He then sat next to her and began massaging her shoulders in an attempt to relax her too. "We have to keep everything normal . If you just run off, things will look suspicious."

Recognizing that he was taking the bait, she backed off her act a little.

"Even though you and I both know there's nothing going on," Bullock continued, "let's just carry on with our regular routine. They don't have a thing on us at the station; and if they did, you wouldn't have to worry about nothing. Now, let's have a nice meal, go back to your place, and get it on," he smiled picking up a menu.

"No, no, no, Theo! You don't understand. They told me if Ortiz mentions my name, it's over."

"Who did you just say?"

"Ortiz. They've approached him and it's a possibility he's working with them. So, I have to go because if he mentions my name, or if I'm mentioned by one of their witnesses, I'm going to prison. And Theo, let's face it. I love you dearly; but not enough to lose my freedom. So, goodbye." She leaned over and kissed him on the cheek just before going to the exit.

Bullock was left awestruck as he watched her walk out of his life. However, he believed she was making the best decision concerning both of them. He was even happier that she gave him the heads up on what was going on.

Damn, Bullock thought to himself, *they got to Ortiz's weak ass, huh? And that son of a bitch didn't even tell me after all I've made possible for him and his family. Hmmm, I wonder who else is working undercover on me.*

Bullock stepped up to the waitress at the counter. "Hey, Kathy, let me use the phone. It's urgent." He dialed Josh's number.

"Yo', whaddup?" he answered.

"This your uncle boy."

"What up Unc? What now?" He asked. "Wait, hold up. Let me guess. Ya'll took something else from me and you're about to make me work it off for free."

"Listen Josh, I don't have time for your bullshit. I have a problem, and that means *you* have a problem. Now, meet me in thirty minutes at our place so we can figure out how we're gonna fix *our* dilemma."

"Yeah, aight. I got you." Josh hung up wondering what the hell was going on.

CHAPTER 12

Tone turned down the tunes of Tupac Shakur's, "Picture Me Rollin" just before he answered the phone. "Hello…"

"What's the demo? I'm tryna do one and a half with you…"

Tone interrupted his client before he got too reckless with his tongue. "Hold fast fool. One and a half will be good knowing who this is. But, how many times I gotta tell you to stop doing that dumb shit?"

"I know. I know," Shoestring repeated feeling a little guilty.

"Anyway, I'll be there in a couple."

Tone gave him the dial tone. He turned to Robby. "Man, these be some stupid muthafuckas! No matter how many times you tell them to just pull on the block, they wanna keep callin' me on these souped-up ass phones."

"I know that's right," Robby agreed. He had his eyes glued on a blue Lesabre which just pulled up. He jumped out of the car and told Tone, "Hold that thought. Let me serve my peoples this last 63 right quick."

"This shit is crazy," Tone mumbled, watching Robby hop into the Lesabre. He then switched the song selection on the Tupac CD to, "I Ain't Mad At Ya."

*****

"What you mean, 'ain't nothin' right now?'"

"You heard me. I'll call you when we're back in route alright?" Sergeant Phillips hung up to do roll call without giving a second thought to his son's whining.

Doc was extremely frustrated. "Damn! How am I gonna get work now? Spook ain't gone fall for me telling him I dumped off the last package in two days. Plus, I only got money for seventy," he sighed. He whipped out his cell phone.

"Yo' Spook, where you at big homie?"

"I'm at the barber shop. Come on through."

"Aight," Doc cheerfully replied, turning off the mute button. Jay-Z's, "Coming of Age" continued to bump.

When Doc arrived at the shop on 69th and Western, he was unaware that the place was split in two. A beauty salon was up front, and a barber shop in back. He was aware, however, of the fact of word of mouth. His reputation was everywhere. He stepped inside, gallantly greeting everyone.

"Hey, Doc," Tiffany greeted flirtatiously.

"What up Ma?" Doc replied with confidence. He headed straight for Spook's office toward the rear of the building and knocked.

"Come in." Spook leaned forward in his recliner when Doc entered. "What up, playboy? Don't tell me you had a problem, because I always triple check everything before taking off."

"Naw, naw. It ain't like that big homie."

"Then what is it Doc?"

"Man, big homie. It's a long story."

Doc paused when Spook opened his two-way pager, looked at the screen and began typing in letters.

Spook was satisfied that Doc wasn't bugged up with a wire. "Okay, now tell me your long story and how you think I can help you, 'cause I know that's why you're here; right?"

"Yeah." Doc replied. "Well, first off I'm through with the one, but I only got money for seventy left."

Spook gave Doc an evil eye. "Already? What you do, eat that shit or somethin'?"

"Naw. My pops took care of it; but he didn't give me none 'cause he needed it for some type of police operation."

"Police operation?" Spook quickly grew agitated. "What da fuck you talkin' 'bout Doc?"

He quickly searched under his *Rocawear* fleece hoodie, whipping out his .357 *Python* hand gun and aimed it at Doc. Then he silently wrote on a piece of paper, *Take your clothes off.*

Doc knew that his confession would more than likely further Spook's frustration, so he quickly obliged and stripped down to his underwear.

"Listen man. My pops is a police Sergeant. The one I bought had to go back to him because it was time for the Feds to pick it up from the evidence room; you see what I'm saying?"

"No. No I don't," Spook said coldly.

Doc swallowed hard, "Well, do you remember when Tre got murked?"

"Yeah," Spook was on high alert.

"I turned my pops on to him, and he had him whacked in order for me to get on." Doc paused to check Spook's reaction, but Spook looked more intrigued than anything else.

"It was smooth, but the other police station turned in the hundred to cover their asses. I had to flip it a couple of times with Tone. He doesn't have a clue big homie. Trust me. He just moves forty to fifty a month, including the orders he gives me…"

"Now, I'm through with my pops, and I'm dealing with you so; I need that push big homie. I got the paper for majority of the portion like I said. You can look out and hit me with the thirty to make it a whole one. So, what you think?"

"Damn, you deep Joe." Spook responded. He couldn't believe that Doc had enough balls to admit to his face that he was bogus. More importantly, that he had his associate and so-called best friend knocked off by the cops, just so he could get in the game.

Spook smirked. "Now, how can I trust *you*?" he asked, fighting back the urge to blow Doc's brains all over the office walls.

"'Cause, I didn't get you popped off when you served me the one. I'm not like that Spook. It was also personal between me and dude. I didn't even know my pops was going to knock him off."

Spook sighed, "I see," he said, tossing Doc the alarm key pad again. "You know the procedure."

"Thanks big homie." Doc was relieved. "Thanks."

"It's cool, lil' daddy. Just take care of your business aight." Spook wished Doc the best and watched him like a hawk as he redressed himself and left.

*****

"Aight, team. I got about a hundred ridin' on this game!" Tone shouted from the bleachers to the teen basketball crew he managed to form while working his magic in the streets. This was his way of helping the kids duck the environment of the ghetto. Lindbloom Park's field house was about to witness another victory.

"Ya'll win and I got five bucks for each of you. Now, ya'll go kill them niggas!"

Prior to tipoff, Tone yelled, "Dawon, pass the ball!" He leapt down the stands toward the side line.

"Excuse me. But you lil' Robby's man Tone; right?"

Tone recognized the suave individual from Tre's funeral. "Yeah," he said reaching out to shake his hand. "And you Spook; right?"

"Everybody around here calls me that, so you might as well too."

Tone returned his attention to the game. "I see you diggin' my team," he cleverly stated.

"Nah, lil' homie. Actually, I'd like to bet a hundred to your twenty-five dollars that my team sweeps yours off the floor." Spook challenged, hoping to break the ice.

"Bet!" You ain't said nuttin' but a word." Tone quickly jumped at the chance of winning an extra seventy-five bucks. He was confident in the athletic killers he recruited for his squad.

In the final twenty seconds of the game, Spook's team had the ball, walking it to the hole.

"Stephen, stick yo D. D-up! D-up! No sooner after Tone yelled to his point guard, Stephen stripped Spook's player of the ball.

"That's what I'm talkin' bout Steph! Go in, baby. Take it in!!!"

When Stephen jumped up and released the ball from half court, the entire gymnasium of spectators froze like mannequins as they watched the basketball twirl around the rim. The buzzer sounded off as soon as it fell through the net as cheers filled the gym.

Tone ran up to greet his team. "Aye, Black Jack, Ginarus, Stephen, E-Smooth and the rest of you cats slide on me later at the spot to get ya'll cheddar." As he continued dispersing his congrats to his players, Spook slid over to him with a bag.

"Here you go Tee; if you don't mind me callin' you that."

"No, thanks," Tone declined. "Man, just give me half and call it even."

"Naw, naw. When I make a bet, I pay. So take it." Spook insisted, "There's an incentive in there for you."

Tone frowned. "What kind of incentive?"

"A bird," Spook replied like it was nothing. "I want you to sample it, and get back wit me; aight?"

"Tone glanced inside the bag and noticed the brown taped square stamped with googly eyeball stickers. "Oh, yeah?" He passed the bag to Ross. "Here, take it to Robby, and tell him to test tube that."

"People say you're the best thing on your side of time since my man Tre's untimely departure; you know."

Tone's ears went up like a canine's when Tre's name was mentioned. But at the same time he instantly became leery. *Does this nigga know who I really am*, he wondered.

"Look Joe. I'mma give this to my guy," Tone said. "If he hits me and say it's good, you can keep this hundred and I got another one-and-a-half in my trunk for you. So, if you don't mind, we can drink while we wait."

"Come on," Spook replied leading the way out front to his money green Cadillac DTS. Tone took special notice at the 22 inch *Oasis* rims it was sitting on.

"Nice whip."

"Thanks." Spook proudly replied as they hopped inside.

"Man, shorty, if you hit like my man Tre, whooo weeee! Me and you are gonna have a long, long, friendship; you know?"

"I really miss my nigga. He used to spend a mil or more every month faithfully. But it ain't the money shorty. I miss kickin it with that nigga the most. Me and him been all over the world and back; straight up. It'll never be another nigga like Tre." Spook shook his head despairingly.

"Yeah, man. I've heard," Tone said contemplating Tre's reputation.

Spook pulled into the liquor store parking lot on 63rd and Damen. "Whatcha' drinking on lil' man?" he asked Tone, turning to accommodate a clucker hustling for spare change.

"*Moet* and *Remy V.S.O.P.*"

"Aight." He then turned to the crack head, "Hey, go in there and get me one Remy, one bottle of Mo, two *Red Bulls,* a pack of *Newport* shorts and get a box of *Cigarillos*. Gon' head and keep the change which should be a saw buck or better.

The oily beige, *Carhart* coverall dressed, dope fiend smiled ear to ear when Spook placed the $100 bill in his hand. He happily strolled away.

Tone's cell rang. He answered after receiving Robby's code. "Yeah, what's the demo sir?"

"It's good."

"Aight. I'mma hit you later." Tone hung up, satisfied with the results of Spook's product.

The dusty looking man shortly returned to the car and told Spook, "Here's yo' drinks and thanks for the change."

"No problem Cooley. You be easy out here." Spook pulled off. "Yeah, man. Like I was sayin', dude was my man; straight up. Even though he physically departed, he still watchin' over me."

"Yeah. I knew ya'll had to be close when I saw you at his wake. You was crying over his casket like you had just lost your mom or somethin'."

"I saw you there too with yo' mans and 'em. So you knew my nigga too; huh?'

Tone nodded, "Yeah man, I did."

Spook nonchalantly, pulled out a 40 cal., and gently sat it on his lap. "Friend or foe?" he asked.

Tone replied cockily, "Friend."

"Man, how I'm s'posed to know fo' sure?"

"Because right after you had finished speaking with our father, he and I started to leave together before anyone noticed."

Spook was baffled. "Wait, wait, wait. See that's where shit just took a left turn. You can't be Tre's brother. He didn't have no brothers. I've been knowing my man damn near my whole life. He ain't never mentioned anything about a brother, and he damn sho' ain't mentioned you."

"Yeah, I know he didn't. We just found out about each other before he got killed. We never met on family terms though. But, when he did find out we were brothers, our old man thought it was best we waited 'til I got out the joint. That way pops wouldn't have to be feuding with either of our mothers. Seriously, if I'm a friend, I ain't gon' lie about no shit like that. He left me his Benz and everything."

Spook had a hard time absorbing everything. "Damn, it's a small, small world, my nigga. So, you Tre's lil' bro; huh? Then, why you hangin' with that stud Doc?"

"What you mean?" Tone defended. "Doc been hittin' me since I got out the joint."

"Does he know you're Tre's brother?"

"Hell naw! Don't nobody know. The only reason I let you in is because you sounded sincere when you spoke about him and plus, I've been wantin' to get that shit up off my chest straight up."

"Yeah, that's cool. I feel you a hundred percent my man. So, listen, I'mma front you fifty bricks. Fuck Doc! Understand?" Spook resolved.

"Yeah, I hear you…"

"I'm not playin' around Tee. You don't know this dude. If you did, you wouldn't be caught dead with him."

"Why?" Tone frowned. "What is it you tryna insinuate Spook? 'Cause that's my man." Tone sighed, "I can't deal with you if you on some hatin' shit."

Spook spontaneously slammed on the brakes. "A hater?! Nigga, you just need to take my advice before you end up like your brotha."

"Take yo' advice?" Tone couldn't believe his ears. "Nigga, who the fuck you supposed to be; huh? Take my advice," he chuckled. "You must ain't heard the part when I told you Doc been lookin' out for me ever since I been home from the joint."

Spook stepped on the gas. He let his window down for fresh

air to help calm his nerves. *This nigga don't have a clue*, he thought. *Fuck it!*

"Look, Tee. I'm about to put you up on somethin'. But after I do, I need you to follow my every step 'cause I can't afford for things to backfire."

"What? What you gon' put me up on that I don't already know?"

Spook ignored him. "Listen man," he said, "Doc, just admitted to my face that he had Tre bumped off by some dirty ass cops his father knows."

Tone was struck with alarm. "What?! You mean this Vick been in my grill all this time, and he the one? Oh, hell naw. I swear I'mma slump that bitch."

"Chill out," Spook interrupted. "Just chill. Don't even trip. We gone play our cards and get him clean without any casualties. You gotta think. That mark got police backing him. We have to be discreet with the whole demo fam. You understand?"

Tone bit his lip to suppress his anger and reluctantly agreed.

"Now, I'll hit you later so we can discuss the details; aight?"

Tone sighed, "Sure. Whatever you say."

Spook drove Tone back to his car and handed him a remote pad. "My Denali is on the corner of 65th and Damen right by Granny's crib. Don't worry 'bout my folks being on bullshit. They ain't on no gang bangin' or stickup time. So just pop the trunk, get the bag and put that remote alarm in there."

"I got you." Tone got out and jumped inside his ride. Then he headed down to Spook's stumping grounds. The thought of how his brother's killer had been under his nose for the past few months enraged him. *How the fuck am I gone merk this fool?* He pondered to himself.

Tone parked his car and hopped out, heading for the SUV. He popped the hatch and grabbed the bag. He then tossed the controller inside and jumped back into his vehicle. As soon as he heard his phone ring he answered.

"Yeah, whaddup?"

"Hey, sweetie. How are you today?"

"Not good," Tone replied, sounding down. But it was just a ploy. He knew Jennifer would be at him.

"What, you lost the game you told me about?" she asked concerned.

"Naw."

"Well, if you come meet me at the Drake, I promise to make it better. On top of that, my mouth been feeling a little naughty."

"I like the sound of that," Tone snickered. "Just be ready when I get there," he declared.

"Okay, sweetie. Hope you're ready to quench my thirst," she added in her sexiest voice.

"You know I am." Tone hung up. "Man, I'm 'bout to punish this white chick."

He headed out toward his stash house on 72nd and South Shore Dr.

Twenty minutes later, Tone exited the Dan Ryan via Roosevelt Road, making his way to the hotel parking lot. He dialed Jennifer's number. "What room are you in?"

"315 hun."

"I'm in the elevator, so have the door open."

"Okay. Bye-bye baby."

Tone exited the elevator and strolled down the hall. He soon found the room and stepped through the door. To his surprise Jennifer greeted him posted on her knees. Without hesitation she began to unzip his *DWC* jeans.

"Damn, baby!" Tone was awed by the way she snatched out his penis and shoved it into her mouth. He jerked when she began mumbling. He reached behind him and pushed the room door closed.

"Man, baby. Let me get on the bed," he managed to whisper. But she ignored his request as she continued going to work licking up and down his dick and simultaneously massaging his testicles.

She begged, "Give it to me sweetie. Give it to me now!" Jennifer pulled down his pants and gently circled the tip of his penis with her tongue.

Tone couldn't hold back any longer. When he burst his first nut, she swallowed every bit while vigorously sucking on him nonstop. His erection was stronger than ever.

"Damn, baby. Stop," Tone teased. Alicia never made him feel that way. He had never remembered oral sex feeling so good.

Jennifer licked and sucked around and around his tender dick's head. "You like that daddy?" she asked between rotations.

"Oh, yeahhh." Satisfying moans were all he could muster as a response.

When she saw that he was ready, she jumped up around his waist and gyrated her hips as Tone walked her over to the bed and laid her down.

When she begged for Tone to fuck her, he immediately threw her legs up to her ears and thrust himself inside of her. Strong and hard. He intended to make sure she walked with a limp after he was through.

"Ohhhh, daddy. Fuck me...uh huh. Fuck me. Fuck me!" she screamed, enjoying how he felt stroking her walls.

"Give it to me from the back!" She was insatiable and didn't miss a beat when he flipped her over while keeping his stiff member inserted inside her pink prize. She screamed out when his nine inches went deep, pounding her G-Spot.

"Yessss! Fuck me harder! Fuck me, daddy!" Jennifer began to experience multiple orgasms and the sight of ecstasy all over her face turned him on more.

Tone spread her ass cheeks, and started pounding even faster as he grew close to shooting off his second nut. When he felt her grip and release her pussy muscles around his dick, he couldn't help himself any longer, he exploded. Jennifer quickly turned and hungrily sucked him dry.

"Ohhhh, shit!" Tone moaned and fell over on his back; exhausted and satisfied. Her blowjob technique was the best he had ever experienced. Jennifer didn't know it, but he was stressing and her skills gave him a bit of comfort; but only momentarily.

Damn, this chump killed my brother. How the hell am I gonna get back at him? Tone was thought as Jennifer rode him cowboy style, swinging her hips in circular motion.

Tone snapped back, focusing on the situation at hand – fucking the shit out of the sex-crazed white girl working his dick.

"Yeah. Ride this dick baby! That's right. Ride the head," Tone cheered on, watching her shoulder-length, blonde hair shuffling all over her face.

Jennifer took charge as a woman who had never been fucked the way she wanted. She became even more aroused by her lover's words to her. She began bouncing up and down faster and faster on his shaft.

"This....huh....dick....is....is....huh good daddy! The best... I've ever...huh...had...Oh, my god!!!"

"You like it; hun?" Tone asked.

"Yes!"

"Turn over and arch your back," he instructed her.

Jennifer desperately submitted, hiking her ass in the air. She didn't expect him to try driving his erect penis into her anal hole, but that is exactly what he did.

"Ohh...ohh...owww!" she screamed. "Daddy, it hurts. Take it out please! Take it out!"

"Just relax baby." Tone began rubbing her clit while slowly stroking her ass hole. She was more open and receptive to allowing him to do what she knew he wanted to do.

"Ohhh, daddy. Ah, ha...Give it to me," she moaned, feeling herself getting into the motion. But suddenly Tone switched into over drive and began wildly banging her insides.

"Stop! Pleeeze daddy. Please stop!!"

Tone blacked out. He could no longer hear her pleas as he did what he came to do, which was punish the hoe. She continued screaming until she felt herself beginning to climax.

"I'm cumming...Yes daddy. Bang this ass. It's yours! It's yours! Bang...it...ba...by!!!"

Tone was so caught up in the frenzy of their fucking that he was victim of the trance of the biggest nut he ever had. When the condom was completely filled, he pulled out and rolled on his side. He was exhausted.

"This broad can go," he mumbled, "and I haven't even put my tongue game down." He turned to her and asked, "You like that?"

Jennifer caught her breath. "I loved it, daddy," she replied, watching his cheeks as he headed toward the bathroom. "I love you," she blurted, not realizing she had just disclosed her true feelings.

Tone chuckled. "You just love my doggy style." He stepped through the door and closed it. He stared into the mirror. *How she gon' love me after the first time? This bitch is trippin'*, he thought.

CHAPTER 13

"I'm pulling in now," Bullock said into his phone as he slowly drove into a darkened lot stacked with truck trailers. He timed the grayish steel garage door, which seemed to automatically open and rolled into the vacant *United Postal Factory*. He was pleased to see the black Escalade parked diagonally in the middle.

"Hey, hey, Unc." Josh said proudly greeting him as he exited his trunk. "What kinds of problems do you — I mean — 'we' have now?" he asked just as Bullock jumped out of his squad car. Josh loved the fact that his so-called gangster cop uncle, could finally feel the wrath just as he had all his life growing up in a poverty-stricken neighborhood. He smirked.

Bullock snapped, "Listen punk! I don't have time for your shit right now. The Feds are closing in on me; which means they'll be coming for you also. That is if we don't tie up these loose ends."

Josh squared up. "Damn, Unc! Fuckin' with you and those cadets finally got all of our asses in a slinger. Now we about to get snatched by those people. Tell me, with yo' smart ass, how we gon' duck the Feds; huh? Just tell me that!" Josh was infuriated as he began pacing back and forth.

"Look lil' muthafucka. I got word before it got started all the way. Now, if we act fast, we can still control the situation."

"I hear you talking," Josh replied. He wasn't feeling the whole scenario.

"You can also keep whatever money and merch that's left around for your services. As a bonus, you can get back at Kruger and them for all the hassles over the years; especially for him killing that boy, Munch, you were troubled about."

Josh was now intrigued. "Oh, yeah? I might like what you have to say after all, so, keep talking."

Bullock went deeper in detail. "We have to move quickly, silently and clean 'cause Kruger, Ortiz, and Canal have to go. They know too much, and I'm not about to sit around tryna figure out who's loyal and who's not."

"What about that chick you were fucking?" Josh asked, inquiring about Ms. Singleton. He had witnessed his uncle bring her through granny's house on special occasions. Bullock said she was a coworker. But Josh knew better; especially after seeing the two creep off into the bathroom for a quickie once.

"Did I say her?" Bullock retorted.

"Naw, man. But she was always present. Don't you think the Feds will try to get at her?"

"Don't worry. Victoria's straight. Trust me. I talked to her today and she's left town. That's how I found out about everything; what we're looking for, and who they've talked to already. So far it's only Canal and Ortiz's bitch ass.

Now this is how it's going to work. I need you to gather up a few of your guys who aren't scared and who will keep their mouth shut if they get knocked. In the meantime, I'm gonna call Ortiz and have him get Kruger and Canal together so they can bring you the product they got off the lick.

"I'll call you to let you know what car they'll be in, and from what direction they'll be traveling. That way, you can have your team ready to intercept. But ya'll have to kill everything in sight. We can't afford no mess ups J.B., do you understand?"

"Yeah, Unc." Josh could tell it was going to be a blood bath. "I'll oversee the operation myself, and call you once it's over; aight?" He knew that it was time for Solo to come through on what they had discussed.

Bullock jumped back into his squad car. "Hit me later, Josh." He pulled off and dialed the number to the station. Ortiz picked up right away.

"Hey, Ortiz. Just the man I wanna speak to. I need you to call in Kruger and Canal. I need the three of you in my office, pronto! I'll be there in five minutes."

"Ten-four, Captain."

Moments later Bullock entered his office thinking about all the events that had taken place. He could remember ten years back when he actually used to serve and protect. There was great influence through his eloquence and achievements. But now, the Federal Government was out to ruin everything he worked hard for, including the bust they made on "Fly Guy Bradley." That was the case that elevated him to the position he currently held. Nevertheless, looking back on it all, he strongly resented his interference with helping the government in any type of way.

Three knocks on the opposite side of his office door snapped him out of his train of thought. When Ortiz, Kruger, and Canal walked in, he decided to give them the benefit of the doubt. Bullock smiled.

"Anything new under the sun you all want to tell ol' Captain Bullock?"

"No sir, Cap," replied Ortiz. "Everything's still everything." He looked to Kruger and Canal.

"Yep. Nothing new with me," said Canal.

Kruger shrugged his shoulders. "Different day, same shit."

Bullock nodded, "Alright anyway, it's time for J to pop off that stuff you all picked up from the building."

"Excuse me Cap..."

"What is it Ortiz?"

"Are you telling me that you also want me out in the field?"

"Yes. I'm sure Turner could handle things down in the evidence department." Bullock knew that Ortiz would be leery about working the streets; especially since he had been on the inside for thirteen years. "Also," he continued, "you've been making the same share as my officers who've been risking their lives to make things right for you and your family. So, it shouldn't be a problem with you assisting the home team this one time I ask you." He thought he'd play on the debt Ortiz owed to the rest of the men.

"I...I see sir." Ortiz uttered, biting the bait.

Not wanting to waste time, Bullock ordered, "Ya'll three pull it out and be careful on the way."

"We're always careful Cap," Kruger replied.

Canal wondered, "So Cap, where are we meeting them?"

"Over by the lagoon at the Golden Dame. He'll go from there... Here," he said tossing his keys. "Take my truck."

"Sure Cap." Kruger caught them midair. "Alright boys, let's get moving!"

After the three left, Bullock called his nephew. "They're on their way."

"Aight." Josh hung up and hit his people on the walkie-talkie. "Yo', ya'll in place?"

"Yeah," Solo replied.

"Good. You should be able to see a blue police truck coming your way in about three minutes."

"I got you lil' bro, over." Solo clicked off the transmitter and posted up.

Once outside, Kruger told Canal to drive. They pulled off towards Sacramento to jump on the expressway.

"Man, how much do you think we're going to check off these bricks Mike?" Ortiz asked from the backseat.

"Maybe between five to six hundred stacks. Ya'll know the Captain's punk ass nephew is also getting a piece of the mon..."

Boom!!! The impact from a black dodge pick-up truck caught everyone by surprise; ramming them on the edge of the ramp.

Kruger was shook. He blinked a few times, trying to focus. "Is everyone cool?"

"Yeah." Ortiz lifted out of his seat.

"I...I think I'm good too." Canal replied rubbing the back of his neck.

Kruger growled. "I'mma beat that stupid son of a bitch's ass!" He opened the door. Just as he stepped out, a champagne colored Cadillac STS pulled up from nowhere and began firing. Two of the bullets caught Kruger in his shoulder; propelling him back into the truck.

A man dressed in black rushed from the Sedan, raising and Aiminga M-16 and commenced to firing multiple shots. It was obvious he was trying to mutilate whoever was inside as he emptied ammo into the truck; but his destruction ended abruptly when he heard the sounds of sirens quickly approaching. He jumped back into the Cadillac and sped off.

Kruger screamed, "Canal! Ortiz!"

Miraculously, both officers stepped from the truck dusting shattered glass and interior particles from their clothing while rushing to Krueger's aid.

Ortiz freaked out when he saw his fellow man covered with blood. "Mike! Are you okay?!"

Kruger grunted, "Yeah, asshole! It's only a hit to my shoulder. I'm good, but you and Canal need to get the dope and get the hell outta here," he demanded, holding on to his wound.

They did as they were told and fled the scene in the same bullet-ridden truck, leaving Kruger stretched out on the side of the street.

Canal was hysterical, "Dammit, Ortiz! What the fuck was that all about?"

"I don't know Ron! Phone the Captain and let him know somebody tried to kill us, and we're on our way to dump his truck and stash the dope somewhere until we figure out the next move."

"Well, first we can take the narcotics to my house. Then we'll burn this truck out south somewhere too."

The paramedics rolled Detective Kruger on a stretcher through the entrance of the hospital emergency unit at *Bethany Memorial*. There were other officers on the scene towering over him asking questions.

"Sir, I'm officer Borat. I'm from the precinct on Clark and Division. I understand that you were just assaulted. Can you give me a brief description of the individual or individuals responsible? Any attempt to kill a police officer makes the perpetrators a total threat to the community and society at large."

Kruger snatched the oxygen mask from his face. "Look, I already told your other partners, I didn't see who the fuck did this to me. The bastard was dressed in all black and was wearing a damn ski mask." Kruger groaned out in agonizing pain just as the staff wheeled him into the operating room.

*****

Captain Bullock was enraged to find out the hit he planned was a failure. Kruger was still alive with only a shoulder wound. He wasn't sure about the others until they called.

"Hey Cap. It's me Canal."

Bullock pressed the receiver to his mouth, "Where the hell are you and Ortiz?"

"We came to my house 'til you give us further instruction; sir."

"So, what the fuck went down?" Bullock asked aggressively. But he remembered that the phones could possibly be tapped. "Never mind, I'll be over there once I check on my officer at Bethany and take a report. So stay put. Ya got that?"

"Yes, sir." Canal hung up.

When Bullock made it to the hospital he didn't shoot straight to the trauma unit. Instead, he stopped in the lobby to make a call on the pay phone.

"Yo', whaddup!!!"

"Why are those sons of bitches still alive?! I thought you were going to personally supervise this one?"

"I did, but some patrol car started coming before we finished," Josh explained.

"I see, but we still have to finish this. If not, they'll be at your ass real soon. Kruger's in surgery getting those bullets removed from his shoulder. Get some guys together and be ready once he's released from Bethany."

"Got you." Josh hung up, and turned to Solo. "We 'bout to finish this muthafucka off! Let's go."

Ten minutes later Josh pulled up on the side of the hospital and sent one of his sisters inside to see if Kruger had been released. When she realized there was a male receptionist she began throwing her hips. She squinted her eyes at his name tag.

"Uh... Mr. Jones is it?" she asked seductively licking her lips.

The young African American instantly responded at the sound

of her voice. "Yes, ma'am. How can I help you?" he asked, wondering what was behind her tight-fitting *Baby Phat* jeans.

"Well, I was one of the witnesses to the attack of an officer that happened earlier today, and I saw the car that fled the scene. Some other officers tried questioning me, but I declined to answer anything. I'd rather speak to the officer himself who was wounded."

"Say no more sweetheart. I'm aware of the situation already. As a matter of fact, he should be coming out any minute. I think he just called a cab."

"Thank you so much." She batted her eyelids, turned and walked away.

The receptionist smiled as he gawked at her bootylicious figure.

Josh's sister jumped into the backseat of the truck." He should be out here any minute. They say he called a cab not too long ago."

"Perfect, Niecy baby." Josh stared intensively at the emergency exit. A few minutes later he spotted the target coming out with his left arm in a sling. He grabbed the walkie-talking and clicked it.

"Ya'll peepin' the mark?"

"It's on…" Solo stated. "Here he comes Lotti G."

Kruger hopped into his cab. "31st and 15th Avenue," he told the driver. As the cab began to roll, he leaned into the backseat and sighed, "What a day." Then he pulled out a *Newport* cigarette and lit it.

The driver stared into the rearview mirror when he smelled the burning tobacco. "There's no smoking in my…"

Boom!!! He was cut off midsentence by one hell of an impact. The cab jerked forward after being hit from the blindside.

For Kruger, it was a moment of déjà vu. "Fuck! Not again," he snapped, shaking his head to regain his composure. The door near Kruger was snatched open by another male dressed in black, masked up and wearing leather gloves. Kruger screamed as he was snatched from the cab.

"What the fuck you want with me? I'm the police. I'm – the – Po – lice!!"

Without skipping a beat, he was thrown into the back of a van and punched in the mouth. "Shut the fuck up! This is about revenge; muthafucka."

Kruger grunted in agony, "But I'm the..." his words were cut short by another fist to the mouth.

"I don't give a fuck if you are the President of the United States," Solo said from the front seat.

"Bitch! Yo' badge ain't shit but a metal of dishonor. June, slap duct tape on that hoe."

June and Lotti Go strapped Kruger up like a Christmas gift as the van made a left turn into the Sally Port factory. Solo instructed them to strip the cop butt naked and strap him to the chair.

Josh answered his cell after the first ring. "Hello."

"This is Solo. Slide down on us now."

"Bet 'em up!" Josh hung up and pulled out of the polish stand lot in his grape Lexus 470 with the Snypaz blasting through the speakers.

"Searchin', hurtin' fo' certain, lookin' fo' a come up with da quick fast..."

Josh quickly turned the music down to answer his phone again, "Yo'!"

"I see ya'll got right on it."

"I told you I would," Josh replied, hanging up in his uncle's ear. He honked his horn as he pulled up to the factory. The garage door automatically elevated allowing him to zoom right in.

Josh hopped out, dressed in all black from head to toe. "Well, well, well..." he crooned, watching as Solo administered thin slashes across Kruger's face with a razor blade. "Look at what we got here."

Kruger's eyes widened with glee. "Oh my God J! Please...tell these goons I'm cool. Please! They got my arm tied and I just got out of surgery. Please... make 'em stop. Make 'em stop and I'll forget about all of this."

"Oh, really? Well, I don't think you're in any position to make any kind of negotiations," Josh chuckled.

Solo nonchalantly stepped up and poured half a bottle of rubbing alcohol over Kruger's shredded face.

"Uhhh! Ahhh! Ahhh! Oh my God!....You...you sons of bitches. I swear when I get..." Phoomp! June's foot connected to Kruger's mouth with such force before he could even finish his statement.

"JB, Please!" he screamed, spitting a glob of blood. "Stop them!

I'm sorry about everything…God as my witness. I'm through if you let me go. I'mma pack my shit and leave town. I swear!"

"Shhhh…," Josh callously responded, "'Sorry' didn't do the things you did, Kruger. Now it's time for you to pay the piper, my man. But how you pay is totally up to you. Hard or easy, your call. Just tell me you've got the money and we'll let you go."

"I'm not telling you shit!"

"Ohhh. So I see you want this to go the hard way; huh? Okay, then…" Josh snapped his fingers, motioning to June. He stepped up to Kruger, removing his ski mask and gave the victim a hard stare.

Josh snickered. "You remember my man June don't you? Take a good look at him. It was about a month ago when you hit him on the block for all he had and killed his cousin in cold blood."

Kruger's squinted eyes widened with terror as he suddenly recognized the one holding the 2x4 in his hand. "Arghh!!" he bellowed after receiving a hard whack against his injured shoulder. He surrendered.

"J! Okay, man. Okayyy! I don't have any money…ahhh… that's…that's why I've been prowling," Kruger replied.

Josh wasn't buying it, so he signaled June to strike again.

"Ahhhh shit!!! Please, J!!!" Kruger screamed. I'm sorry to you, him, the whole fuckin' world. Just pleeease…stop it!" he begged for mercy, breathing hoarsely from dehydration. "Please. Just give me something to drink and I'll tell you everything."

Solo pulled Kruger's head back, while June poured a cup full of dog feces and urine down his parched throat. Kruger vomited instantly.

"Muthafuckas!!!"

"I got yo' muthafuckas," Solo replied, throwing more alcohol into Kruger's face. He chuckled like a mad man, and then tossed a lit match on him. Kruger squalled like a pig as he tried shaking his head free from the flames.

Kruger violently coughed after being doused with several buckets of water. "Fuck you!" he finally managed to blurt out; catching his breath.

"No, fuck you!!!" Josh turned Kruger over in the chair snatched his pants down. Kruger was now face down on the ground with his ass in the air still strapped to the chair. Solo grabbed a broom stick and plugged it straight through the bottom of the chair, penetrating Kruger's rectum.

"Owwwww! Shit! Mutherfuckerrrsss!!! Why? Why?! Why are you doing this J?!! Stop! Please stop!"

"Stop?! You want me to stop? Well, where's my money?" Josh demanded towering over him.

Kruger suffered excruciating pain. He knew they weren't going to let him live. Not after what they had already done; especially not after all he had done to cause their act of retaliation. He used his last nerve to force a smile upon his face.

"Suck my dick; bitch," he said with a slight chuckle.

Solo instantly fired two bullets into Kruger's skull from his .45 Desert Eagle.

Josh shook his head. "Clean this shit up and dump him on Central." He got into his truck and left the factory.

*****

"Good morning. This is Kathy Connor. I'm here with the latest Channel 7 news. We're here live at the scene where Detective Michael T. Kruger was found this morning with two bullet holes in his head;, a severely burned face; and what appears to be a broken broom or mop handle hanging from his rectum. This all occurred shortly after he had been released from *Bethany Memorial Hospital*, following surgery to remove two bullets from his shoulder after an earlier gun battle yesterday. Witnesses say he was snatched from a *Yellow Cab* taxi by two assailants, dressed in all black, who forced the detective into the back of an awaiting van which sped away.

There are no leads on the suspects, and no further details in this case right now as police are diligently searching to bring justice to one of their own. This is Kathy Connor, coming at you live, from CBS Channel 7."

Bullock dropped his spoon in disbelief. What he saw on his kitchen television set blew him away. He had to force his feet to move in order to answer the phone. "Captain Bullock here…"

"Sir, have you seen the news?!" Canal sounded frantic.

"Yeah…"

"They killed Mike sir. Those sons of bitches killed him," Canal cried.

"Calm down. I'm headed to the crime scene right now to see what happened. Just stay with your family. I'll call you later, understand?"

Canal sniffed, "Yes, sir…"

"Good. Stay by the phone." Bullock hung up and headed out the door. His cell phone began buzzing in his pocket. He checked the caller ID then headed straight to the pay phones in the front lobby of his building.

Josh answered as soon as he heard his cell phone going off, "Who this?"

"It's me, Theo."

"Ay Unc. Did you see the news?"

"Yeah. But didn't I tell you to keep it clean muthafucka!"

Josh frowned. "Wait a minute Unc. You've been relieved of duty because of me! I'm calling the shots now. Just enjoy yo' bitch and whatever money you have 'cause it's a wrap for you…you got that Unc? Your services are no longer needed. Thank you and have a blessed day!" Josh slammed the phone.

Bullock was stunned. "I know this lil' punk ass boy didn't just tell me no shit like that!"

Twenty minutes later when Bullock walked into work, the DEA and IA were there to greet him. An African America woman with short dreads stepped forward.

"Good morning Captain. You look like you've seen a ghost."

Bullock quickly regained his composure. "Oh, a ghost?" He smiled. "No, not at all. I just didn't expect to see you guys. How can I be of service to you?"

"We're here to discuss what happed to Detective Kruger. Did he have any enemies that you knew of, sir?"

Bullock smirked. "Enemies? He was a cop… of course he had enemies," he replied casually strutting towards the office.

A white male DEA agent cut in, flashing his badge. "Well, can you think of any in particular?"

"No, I can't. Look, do you think that you all could come back at another time. I'm not feeling myself after this tragedy." He stated madly with tears running down his face. Then he slammed his door in their faces.

He thought to himself, *what have I gotten myself into? The media is all over the place as well as the FBI and IA. Kruger's dead, Vicky's gone, and Canal and Ortiz are marked. What am I going to do now?*

Bullock felt like the world was caving in on him. "Lord knows I can't keep being the Captain, especially after these other two fuckers get whacked," he sighed. "Well, Theo, it's time to stop beating around the bush." Bullock sat up in his chair at his computer and began typing his resignation.

When he finished punching the last strokes on his keyboard, he stood up and exited the door. He was bombarded by the media, but he pushed straight through the crowd in search of the Chief.

CHAPTER 14

Tone rolled over and hit the snooze button as soon as he heard the alarm clock going off. He turned on his back to catch a few extra winks.

"Rise and shine, big daddy," Alicia whispered into his ear.

"Huh? What time is it Boo?"

"It's the same time you told me to set the clock for; 9:52 a.m."

"Aight," he mumbled, still drowsy. He soon gained full consciousness after feeling the warmth of her mouth wrapped around his manhood.

She periodically stopped between sucks asking, "You like that?"

"Hell yeah!" Tone responded, barely able to get the words out. With his eyes tightly closed, he continued to enjoy the pleasure for as long as it lasted. "Now, that's an alarm clock!"

Alicia took one last lick and sat up on the bed next to Tone.

"Why'd you stop Baby?"

Alicia smirked, "I just wanted to get you up Babe."

"Aw hell naw! Bring yo' ass over here and finish the job."

"No, no, no! I have to leave for work, and you need to get up so you can make your meeting by 10:30 a.m. like you told me."

"Yeah, aight," Tone said, tossing the sheets back. "It's cool. I'll just punish that ass later; so make sure you take the kids by yo' mom's crib."

Alicia flirtatiously smiled, "Yeah, whatever!"

Tone jumped out of bed and headed for the bathroom. Right before getting in the shower he called Spook to make sure they were still on. With plans confirmed, he jumped into the shower, dried off and sprayed on his *Jean Paul* cologne. Afterwards, he threw on a *Presidential* sweater and jeans and a pair of white *Air Force Ones*. *Perfection*, he thought as he looked at himself in the mirror.

When he stepped from the bathroom Alicia was sitting on the couch, watching *Good Morning America*. The boys were all dressed and ready to head out.

"What up baby?"

"Nothin'," she answered nonchalantly.

Tone shook his head. *She must be coming on her period*, he thought. "Dion…Mario…go and put on yo' coats man!" he told the boys.

Little Dion looked up. "Tone, are you still gone buy me the *Power Ranger* game for my *Play Station*?"

"Uh-uh," Mario interjected. "It ain't just yo'game. That's both our *Play Station*."

Tone smiled at the boys, wishing he had a brother to argue with when he was growing up himself. He laughed, "Ya'll chill out. I'm takin' both of you to *Toys R'Us* after school."

"Yay!" The boys cheered in unison.

"And Mario is right, Dion. The game is both of you all's. Now, grab your coats, so we can get outta here."

"I told you!" Mario teased.

"Shut up, big head!" Dion shot back disappointed.

Dion ran off toward their bedroom. As soon as the boys were out the picture Alica spoke what was on her mind. "Tone, you said once you got certain things out the way you were done. I mean we got everything we need and more. Let's just move out and start a business in another state. For real, baby, 'cause I worry about you a lot – day in and day out," she sobbed. "Let's just leave…please!"

"Calm down, baby." Tone said as he stepped closer to her. He wiped her tears from the corner of her eyes with his thumbs. "I promise after this last move, it's over Boo. You, me, and the kids' gon' move down to Texas."

He put his arm around her. "I'mma let Robby take over everything here, of course with my dad still overseeing it all. Then we can carry on with our lives; okay baby?" He embraced her with a reassuring hug.

Alicia laid her head against his chest. "Yeah, daddy."

"Good. Now get up and take yourself to work with yo' gorgeous ass. Oh, and remember tonight too."

"Mmm hmmm," she replied, curling up her lip. "Come on boys. Let's go!"

Thirty minutes later Tone pulled up in front of Spook's shop, wondering how to tell him the next hit would be his last run. He wondered if he should even tell him at all. He hopped out of his car and stepped through the door.

"What up Joe!" he said speaking to a few of the barbers. "Ralph, I'll see you tomorrow 'round noon."

"No doubt. I'mma get you right too." Ralph bragged as Tone headed for the office in the back.

As soon as Spook heard the tapping at his door he yelled, "Get in here man!" He and Tone greeted one another with firm handshakes and a hug. Spook backed away.

"I knew it was you. I saw you on camera. Here," he said as he handed Tone the alarm. "The car is parked down the street."

"Cool." Tone turned and walked out the door.

The time was 6:35 p.m. and it was warmer than usual for an evening in March. Doc was waiting on the light to change at 59th and Western in his brand new purple Dodge Plymouth Prowler. The top was down; the heat was turned on low as he puffed away on a Cuban cigar.

"It's just me against the world," he mumbled wondering why he hadn't heard from his chief customer Tone. He vowed to never let another man think he was in need of him. Besides, he didn't need anything ruining his evening. And that's exactly what was going to occur if Tone happened to say something slick in response to his absence.

Doc sparked up a blunt as he headed down to *Extremes* to play boss with a few strippers. He steered steadily long while reciting the lyrics to Naz's, "The Life Is Mine." His car speakers pounded as he eased onto the Dan Ryan expressway, planning to have a good time. His Prowler's racing engine under the hood got him to the club in ten minutes flat. He eased up to the curb.

"Man, that bitch is nice," an older slim valet jocked as Doc pulled up.

"Yeah, I know," Doc spoke confidently as he proudly stepped from his ride. He entered the club and strolled straight to the bar.

"Ay, yo'," he said motioning to the bartender, "All the drinks are on me tonight," he told her. "And send all the top hoes over to my table."

The bartender's eyes lit up like the 4th of July when she was tipped with a hundred dollar bill. She nodded her head and went straight into action.

As Doc sat in the VIP section, he was approached by two stallions. One wore a neon green thong with glittery stars taped over her nipples. The other was dressed in a nurse's outfit and six inch *Prada* heels.

Doc smiled, "Just what the doctor ordered," he said, rocking hypnotically to the sound of R. Kelly's, "Ghetto Queen."

Both women smirked at him and began popping and rolling their asses in Doc's face.

Suddenly the song switched to Juvenile's, "I Got That Fire." The 'nurse' told her partner to give him a personal lap dance so she could take her turn on stage.

"What's ya'll names?" Doc asked as his slid a $50 bill into her crotch.

"Pleasure," she replied. She pointed to her partner, "And that's Pain," she said grinding her nakedness in his lap. It was as though Doc's hardness was trying to bust through his pants. It caught Pleasure's attention. She looked back.

"Damn, baby," she remarked, "I see you twirkin' real good under there." She straddled him even harder, provoking him to want a piece of her badly.

Doc opened his zipper and poked out his rock hard penis. "Do you mind?"

"Only if you got two bills and a condom…" she inclined,

stroking his member as she wobbled her ass in perfect harmony with the music. "But we have to be finished before Pain comes back."

"Not a problem," he casually stated, slipping on a magnum.

Pleasure wasted no time pulling her G-string to the side. She jumped on him rodeo style. She mounted his stiffness nice and slow, squeezing every inch of him up her tight sugar walls. She rolled and flexed her vaginal muscles while simultaneously bouncing up and down; and like clockwork, Doc ejaculated.

"Aw sh-sh-shit!!!" he bellowed.

When Pleasure felt his dick soften she rose off of him, removed the condom, and sucked him clean. In doing so, she felt his next erection. She knew she couldn't finish what she started so she stopped.

"Mmm," she uttered, smacking her lips. "I'm...I mean me and my sister are available tonight...if you think you can handle a little Pleasure and Pain." Pleasure stood and placed the condom in a napkin before walking off.

Doc noticed that the 'nurse' was stepping off the stage. He smiled and thought, "This might turn out to be a nice night." He signaled for the waitress.

"Bring me another bottle of Cris and tell Pain to come and give me a dance." After having a small portion of Pleasure, he was inquisitive as to how her partner's head game was, especially since she had the nicer pair of lips.

Moments later Pain strutted up on his booth in a crimson thong, garter belt, bra, and a pair of *Versace* whip snake sandals. She stopped directly in front of him and started dancing in perfect sync to Donell Jones', "What's up."

She had Doc in awe, staring at her with his mouth wide open as she slowly gyrated her pelvis and removed her bra. He couldn't hold his composure any longer.

"Damn, baby! I got two buck fo' some head and later I'mma hit you and Pleasure up with a lil' somethin' somethin' for a lil' mo' action."

"I'm sorry, but I ain't doin' nothing in this place. That's against policy," she replied.

"Man, fuck that shorty. Ya friend just did that damn thang. So what's up wit' you?" he asked aggressively.

Pain snapped, "I don't give a fuck what she did. I'm not her! As a matter of fact this dance is over." She tossed his money in his face and turned to exit the booth.

Doc quickly snatched her up by the arm. "I'm not through with you," he ordered. "I'll give you three then for some of that sassy mouth of yours. Now quit playin' hard-to-get hoe!"

Pain's eyes bucked. "Hoe?! Oh, yeah! I got yo' hoe!" She picked up his glass and threw the liquor all over him.

"Stupid bitch!!" Doc raised his hand to slap her, but a bouncer appeared out of nowhere and grabbed him just in time.

"Is there a problem Ms. Pain?" he asked squeezing Doc's wrist.

She looked at Doc and smirked. "Naw, Goob. Ole' boy just a little tipsy."

Doc blurted, "Hell, yeah, it's a problem. I want that bitch kicked outta here for throwin' liquor in my face with her stupid ass!"

"Stop it with the names sir. Obviously, she had a reason. So if anyone will be leaving, it's gonna be you; understand?"

"Naw, I don't understand!"

Pleasure could plainly see that it was about to get ugly, so she quickly dialed up Doc's people.

"Hello."

"Hey Rob. It's Pleasure. I think you and yo' guys need to come up here and get Doc before security beats the hell out of him."

"What?!"

"Yeah. He's drunk as a skunk, tryin' to fight my girl Pain, and whoever else gets in the way. Hell, this nigga didn't even realize I was the same bitch that fucked him at Stevey party! Thats how us women know all pussy aint the same."

"Aight, Pleasure. Hold on. We'll be there in a minute. Just tell security to relax."

"Okay, but you better hurry."

"Where yo' mutha fuckin' boss?!" Doc yelled with hostility. "I want all ya'll outta here!" he screamed.

Pleasure stepped up and told security that someone was coming to get him.

"So, just turn the music up louder, take Pain somewhere else, and let him finish bumpin' his gums…"

*****

"Man, who was that? Tone asked as he and Robby headed to the car.

"That's Pleasure."

"What that hoe want you to bust her down or somethin'?"

"Naw, man. She said Doc is up there trippin on Pain and security."

"Oh, yeah?" Tone responded smoothly. "Man, let that nigga get fucked up then. He need it," he said coldly.

Robby frowned, "What you talkin' 'bout? That's our man."

"That nigga ain't shit to us no more Robby. Straight up!" Tone sighed. "Man homie, I ain't been totally honest with you lately but Tre was my brother."

"What!"

"Yeah, man. I recently found out that Doc had his pops and 'em take Tre out just so he could get on. His pops is the Sergeant for the 7th District police station."

"What!" Robby couldn't believe his ears. "Nigga, you trippin' right?"

"Naw, nigga. I'mma explain everything a lil' later, but let's go and scoop up Doc right now." Tone had a change of heart. "It just dawned on me how I'm gonna get back at him for whackin' my brother. Don't repeat this conversation Robby. You got that?"

"Yeah. But you gotta holla at me later."

After they arrived at the club, Tone went to find Pain while Robby checked on Doc.

Doc's bloodshot red eyes widened with joy. "Ay, Rob. What up, Chali!" he screamed excitedly. "Waiter, bring us six doubles of *Remy VSOP*," he slurred.

"Doc, how long you been in here?" Robby asked.

"'Bout two hours Joe. And I almost had to whoop one of these snobby ass hoes and security. Lucky fo' them they backed down. But what about you Moe? What you doin' way out here?"

"Aw me and Tone was just tryin' to get us some air tonight. That's all." Robby lied not wanting him to get the misconception that they were there to baby sit a grown man.

"Oh, yeah? Tone with you too?" Doc glanced at Robby's shoulder. "Where that nigga at? I've been meanin' to talk to that mister."

"He went straight to the bathroom when we came in. He'll probably be out in a minute."

"Yes, sirrrr! 17s in the front, 20s on the back; it's off the chain baby boy," he bragged as he laughed.

"Hey, Tone." A female voice called out.

He turned to see Pain standing in the dressing room doorway, wearing a skin tight body suit. He smiled. "What up shorty?"

"Naw, that's still, secretly big sis T." She said sarcastically. She remembered how Travis and Tone explained to her that it was best to keep their relation undercover.

"Cool out baby girl. What's in the dark will come to light soon enough."

Pain slyly smiled. "Yeah, yeah…I hear you. But what you doing here anyway?"

"I came to get Doc's drunk ass before ya'll hurt him in this piece."

"Yeah, you better! That nigga came at me like I was a bust-down broad. He had the nerve to try slapping me because I told him I wasn't gon' suck his dick up in here. I swear you all need to teach that nigga some manners…"

She sighed. "It's times like this that I wish my husband was still alive. I wouldn't even be doing this shit Tone." her voice broke. "I miss Tre so much," she cried, "Why? Why him, Tony? He never hurt nobody!"

Tone handed her a few napkins from the nearby table. "It's cool big sis. As a matter of fact, that's what I'm here to speak to you about. Come on. Let's go to my car to talk in private.

Doc spotted Tone and Pain heading toward the door. "Yo' Tone!" he yelled, "That bitch ain't on nothin'. She just a waste of time." He turned to Robby, "Yeah. That's the hoe I was finna smack down. To me she look like she got a good head and fuck game on her."

"Yes, Sir. I feel you Moe." Robby agreed as he gave his attention to the eye candies trotting across the stage dancing to Missy's, "Hot Boys."

"It's cold out here Tony. Why we couldn't talk inside?" Pain was shivering.

"Because I don't want anybody to hear this but you. I'd like to keep it that way until I'm able to tell you different; okay?"

"Yeah, Tone. Whatever you say. But what the hell you talkin' 'bout?"

Tone popped the locks on his Lincoln. "Get in and I'll tell you."

Pain snuggled into the leather seats. "Okay. Now, what's up T?

Tone stared hard into her eyes and said, "Candace, Doc is the stud who had Tre merked."

Pain's eyes almost popped from their sockets. "What! And that muthafucka all up in my grill?" She snatched off her earrings. "Just take care of our baby Tone, 'cause I'm finna go in there and kill that bitch!!!" She reached for the door but he grabbed her shoulder, stopping her in her in place.

"Whoa! Slow down baby girl. I got it all worked out. Still I'mma need your help and yo' friend's too if she up to it."

"That muthafucka murdered my husband Tone; and he's right in there!" she emphasized. "I promised my baby that whenever I found out who killed him – whether police or whoever – I got to do it now Tone! This might be my only chance."

Tone slammed his hands on the steering wheel. "Okay, then; fuck it! Go all out with yo' bad ass!" he shook his head. "Now all of a sudden you a killer over night?"

Pain was shaken. She burst into tears, jumped out the car and stormed her way into the club. Tone was right on her heels.

"Let me get off in here before she do some ole' stupid shit," he mumbled.

After they entered the club, he smacked her on the ass and told her to hurry up. Pain headed straight towards the dressing room, pouting like an immature child. Tone advanced to the VIP booth. He smiled.

"What up, Joe?" he said as he sat down.

"Me and Robby was parlaying, playboy." Doc still slurred his words. "I ain't heard from you in a few weeks. What? You don't fuck wit' us no mo'? he flared.

"Naw, big homie. Somebody been tryna set me up. I heard that detective stud Diesel was workin' and he laying on the block since the last time I got at you. I felt it was best to shut things down until that Vick disappeared," Tone lied.

"Which he did this past Monday; somewhere in the wild hundreds. That's why I'm ready now, straight up. Just get at Robby. He got the money. I'm finna dip those sistas who work here," Tone schemed. "Pleasure and Pain, as they like to be called. I'mma fuck they brains out and get some more of that excellent head out that hoe Pain. Shit, she just got down in the car, I can imagine being with her in a room where she can move around and maneuver. It's about to be on and popping!" he bragged, tossing his keys to Robby.

"Take my car home."

Doc caught the drool in the corner of his mouth. "I'm goin wit' you!" he exclaimed.

Tone shook his head, "Naw, not tonight Doc. I'm rollin' solo. But, she did tell me to tell you she apologizes about earlier. She also said she would like the opportunity to make it up to you whenever they finished with me. So here," Tone handed Doc a card. "That's her number. I'mma demonstrate with you in a couple of days." He turned to Robby.

"Robby gon' get that lil' paper to you sometime tomorrow. If you don't mind, my nigga," he tapped him on the arm.

"Right, right. I got that." Robby caught on, but was still somewhat puzzled. "I'mma park your whip in our driveway."

"That'll work," Tone replied, standing up to leave. "I'll see you later then. Peace."

Tone left the club, hoping Robby could keep a tight lip. But he thought, "Oh, well, only time will tell," then he hopped into the backseat of Pain's royal blue Cadillac truck.

"Hey, Pleasure, what you been up to lately?" he inquired.

"Nothing much Boo. But guess what? I talked to Sheree the other day and she enrolled in school and everything. She also told me to tell you that she misses the fuck out you and still loves you like crazy."

Tone raised a brow, "Oh, did she? Well, make sure you tell her I said, 'what's up too,' the next time ya'll talk." He sank deeper into the back seats and started to relax. He sighed and thought, "It's always a method to the madness. Patience is definitely the virtue."

CHAPTER 15

Canal had been distraught ever since Krueger's death and Bullock's departure. He knew he could have ended up just like his partner on that drastic night three weeks ago. But he believed that God kept him on earth for one purpose; to finish his duty as a father to his baby girl. With that understood, he was going to announce his final decision of the transformation he was making with the force as soon as he got to the station.

"Elizabeth!" Canal yelled impatiently from the front door of his attractive family home on 58th and Hamlin.

"Yes, daddy?" Canal's daughter replied as she stood in her bedroom mirror combing her curly ponytails.

"Hurry up honey or you're going to miss the assembly."

"Okay, dad. I'm on my way down now." Elizabeth threw her *Barbie* backpack over her shoulder and darted down the stairs.

Canal looked at his little girl, his eight-year-old angel, and realized that being the best father in the world to her was all that really mattered. Everything else was secondary.

Elizabeth looked up at her hero.

"Are you gonna stay for the assembly daddy?"

"No, baby. Daddy has to work, but mommy will meet you at the school. Alright darling?"

"Okay!" she happily replied as they stepped into Canal's forest green Volvo. Ferdinand Elementary was just up the street on Springfield so they arrived in a matter of seconds.

"Bye, daddy. I love you."

"I love you too cupcake," he kindly replied, kissing her on the forehead. He watched to make sure she entered through the front door safe and sound.

Elizabeth stepped into the auditorium and took a seat in the third row with her classmates. All the students had given their attention to a bald and chubby white police officer sitting up on the stage.

"Alright children. My name is Officer Friendly. How is everyone today?"

"Fine!!!" a few students screamed.

"I can't hear you! How's everyone doing?"

"Fine!!!" the audience roared in response.

"Okay, that's what I was waiting for. Now we're going to talk about some serious things…bad drugs; okay?" he said as he maneuvered around the stage. "How many of you know about drugs? The kind that are bad for you?"

The majority of the listeners raised their hands.

"Great. Now those bad drugs are things like marijuana, cocaine, harmful pills and heroin. These are the kind of drugs that hurt people in their bodies and their minds." He removed the first page of the easel on the stage which had three large pictures of different types of paraphernalia.

"Here they are," he said as he pointed and named each one. "This here is called cocaine. This is marijuana, this is heroin and these are a small variety of pills that you should not see in your medicine cabinets at home."

The officer focused mostly on the minority students. "Now, does anyone know the number to call, in case of an emergency, or with regards to some of the things I've shown you?"

"9-1-1!" One child exclaimed.

"That's right. 9-1-1 kids. Repeat after me, '9-1-1'!"

"9-1-1, 9-1-1, 9-1-1!!" everyone shouted in unison.

"What number will you call?" he asked again.

"9-1-1!!!" they screamed, applauding as Officer Friendly was exiting the stage. Hearing the children chanting 911 was music to his ears.

*****

"Sergeant Phillips," the clerk spoke into the phone, "Captain Bullock is here to see you."

"Good. Send him in Dorothy." Phillips cracked a smile at his old friend when he stopped through the door.

"Theo, how are you and what made you travel from out west way over here? I know you don't miss this place." he joked.

"Nah, I don't miss this rat hole one bit." Bullock looked around Phillips' office and closed the blinds. "In fact, that's the reason I'm here. I retired from the force today."

Phillips was shocked. "What?!" he exclaimed. "Why would you do a thing like that Theo? Are you crazy?"

Bullock sighed, "We already went over that Duke. I don't feel like doing it again."

"That whole 'we're getting hot' shit wasn't good enough for me Theo, and you know this."

"You're absolutely right about that Duke, but we're this close to being caught up," he said demonstrating the distance between his fingers. Look at what's happened thus far; Kruger's dead, the DEA has Ortiz cooperating and – not to mention – I haven't heard from him or Canal since the shooting. I strongly believe you should also hand in your papers."

"Theo, I think you're overreacting my friend. Even if that's all true, they can't tie us together. So, I don't have a thing to worry about old friend. There's no reason for me to resign. Plus, my pension doesn't kick in until I finish a couple more years. I'd be a damn fool to quit now without being compensated for my years of hard work on this force."

Bullock sensed his stubbornness. "Compensated? We already own a nice percentage of the new –construction condominiums in Brownsville area. That alone will keep us and our kids paid for quite some time. Listen to me Duke. Let's quit while you and I are ahead before things get screwed up any further."

Phillips propped his elbows on the desk and began twirling his thumbs. "I'm sorry ole' friend, but it's not gonna happen any time soon; at least for me. You're just paranoid. And even if you're right, there's no way they can link us together, so relax. Take a vacation and pray the FBI or the DEA doesn't pick yo' old ass up; alright? And, I suggest you give me some air for a few months; just in case you're being followed under an investigation."

Bullock shook his head, "Yeah, okay, old friend." Then he turned to leave. Just before he could exit, Phillips called out to him.

"Hey, Theo!"

"What is it Duke?" Bullock asked dryly as he stood in the doorway.

"Be careful...and enjoy your vacation."

"Yep. You be careful also."

*****

"Mommy, I'm going to be a police like daddy and Officer Friendly when I grow up." Elizabeth was excited. Ever since her mother picked her up from school she had been inquiring about her father and Officer Friendly's line of work.

Mrs. Canal pulled into their garage and stepped out of her most recent anniversary gift, a brand new white Toyota Camry. "That's great honey. I'll make sure to have your dad tell you a police story later. But for right now, go upstairs and get yourself ready for dinner."

"Okay Mom," Elizabeth dashed upstairs. On her way to her bedroom she spotted her father's gym bag lying next to the hallway closet. She tried moving it to put it away, but it was too heavy. She decided to take out the contents and put them up one by one.

"Daddy's gonna be so proud of me," she whispered to herself smiling upon seeing what was actually inside the gym bag. Instead of informing her mother first, she ran to the phone and dialed 9-1-1.

"Chicago Police....what's your emergency?" the male dispatcher answered.

"I need to talk with my dad. He's an officer."

"Alright, sweetie. Who is your dad?" he replied hesitantly.

Elizabeth took a deep breath, "His name is Ronald Canal."

"Oh, Officer Canal. Yeah, I know who he is. He's got some character," he said realizing the call wasn't a prank, "I can try and locate him for you, but if by any chance I don't reach him, would you like leave him a message?"

"Mmm hmmm," Elizabeth nodded. "You can let him know he left his bag of drugs at home, instead of taking them to work this morning."

The dispatcher removed the receiver from his face and stared at it. With a bewildered look he placed it back to his face. "Did you say, 'drugs' young lady?"

"Yes."

"Okay, how do you know what kind of drugs they are?" He asked in assumption that they could just be simply some prescription drugs and she's just an anxious kid.

"Because, Officer Friendly spoke to us today at school about drugs and showed us what they look like and Dad left some giant white cubes wrapped with the saran-wrap mommy uses to cover food after she cooks. And he also said that if we ever see any we should dial 9-1-1."

The dispatcher was convinced, "Well, it sounds like you are a very smart girl. Hold on for one moment okay honey?"

"Okay." Elizabeth patiently waited for her dad to pick up the line. She was surprised to hear a pleasant yet unfamiliar voice.

"Hello? Is this the young lady who called about her dad's bag?"

"Yes, I am."

"And what's your name?"

"Elizabeth Canal," She responded dignified.

"Aren't you smart," he chuckles. "Well, since we're exchanging names, you can call me Agent Tinley; okay? "

"Okay, Agent Tinley. Is my daddy coming to the phone?"

"He's not around right now, but we'll catch up with him soon. Listen Elizabeth, does your mommy know you called us?"

"No."

"Okay. Is she home?"

"Mmm hmm. She's downstairs and my daddy's at work with you guys catching bad people."

Agent Tinley chuckled. "Oh, that's great," he replied. "Elizabeth, I'm sending some more police over to get your daddy's bag of drugs; alright?"

"Yes, okay."

"Good. Now give your mommy the phone and thank you for dialing 9-1-1. We'll let your daddy know how much of a good girl you've been. I know he's going to be very proud of his daughter. Good bye honey."

"Bye-bye." Elizabeth said, smiling ear to ear. Then she raced the cordless phone to her mother like a baton. "Mommy, mommy, mommy!" She chanted rapidly.

"Yes, honey! What is it?" Mrs. Canal thought something was wrong.

"Telephone. It's 9-1-1."

Mrs. Canal looked baffled, "9-1-1? Did they call here?"

"No, mommy, I called them."

Mrs. Canal was stunned, "Oh, my god," she said snatching the phone. She placed it up to her ear, "Hello? I – I am terribly sorry that my daughter called you guys but…"

"Mom," Agent Tinley said, cutting her off, "Not a problem. Kids do it all the time, but here's the deal. Your daughter tells us that her father left his bag of drugs at home."

"Drugs?" Mrs. Canal wasn't buying it. "There must be some sort of mistake because…" Little Elizabeth ran to her interrupting her sentence.

"Mommy, look." she said standing there holding up a kilo of drugs.

"Oh, my gosh!" Mrs. Canal quickly hung up the phone. "Elizabeth, where did you get that from?" she nervously asked.

"Out of daddy's work bag with the rest of his stuff."

"Give me that honey, and go to your room; okay?"

Elizabeth walked upstairs feeling like she had done something wrong. Tears welled in her eyes as her proud moment was converted to guilt and shame. She ran to her room lamenting.

Mrs. Canal took the square package and placed it on the kitchen counter top. Then she tried calling her husband's cell. To her surprise, she heard his phone ringing in the dining room. She quickly walked to it, wondering why he left it. She stood there mystified as three rapid, loud knocks on her front door startled her back to reality.

"Open up… DEA!"

As she walked towards the door, her heart violently pounded.

Her hand reached for the knob. "May I help you?" she timidly asked upon opening the door.

"Go, go, go!!!" The agent ordered. Fourteen other officers rushed inside the house shoving Mrs. Canal to the side.

*****

Canal was just finishing up some paper work when he decided to head on over to the evidence dept. to speak to Ortiz and Turner.

"Hey Ron, what's up?" Turner greeted him.

"Did you all see old Captain Bullock tuck his tail and run?"

"He had to do that before IA came down on him Canal," Ortiz claimed from behind his desk. "Anyway, we don't need to be worrying about the Captain. We got to figure out how we're going to play this out; especially since we haven't got a clue as to who killed Kruger, or why. Besides, the Captain's gone so we don't have anyone to cover our bullshit. Now, do either of you have a suggestion?" Ortiz inquisitively stared at them, waiting for feedback.

Turner shrugged his shoulders. Canal said, "Maybe we should all relocate to separate precincts."

Turner snapped his fingers. "What about the narcotics?"

"Don't worry about that," Ortiz replied. "We can't afford to do another damn thing right now or anytime soon. The game at this point is definitely over boys. It's been extremely too much blood shed and…"

"Everybody down!" A man commanded before Ortiz could get out another word. The trio almost shit in their pants when a dozen FBI agents swarmed in on them.

"This is the DEA; Officer Ronald Canal, we have a warrant for your arrest!" Ordered the agent. "Take off your weapon and slide it out under the gate." He turned to his agents and told them to cuff Canal.

Canal was spooked, "Wha – Wha – What's this about?"

The leading agent stepped forward and said, "You have the right to remain silent. You have the…"

"What did I do?!" Canal responded. "Turner, call my lawyer," he yelled as he was being carried from the evidence room and up the stairs.

Ortiz confronted one of the last agents. "What did he do?"

"We found twenty-five kilos of narcotics at his home. If I were you fellas, I wouldn't disappear."

Turner frowned, "This has to be a mistake! I've known Officer Canal for fifteen years. He's never done a damn thing wrong Agent, Agent…"

"Tinley, Agent Tinley. Here's my card."

Turner took the card in his fingers, "But where are you all taking him?"

"The Dirkenson Building. Canal has to be interrogated, of course." Agent Thompson left their presence.

At 3:20 p.m. Canal sat petrified in a wooden chair at a table inside a small dimly lit room with two Federal Agents hovering over him. They humiliated him over and over again.

"Okay, Canal. Let's try this again, and you better answer us truthfully this time, or at least make it sound good. Where were you two evenings ago while your partner Kruger was being murdered?" Asked the first agent.

"I swear. I was home. I hadn't seen Kruger in six or seven days."

Agent one spontaneously smacked Canal upside the back of his head with a *Yellow Pages* phone book. "That's a lie!" Several officers say that they saw you, Ortiz and Kruger leaving the station together on the day he was killed! Now, help us Canal, and we'll help you."

"I already told you. I was at home dammit! Now get me my lawyer, you son of a bitch."

Both agents laughed, "You know better than that. We're the DEA. That lawyer shit doesn't work with us. You'll be better off representing yourself in our courts," Agent one assured. "You're facing a life sentence to death row if you don't cooperate with us now."

Canal rolled his eyes, "Yeah, right."

"Oh, so you think we're bullshitting ya? Look Canal, we went to your home and confiscated those twenty-five kilos of heroin. How do you explain that?"

Canal's heart dropped, but he played calm, "You all are framing me. I don't know nothing about no heroin."

"Oh, yeah?" The agent looked at his partner and nodded. He pulled a small tape recorder from his portfolio and sat it on the table in front of Canal. He pressed play.

"Okay, Elizabeth. What did you say?"

"My daddy left his bag of drugs at home."

Click.

"That's a smart little girl you got there Officer," The first agent said after his partner stopped the tape. "She and your wife must care a lot about you. Now, do you still wanna play dumb, or do you wanna play right? Help us and we'll do what we can to help you. We know you weren't acting alone in this. Tell us everything if you want a possible deal."

Canal hung his head low and burst into tears. "Can I get a cigarette?"

Agent one smiled, "Sure…"

Canal was traumatized, "What have I done?" he asked an invisible power.

He lit his *Camel Light* and took a long hard drag. Then he exhaled a giant cloud. "What's going to become of my family? I can't go to jail."

"That's totally your decision," the agent coldly stated. "But this is a one-time offer. Let us know now. What are you going to do Officer Canal?" he asked, staring directly into his eyes.

"Let me see my daughter and wife first. Then, I'll do whatever you want…please."

The agent sighed and nodded to his partner. "Bring 'em in." Minutes later Canal's family stormed through the door.

"Daddy, daddy, daddy," Elizabeth screamed, running up to her father. She leapt into his arms. "I called 9-1-1. Aren't you proud of me?" she asked gleefully.

"Yes, I am angel. I'm real proud of you," Canal replied sorrowfully. He forced a smile. "I love you."

"Ron," Mrs. Canal tearfully interjected, "What have you done?" She was hysterical.

"Nothing darling. This is just a big misunderstanding. Let me speak in private with these gentlemen and then I'll be right out."

Canal kissed her and waved as they stepped out.

The first agent jumped in,"Okay, Canal. My name is Agent Tinley and my partner is District Attorney, Mr. Tussman."

Tussman cleared his throat, "How are you Mr. Canal? You were not aware of the fact that we've been investigating your station for the past two years. Our main focus has been on Captain Bullock. Now, you and I both know that what he has is too much power for a negro to have; especially over the largest precinct in the city."

Canal thought fast, "No, Captain Bullock didn't have a clue. He even mentioned that if he ever got wind of any of his officers being involved with criminal activity he'd testify against them in a court of law. I just came into the picture a few days ago, after a minor raid on this spot off Kostner. Ortiz suggested that I should put the kilos up for a rainy day. Usually, he would log in the evidence before phoning Sergeant Phillips to pick up the load."

Agent Tinley pressed the recorder as Tussman grew all ears. "And what would he do with it?" he inquired.

"Well, first of all, he sent two officers by the names of Choice and Simmons. Then they'd drop the narcotics off to Phillip's son, Duke Jr., known as Doc on the streets."

"And what do you estimate they've made over the current time frame of their operation?" Tussman questioned.

"Hell, I'd say they probably made a few million."

"Would you get on the stand and testify to that? 'Cause that's the only way we can promise you immunity."

Canal looked Tussman square in his eyes. "As long as you relocate me and my family some place and safe."

Agent Tinley states very seriously, "Don't worry, that's already being arranged."

CHAPTER 16

"Bet I beat you for a buck," Doc challenged his boy Sleepy. They sat on Doc's leather couch playing *NBA Live* on his 52' plasma television. Smoking honey dipped blunts of dro and drinking *Coronas* added to their leisure.

Sleepy paused the game to clash his knuckles against Doc's. "Lets roll, nigga. You on, but no All Star teams or special players; alright?"

"You ain't said nothin' playboy. It's on!" Doc remarked competitively. He took a tote from the blunt and began uncontrollably coughing. "This that number Joe, straight up. Roll another one before we get started." He pushed the words through, trying to regain his composure from damn near choking to death. He got up from the couch and headed for the kitchen. "You want another *Corona*?"

"Yeah," Sleepy replied, removing the blunt from his mouth. He blew out the smoke. "In fact, you can bring me…"

Bang, bang, bang!!!

The beating on the front door stopped Sleepy mid-sentence. "Open up! DEA!!!" he heard. "Open the door, or we kickin' it down!!"

Bang!!! Bang!!!

Sleepy immediately dropped everything and ran into the

kitchen. "Joe! The police at the door!"

Doc didn't look worried. "Don't trip. Ain't nuttin' here. Just sit down and chill; alright?" Doc headed toward the door. When he opened it, to his surprise, agents poured into his place, bombarding him and knocking him to the floor.

"Are you Duke Phillips?" One of the agents asked with his weapon resting against the Doc's head.

"Yeah, why?" he replied with his hands up. "What the fuck's going on?!"

"We have a warrant for your arrest!" The agent informed him as he began reading him his Miranda Rights.

Doc screamed, "This is a mistake! My father is Sergeant Phillips of 7th District. Call him! Call him and he'll clear all this up!"

"…you have the right to an attorney. Anything you say…"

"Sir," another agent interrupted, "What about this guy?" he asked pointing to Sleepy.

"Just get his name and address and let him go."

The agent followed orders. Moments later, Sleepy was released.

"Hey Sleepy," Doc called out. "Call my pops and my lawyer."

Sleepy nodded as he left the house.

"that's not gonna do you justice punk. We have your daddy in custody also. The lawyer is speaking on his behalf as of now."

"What?!" Doc shouted in disbelief.

The agent grinned. "Don't worry Jr., we'll explain it all to you later." His attention was diverted to his walkie-talkie.

"All clear here sir. But we did find some money."

"Okay," the agent said into his headset before he cuffed Doc. "Alright, buddy. We're headed downtown. Oh, yeah…" he said, pausing as they reached the door, "…if you think of anything that might convince me to leave you here, feel free to say it now. Your father is playing games, but one of you better get some sense and get it fast."

Doc's instincts kicked in right away. "Alright, let's holla."

"Thatta boy!" The agent was satisfied at Doc's response. He turned and signaled the others to shut the door to Doc's three-story home.

The agent took a seat. "What do you know about the dirty

cops?"

"Look man. Before we start, are me and my old man gonna be able to walk away from this clean?"

"Unfortunately, your father may have to do some time in prison, but that depends on the information you give us. He probably won't do more than a year. But again, it all depends on the info; the juicier the better. So, do we have a deal?"

Doc nodded his head. "Yeah."

"Now, what do you know about the dirty cops your father deals with?"

"Nothin'. I ain't ever messed with them on no business. My pops don't talk to me about none of that shit. Let's get that straight right now." Doc clarified.

"Well, if you have no knowledge of those matters, how can you help us?"

Doc deceptively replied, "I can set people up. I got cats who buy twenty, thirty bricks at a time; hard and soft. I can serve them, and ya'll can pull 'em over and make the arrest. Ain't that how it works?"

Agent Thompson pretended to ponder on his offer. Then he said, "Okay, Doc. Here's the deal; you get me three to five sales for fifteen or better. You got that?"

"Yeah. Three to five. Fifteen or better. Got it."

"Good. Now, we're going to take you in for questioning, and then let you go in a couple hours. That way things won't look suspicious; being that your friend saw us raiding your spot. Here's my card and cell phone number. Call me when you're alone so we can discuss things further and get you hooked up with a wiring device for your deals."

Doc frowned, "Hey, man, but I thought that…"

"You're not in any position to be thinking right now," Agent Booker said, escorting him out the house in handcuffs.

*****

Tone ended up telling Spook that he was hanging up his jersey. Instead of trying to persuade him out of it, Spook respected his decision and looked out by only charging half price on each brick, as a gift to him and Tre.

Spook surprisingly announced that he was going to also be retiring. All he needed to do was find a replacement for his connect, 'cause a smart man quits on time.

"Let's go baby." Tone rushed Alicia as he stood impatiently at the front door of their condo. "You know everybody's waiting for us on the block."

"So, let 'em wait. It ain't everyday yo' man leaves the game alone," she fussed, stepping past him and into the hallway.

Tone's eyes scanned over her from head to toe. The dark purple, custom-made *Barbara Bates* taffeta dress was simple, but extravagantly enhanced with a diamond studded tennis bracelet and iced out hoop earrings. She rocked a pair of whip snake thronged sandals by *Michael Kors*.

"Damn, baby. I think we should stay here and get yo' fine ass outta that dress!" Tone licked his lips and grinned devilishly.

"Don't move too fast Boo. You know what they say."

Tone grabbed her around the waist, "What?"

Alicia smiled. "Good things come to those who wait," she said unclasping his hands and pushing them to his sides. "Now c'mon before we late." She seductively strutted away, stepping into the elevator and silently thinking of new sex positions she imagined them trying later that night.

The couple pulled out the building garage in the Benz. Tone blasted Notorious Big, "Mo' Money Mo' Problems," and smoked on a *Royal* blunt stuffed with purple haze. As he drove, he thought about the way his life was going to be after the game. It had been a rough time coping with all the hardships, but that was what made him a true soul survivor. He figured the average person wouldn't have been able to handle the cards he was dealt. But thus far, he played his hand well.

Tone's cell phone vibrated. He broke from his trance and checked the caller ID. The screen read J-Mac. It was Jennifer's code. He carelessly sent her call to voicemail, but she called right back. He ignored the call again.

Still, Alicia detected the obvious.

"You want me to get that for you baby? 'Cause I'll let that bitch know it's all about me tonight and every other night. She can have you on borrowed time," she said in a sassy manner.

Tone smiled. "Naw, it ain't nothing but Robby and the guys bugging me. We'll be pullin' up in a minute." He wondered if she bought it.

Alicia wasn't really tripping on who was calling. She knew that there would never be any problems as long as he kept bringing his ass home every night. "Tone, I love you."

"And I love you too baby." Tone changed the song to Lauryn Hill and D'Angelo's, "Nothing Even Matters." They held hands, riding the rest of the way in silence.

When they pulled up to the stop lights on 54th and Morgan, Tone's phone began vibrating again. He answered it and snapped. "What the fuck you want now?" he angrily asked thinking it was Jennifer again.

"Man Moe. It's just me, Doc. Can a nigga call to check up on you?"

"Oh, shit," Tone relaxed. "What up Doc? I thought you was Robby and 'em rushing me. What's the deal though?"

"I hear through the grapevine that you're through with the life."

"Yeah, man. It's over for the kid. Time for the good life; you know?"

Doc wished him the best. "All's well with that! What about ya boys? Ain't you gon' give those brothas a going away present for they loyalty over the years?"

"You know what? I hadn't even really considered that. I'll tell you what…why don't you meet me on the block so I can holla at you in person." Tone hung up.

*****

Doc called Agent Booker. "I'm about to call a quick thirty five. I hope this wired up pager workin' right."

"Just handle your business and get back with me," Booker sternly stated.

*****

Alicia was amazed by the trail of fancy automobiles. "Dang, everybody's over here tonight," she said as they pulled up Tone's block on 55th and Winchester.

"You right about that." Tone was just as flattered. They eyed Jaguars, Lexus, Cadillac's, and Chevy's. Up until that point, he recognized what rides belonged to whom. But he was puzzled that he couldn't put a face to the red-tinted Hummer.

Whose shit is this? He wondered. He pulled to the end of the block and spotted Robby, Brian, and Brandon leaning up against Brian's forest green SS Impala which was embellished with a pearl white interior, wood grain paneling and sitting on twenty-four inch *Lowenharts.* "Let's get it in tonight!" he yelled, hopping from his car. He was decked from head to toe.

"You looking real good," Robby responded, checking out the *Gucci* Polo shirt and jeans with grey double G's on the back pockets, and matching black suede *Gucci* loafers Tone wore.

"What's the demo ?" Brian asked.

"Man, Joe. You didn't tell me half da land was comin with us tonight," Tone exclaimed.

"Well. Everybody love you, lil' bruh, and this is how they showing it. They wanna party wit' you and wish you the best. You know?"

Brandon stepped up, "You cool with that ain't you?"

"Ain't no question 'bout it," Tone replied. "But, who the fuck is riding in that Hummer? That's what I wanna know."

Brian chuckled, "That's ya boy Doc, down there."

"Yeah," Brandon said, "That's him sittin' in his shit behind Shawn's girl Mika. That's her gray Lexus."

"He outta his rabbit ass mind, goin' to cop to something like that. This nigga rollin' a big apple red Hummer. He's a bold muthafucka! Lemme go holla at this nigga real quick."

Tone broke off from his guys and headed in Doc's direction. He was somewhat leery of the idea that the Feds were probably following the loud-colored tank. To him, paranoia was full awareness. He pulled out his cell.

"Yo' Doc," he yelled out first just to be safe. "Man, you see me?"

"Yeah, come on in here. I don't want nobody ear hustling?" Doc replied, ending the call.

Tone remained cautious. *I'mma bell in this piece for a hot second, make the transaction and I'm out,* he thought.

Tone got in Doc's truck. "Man, it smells good in this bitch," he said referring to the strong aroma of the weed.

Doc smiled, "Yes, sir. I gotta couple of zones from Tim before I came this way." He reached to turn down the volume on his radio down in order for him and Tone to have a clear conversation.

Tone felt uneasy. "Man, Joe. You ain't scared to drive around in this piece? The Feds don't play when they see cats like us pushin' trucks like these; you know," he said looking around the inside.

Doc shouted. "Muthafuck the feds. I'mma ball till I fall! Now dig, since you looking out fo' them brothas, I got thirty-five for you right now at $9,500 each. But they gotta come cop from me 'cause with you being gone, I'mma need somebody getting off thirty a month. You draw?"

Tone nodded, "I hear you. I'll try to maneuver that when I rotate with the brothas. I'mma send shorty to bring that change to you. Just give me the bags."

"Grab 'em out Sleepy's trunk. He parked two cars behind me in the white Monte Carlo." Doc gestured. "And don't worry 'bout the money. I'll get it tomorrow or somethin'. You go have a good time wit' yo' peoples.

"Aight, fool. I'mma demonstrate wit' you later." Tone got out the truck and hit Robby on the *Nextel*. "Yo' Robby, meet me in front of Fridge's crib."

"Here I come now," Robby clicked off and began strolling down the block.

Doc laid low. He stalked Tone's every move through his night vision rearview mirror. "What the fuck is he doing?" he mumbled. "Naw, nigga. You go and get it out the truck yo' self."

Doc was hoping to put Tone in a trick bag, but when he saw Robby going to retrieve the narcotics, he knew that the Feds wouldn't find anything on Tone if they pulled him over. Doc was mad at the world when he saw Robby toting the bags down to his grandmother's house on Garfield. "Ain't this a bitch?!" he said and angrily sped off.

As much as Tone loved the hustle, he tested his instincts one more time to see if he really had kissed the game goodbye. Even though a part of him wanted to get the product himself, he listened to his conscience that told him, *If you through with it, you through with it. You don't need to touch nothing no more!*

When Robby stepped out the house, Tone was standing there waiting on him. "What's that?" he asked looking down at the *Gap* bag.

"This like $200, 000," Robby replied. "I thought you might want to give it to Doc," he assumed.

"Nah. We gon' need it more so than him tonight. As a matter of fact, take out twenty Gs and put the rest away. We gon' buy every drink at the club, go with that and as far as the work is concerned, hit Stevey with ten, Shawn with ten, and you keep fifteen. Then ya'll, Brandon and Brian, can put ya'll change together and get at Spook G."

Robby embraced Tone with a hug. "Gratitude brotha," He sighed. "So, you actually through with this shit fo' real; huh?"

"It's time. That's why it's called 'the game.' All games gotta end at some point. Like *Monopoly*, the object is play to win, and to quit when you get enough money and property. Or you can play to lose, and the loss ranges from everything, including your life when it comes to these streets."

Robby nodded. "Or your freedom like my old man," he added.

"Yeah, that too. Anyhow, I tried telling Spook that you were a good candidate for my slot, but he claims he only looked out because of Tre. Other than that, he's got someone else in mind. Who? I don't know."

"I ain't trippin.' I know that becoming the man don't just happen overnight. I'mma just play my position until I get called upon. You draw?"

"Ain't no question," Tone replied. He glanced at his *Jaeger Le Coultre* watch. "It's goin' on 9 pm put that up and let's ride." He grinned, "'Cause I know you ain't rockin' those *Moreshi* shoes and slacks for the hell of it!"

"Hell, naw." Robby dashed back towards the house with

nothing but celebration on his mind.

After Tone gave the cue, everyone hopped inside their cars and headed out to the new nightclub, *The 50 Yard Line*. The streets were packed, bumper to bumper, like the motorcade for the President of the United States on a parade day. Tone's freshly washed and waxed, candy apple coupe led the way as he thumped Jay-Z's, "Lucky Me" through his stereo system.

CHAPTER 17

Pain answered her telephone after the third ring.
"Hello, this is Pleasure Palace. How may I help you?" Her words were seductively spoken into the receiver.

"Yeah, this is Doc. Are ya'll free this evening?" he asked smoothly.

Pain's muscles in her body tensed when the caller identified himself. But she never turned down a vic. "Yes, we are Doc. Our address is 11119 S. Aberdeen, apartment 7. Just ring the bell and be ready for the best head and pussy money can buy. Okay sweetie?"

"Yeah, hoe. I'mma see what's popping once I get there. I owe you a bangin' anyway." Doc hung up.

When he arrived at the three-story apartment building he left his cell phone inside the car and grabbed a fresh box of *Magnum* condoms from under the armrest. He strode to the door. When he heard the entry buzz, he eagerly stepped inside. Doc assumed that Pleasure and Pain had just either moved in or were in the middle of remodeling because he could smell the aroma of fresh paint. Their lavender Italian leather couch and loveseat were also covered with plastic. The girls stepped out of the kitchen and into the living room to greet him.

"Damn, ya'll got this bitch hooked up! I see ya'll on some

cleaning shit; huh?" His eyes examined his surroundings and quickly zoomed in on the tantalizing attire of the young ladies. Their enticing French maid costumes insinuated to Doc that he was going to have a wild night with the pair. They both wore old fashioned maid outfits, black *Martha Jackson* lace peep toe pumps, lace garter belts and sheer gloves.

Doc grinned. "But I ain't never seen no cleaning ladies lookin' this damn good," he panted.

Pleasure snatched the plastic from all the furniture. "Sit down and relax baby," she instructed as Pain began helping their guest out of his red *Pelle* leather jacket.

Doc enjoyed their immediate hospitality. "That's what I'm talkin' 'bout. Show a nigga some love!" He moaned when Pleasure gently massaged her hands into his shoulders. "Oh, yeah, girl I need that!"

Pain grabbed the stereo remote control and pressed it, triggering the sweet melodies of R. Kelly's, "Strip for You." She quickly took a role in Doc's massage by caressing his manhood into a full erection.

"Yeah, Boo. Bring it on! I've been waiting for this," he said with his eyes tightly closed. "And I've been waiting to feel those lips."

"Oh, yeah?" Pain continued massaging his penis. "So you think you're ready for this?"

Doc was lost in complete ecstasy. "Like never before," he replied. The mouth he had been waiting for, felt even better than he imagined.

Pleasure stood behind Doc and tilted his head back. She ran her tongue back and forth on his neck, as he quietly moaned in satisfaction. Pain continued to orally stimulate Doc's penis, which was close to erupting. He obviously hadn't realized the razor sharp butterfly knife was between her legs that she had eased from her garter belt. The two girls eyed each other and on signal Pleasure restrained Doc's arms while Pain took a swift whack at his dick with the blade.

"Aghhhhhhhhh!" Doc's moans of ecstasy instantly changed into a roar of agony. His pants stained red as his penis hung by a half inch of flesh. "You…stupid…ass…b-b-bitch! Aghhh!!" He fell to the floor cuffing his hands over what used to be his crotch.

Pain spat on him. "Yeah, nigga!!! Now yo' ass gone think twice about disrespecting me, muthafuckahhh!"

"Please! Get me a towel or somethin'! Please! Call the ambulance! I'm bleedin' to death!!!" Doc pleaded in his attempts to slow down his bleeding. "I'm sorry! I'm... sorry!!!"

"We already know you a sorry ass nigga. But what about my husband? I bet you ain't sorry 'bout him; huh? Huh, you dirty ass bitch?"

"Aghhh...I...I don't even...even...know...know yo' peoples," he managed to squeal through his excruciating pain. "Please!!!"

"Yes' you did know him, you son of a bitch!" Pain kicked him in the midsection, bloodying her peep toe pumps. "Tre was my husband! You left our son without a father!"

The moment Doc heard Tre's name, his eyes widened as if he starred at his own ghost. He blacked out.

Pleasure felt nauseous. "I can't stand this shit girl," she said in disgust covering her mouth with her hands. The grotesque sight of the bloody dangling penis was too much for her to stomach.

Pain looked over at her with a devious stare. "Call Tone and let him know everything went according to plan."

*****

Tone and his people had the VIP section on lock. They had every chick in the club sipping up all the *Moet Rose* champagne they could. Tone sat next to Robby as they watched Alicia, Co-Co, Mika and their friend Princess shake their asses on the dance floor to Mystical's, "Danger."

"Man Tone. I got to get caked up like you befo' I retire and hang up my hustler's jersey; you know?"

"I hear you my nigga," Tone replied, not really giving much thought as to what his tipsy boy was saying. He bobbed to the music while eyeing a familiar face leaving the club.

Tone jumped up, hoping it wasn't the alcohol disturbing his vision, and headed straight toward the entrance. He was just about to close in on the individual when his cell buzzed. He flipped it out and checked the caller ID. He recognized Pain's number and answered it as he continued rushing through the front door trying to get a better glimpse at a ghost from his past.

"Yeah, what up?" he answered simultaneously checking the area for any signs of enemies. But all he saw was a black SUV pulling from the lot.

"Did you hear me Tone? Everything's taken care of." Pleasure repeated.

"Oh, baby. My fault! I'm out here trippin'. I heard you the first time. So it's officially a wrap; huh?"

"Yep," Pleasure replied twirling a roll of duct tape around her index finger.

"Okay. Well, you and baby girl can give Robby a call tomorrow. He'll handle the rest; aight?"

"Aight, Boo." Pleasure hung up.

Robby stepped outside the club to check on his boy. "What's the deal big homie? You raced outta the place like you was on somethin'."

Tone was glad to know his man wasn't too drunk to be on point.

"I'm cool, Joe," he grinned. "I just had to answer my horn real quick."

Robby exhaled, "Oh, aight. 'Cause you know I got Ross and a couple of the goons in the truck. I know you wanted to have a peaceful night. Some of these niggas and bitches still hate; feel me?"

"Ain't no question. Yo'," Tone scanned for eavesdroppers, "Everything taken care of. You'll be gettin' a call from Pleasure and Pain. I need you to give 'em a hundred stacks for me."

Robby waved his hand like he was doing a magic trick. "That's done homey. Now let's go finish partying playboy."

*****

"Look here Candace. That nigga don't know who I am or who you are. Only those close to us know the business. Anyway, in order to get him, all you gotta do is wait for him to call. When he does, give him the address to my spot on Aberdeen. It's a vacant building I purchased in a dead man's name. Once Doc gets comfortable, 'Bam!'"

he'll be dead before he knew what hit him. Make sure you toast it before you leave, though. Cool?"

Pain nodded as he handed her and Pleasure a bag containing $200,000.

"Now take this money and do something smart. If ya'll gone keep workin', buy your own strip club," he advised. "Be the pimp. Don't let nobody pimp you. Don't forget to make sure to call me after ya'll handle that demo."

Pain smiled after reflecting on Tone's instructions. She looked down at Doc and spat on him. He was already half dead sitting with his hands, feet, and mouth duct taped. She slowly pulled out Tre's gold-plated wood grained *Dessert Eagle* and cocked it. She put it to Doc's head.

"Look at me!" she yelled. Then she kicked at the soles of his feet. "I said look at me, damn it!"

In his semi-conscious state, Doc forced his eyes to open just barely enough to glance at her. The last thing he saw was the flash of the gun.

The gun went off splattering his brains all over the wall. "That's for my husband, bitch!" Pain said to the dead man. She turned to Pleasure who stood by holding a can of gasoline in each hand.

"Let's burn this place Candace and get the hell out of here!"

They redressed in their old woman disguises of scarves and wigs and began dousing the apartment with the flammable liquid. Then they left a trail all the way down the stairs to the front entrance and set the cans by the door. Pain struck the match and dropped it.

"This was for you Tre," she dedicated as tears streamed her face. The two of them watched the flames shooting up the stairs. They walked to their cars and drove off, leaving the entire building to burn to a crisp.

*****

Ross and Stokes were still sitting inside of Robby's truck watching the club's entrance from the parking lot as they listened to Tupac's, "Letter to My Unborn Child."

Stokes had the entire inside of the truck filled with weed smoke and he continued to puff away. Ross on the other hand, felt a little uncomfortable being out of the natural habitat of his hood. The only thing that kept him somewhat at ease was his Mac 11. As he wiped it down, he couldn't shake the awkward feeling he had about the particular night before them. He was determined to stay focused.

"Stokes! Roll the fuckin' window down. I ain't tryin to be high like yo' lame ass."

"Fuck you Vick," Stokes retorted, cracking the window.

*****

"Man, this bitch off the chain!" Robby boasted to Tone as Mobb Deep's, "Quite Storm" blared in the background.

"Yeah, Joe. Too bad this boy is about to close." As soon as those words left Tone's mouth the DJ cut in over the music.

"Last call for alcohol!" he announced as he mixed in "Sugar Hill" by AZ on the turntables.

Tone looked at Robby. "Bro, let's go and rotate up outta here befo' traffic gets backed up," he said in a half-drunken voice.

"Aight, Joe." Robby turned to Brandon, Brian, and Lil' B. and called out to them. "Ya'll come on. It's time to bounce. Just tell them broads to meet us at the *Holiday Inn* on 116th in about an hour if they game!"

When everyone made it outside, Tone told everyone he would holler at them later, he relayed to Robby that he and Alicia were going to check out a few cribs in the other areas.

"Yeah, I'm feelin' that." Robby shook his head.

Tone opened the door for Alicia. "You be easy, Rob. I'mma demonstrate with you later."

"Yeah, In the A.M.," Robby replied. He headed over to his black on black Navigator.

Just as Tone was pulling out of the parking lot, Alicia started complaining about being hungry. "Okay, baby. We'll go pick up some breakfast or somethin', but let me call Robby first." He picked up his cell.

"What up, Moe?" Robby yelled into his *Motorolla*.

"We about to go and get somethin' to eat. Ya'll tryna roll?"

"Yes, sir. Just give us a couple of minutes to catch up. Those chicks we bumped about to ride out with us right now."

"Aight, bet." Tone hung up as he pulled into *Shell's* gas station next to the last pump so he could be seen. He jumped out to take a leak. He smiled while relieving himself and thinking, "Man, it's over for me. That nigga is dead. My brother's wife and child gotta few hundred though. My moms and pops straight, Robby and 'em cool; and I gotta couple mil saved up, along with plenty of real estate thanks to Fred. All I need to do now is settle down.

"Whoa!" he yelled, quickly jumping out of the path of a gray Denali. It almost ran him over. "Stupid muthafuckas!!" he spat.

The passenger of the truck looked over his shoulder. He thought he was dreaming. "Yo, yo, yo, Rocko! Stop this bitch!"

"What's wrong fool?"

"Man. I think I just seen that bitch ass nigga Tone," he said eagerly looking back, "and he off his square."

"Man Shane. Forget that shit. It's over between them and us. We out here gettin money. Besides, you not even sure if it is that nigga."

Shane looked at Rocko like he was crazy. "Please G. I ain't gon' ever forget the nigga who gave me the shit bag. On the Boss! Now pull around so I can handle my business, Folks, straight up."

Rocko sighed, "G, I'm tellin' you. Leave it alone. We can get somebody else to whack dude."

"I don't wanna hear that soft ass shit G. We riders, now if you scared, let me the fuck out right here and I'll go handle this by my damn self."

*****

"Baby, me, you and the kids are out; you know?" Tone said.

Alicia smiled. "Yeah, Boo. I just hope you're not mad or feelin' like I pressured you into leavin' the game alone."

"Naw, I wouldn't even let you pressure me. I'm doin this for myself, as well as my family." Tone paused for a few seconds "I was gonna wait until we left town, but…" he continued, "Will you marry me?"

Alicia jerked like she had been struck by a bolt of lightning. Then tears began streaming down her pretty face. "Yes, Tone! Yes, daddy. I'll marry you," she said leaning over to kiss him.

*****

At the stoplight, Shane snatched at both his glock 45's with the infrared beams. "Now listen Rocko, pull alongside that nigga real slow; I'mma knock back his top and whoever else in the car with him."

"I got you G. Let's just do this and get the fuck outta here."

When the light changed, Rocko slid up next to Tone's car. Shane aimed till the red beams were on the driver and passenger's head. He squeezed.

Pop! Pop! Pop! Pop! Pop!

Tone recognized the sound of gunfire right away and automatically fell to the side to cover Alicia. The both of them cringed to remain as low as possible in the car as they were caught in a hailstorm of bullets. He was relieved to finally notice that none of the projectiles were penetrating his car. Not one window was shattering as bullets continuously sounded off. He sighed.

"Thank God. My shit's bulletproof!"

"What the fuck!" Lil' B screamed, astonished to see the gray SUV alongside Tone's car letting loose. "Hurry up Smooth, befo' they whack my man!" He leaned through the passenger window. Ross took positioning through the sunroof and Stokes took the rear passenger window.

Lil' B blasted. As his Tech 9mm rang out, he quickly exited the truck to get a better shot.

Rocko pulled off as one of his windows shattered. "Shane, get in!!"

Ross pressed the trigger to his 40 cal in harmony with Lil' B, turning the SUV into Swiss cheese.

Stokes tried his best to make every shot count, but he missed by inches. The SUV was skidding away.

"C'mon G!" Rocko begged, swooping through traffic. Get in!"

Shane ignored him and continued unloading his guns. I'm

tryna get those bitches up off!" he screamed. Suddenly he was cut off by a riddle of bullets.

Rocko stopped in traffic waiting on the everlasting shooting to stop.

When Ross saw the assailant inside the truck slump over from the last four shots he took, he let off three more just to assure them that he wasn't playing. It was plain to see that his Mac-11 had found its mark. The shooter from the SUV hung halfway through the window.

"Folks!" Rocko screamed from under the steering wheel. "I'mma get us outta here; you hear me?" he turned toward an unresponsive Shane. It was obvious.

"Hell, naw, G!!" he yelled hysterically, snatching Shane's body into the truck. Blood oozed from the two bullet wounds in his chest. "Shit!" Rocko sped off down the emptied street.

Robby, Lil' B and Stokes ran to make sure that Tone wasn't hurt. They were amazed to see that there wasn't any damage to his car. They found him leaned over, hugging Alicia. Lil' B shouted from the sidewalk.

"Moe! Moe! Tone! C'mon my nigga. Let's go before their peoples get here! You hear me?!" When Lil' B didn't get a response he ran up to the car and banged on the window.

Tone finally looked up. He was never happier to see his boy's face. "Man, those niggas just tried to kill me. But they couldn't. Ya hear me?! They couldn't. This muthafucka's bulletproof. Bulletproof!" he yelled excitedly.

"Yes, sir. I'm feelin' that!" Lil' B stated proudly. "What about Alicia, though? She straight right?"

"Yeah, she a little shook up. But other than that, she's good."

Robby yelled, "C'mon ya'll. Let's ride. We gotta find Ross befo' them people get here!" Everybody bailed out.

Upon exiting the gas station, Robby saw that Brandon's S 500 Benz had been hit by a stray bullet as steam was rising from the hood of his car. He cautioned zipping through traffic at a frantic pace. When he saw Ross a block down from the scene of the crime, he swerved onto the sidewalk.

"Ross!" he yelled, "Get in my nigga!" Robby pulled off after Ross hopped into the backseat. Then they hit the closest corner, heading toward the E-way.

Meanwhile, Rocko pulled up next to the cemetery near 115th street. He jumped out and grabbed hold of Shane's lifeless body.

"I told yo' dumb ass not to fuck wit' him," he said in disgust. After taking a second glance, he hopped back into his truck and peeled away. "I'mma make them bitches pay." he vowed.

*****

Tone and his entourage had long gone their separate ways. When he was a few miles from home he decided to call Robby on his cell.

"Ya'll good?" he asked.

"Ain't no question. We're back in the land about to slide with those chicks from the club."

Tone chuckled. "Aight, ya'll be safe. I'mma get up wit' you tomorrow afternoon before Alicia and I leave town."

"I'm drawin'. Whatever you say." Robby hung up.

Alicia was disturbed about everything that had just transpired. "Baby," she began after Tone got off the phone. "Forget that shit. We can leave tonight. I thought I almost lost you." she cried.

"Listen to me. I'm okay and so are you. We all have the money we need. Let's just go find a place to stay. Instead of us coming back for the kids, we can have my mom fly 'em to us; baby, please."

"I'm sorry Alicia, but I can't leave now. It's niggas around here who want me dead. How would you like it if I came back to the city to check on my family and the same cats from tonight came up on me?"

He could tell that she was at a loss for words. "I know you don't have an answer. But I do. I'm gon' find those chumps and give 'em a good night's sleep. Then we can leave and come back to town as we please without having to watch over our shoulders."

Tone continued driving in silence, thinking about the ghost he saw walking from the club. He figured Shane had gone to get Rocko after pulling from the parking lot. Then again, they could've both been on deck for all he knew. He turned to Alicia.

"It's gon' be aight baby."

"I know," she replied reluctantly.

"Well, if you know, come give me a kiss."

Alicia gladly leaned over and began kissing Tone while simultaneously unzipping his pants. Just as she thought, he was already hard. She removed his member, wrapped her full lips around his shaft, sucking him with slow deliberation as he continued steering home.

He switched the song selection to Syleena Johnson's, "I'm Your Woman."

As he observed his main squeeze's oral performance on him he thought to himself, "Hmmm, if pops ain't ever gave me what I wanted, he damn sure saved my life to where I can still marry this beautiful woman who knows how please her man." Tone smiled. *Thanks for leaving me the car,* big bruh! He said to himself, enjoying Alicia's warm passionate sucks that always carried him away.

CHAPTER 18

Even though Tone woke up feeling like a million bucks, stressed still lingered. He had been watching his own back on a daily basis, so he couldn't shake the thought of killing. He had to get down to the bottom of the situation. He called Robby.

"Yeah. What up sir?" Robby answered.

"You know what's up. You find out where them jokers laying' at?"

"Did I? Robby placed his mouth closer to the receiver. He wanted to make sure Tone heard what he was about to tell him.

"Ole' boy, Shane, restin' at the very place that Tre's buried at."

"Damn," Tone was surprised. "That's the fastest funeral I've ever heard of."

Robby chuckled, "Naw, homie. They found his demo at five this morning, gunned up in the chest, right in front of *Mount Hope Cemetery.*"

"So, now we only got one more to go then; huh?"

"Yeah. But this one might be kinda hard. The nigga we need in order to bait him is dead too."

Tone was lost. "Who?"

"Nigga, Doc. Them peoples found him burnt to a crisp in some building out there in the wild hundreds."

"Get the hell outta here!"

"Yeah. They claimed he fell asleep with the gas on the stove still going. The blunt he was smoking caught fire to his clothes. Next thing you know 'poof' shit went up in flames.

"Damn!"

"You know he was demonstratin' with Rocko."

"So I heard," Tone replied.

"Only thing we could do about him was wait till he came around the way. You know he be back and forth outta state. It might be kinda hard to burn playboy."

"Ain't no question. But we'll think of somethin'. In the meantime, I need you to meet me at *Mr. Lee's Customs* in the next thirty minutes.

"Fo' what? You 'bout to switch the rims on yo' shit?"

"Nah, I'mma take off the ones I got on there and change the paint. It seem like everything that happened to me last night was a wakeup call."

"Why you say that?"

"Because, it taught me that if you can be seen, you can be hit. So don't let ignorance overtake you. It'll end up being your death. Now, I'm not saying don't ride slick. Just make sure you're on your square when you're out there flashin'."

It's cats out there who feed their kids off of playas like us, and the people we hurt – those who we starved in order to get to this point. You understand? You gotta stick to your dreams and goals. I see you goin' a long way with the music game Robby. Not the street game."

"I got you big homie. But what you need to be doing is leaving the crib 'cause I'm on my to the shop."

"Aight. I'll see you in a minute," Tone said. He hung up at ease with the fact that Robby's blood was no longer on his hands. He took a quick shower.

After the phone call with Robby, Tone felt that it would be in his best interest to take Alicia's advice and just leave town. He instructed her to pack while he dropped the car off at the paint shop. His plans were to just drive it whenever he visited the city and use her Acura RL until he decided to get one when they reached their new residence.

When he entered the garage he heard the distinct sound of screeching brakes beyond the door. But he wasn't alarmed. He proceeded to hop inside, turning back the ignition. As he reversed out of his parking space, he unexpectedly tailed the front bumper of a navy blue Taurus with dark tint.

"Stupid bitch!" he exclaimed, ready to spit fire from his guns if he got out to see one dent in his car. But before he could get the door open his heart dropped as he soon realized he stared down the barrel of the biggest, blackest gun he'd ever seen.

"Cut the fucking car off now!"

Tone gazed wide eyed at the officer in the dark blue, nylon jacket with yellow letters reading FBI. Tone obliged and exited the car with his hands in the air.

"Get your ass on the ground!" The agent shouted to Tone with the huge pistol pointed at his head. "You breathe wrong and I'll blow your ass all over this driveway." he threatened, snatching Tone's keys from the car. He tossed them to his partner.

"Second floor condo. Don't tear it up looking too hard 'cause the apartment's not in his name. Our search warrant is for him only. But if we do come across something, him and his father could lose it all.

When Alicia heard the door slam she automatically assumed that it was her future husband forgetting his cell phone again as usual. "Baby, I'mma put some of the bags in the car and…"

"Ms. Thompson?" the white deputy presumed, cautiously stepping into the bedroom. "You are Ms. Thompson; aren't you?"

Alicia momentarily froze as though she had seen a ghost. After snapping back to reality, she was infuriated. "Oh, hell naw! I know you muthafuckas ain't just walk into my house without a warrant!"

"Calm down Ma'am. We're just gonna search the place," he said as three more officers entered behind him. "We have a warrant for the arrest of Anthony Wiley, whom we've apprehended downstairs in the garage. We still want to do some looking around, if it's not a problem."

Alicia knew a little about the law. "Hell, no! Ya'll got a warrant for him, not this house. You need a search warrant for that!"

"I understand that Miss, but…"

"But nothing!" Alicia yelled. "If ya'll dirty hands touch anywhere in my house, I'm calling my Alderman." she bluffed. "Ya'll had no right in the first place barging in here if ya'll already place Tony under arrest outside my house."

The officer sighed. "Alright ma'am. No need to make any calls." He began back pedaling towards the front room, gesturing the other officers to do an about face.

Alicia followed, hoping to see Tone before he was taken away. But the only thing she caught an eyeful of was FBI, DEA, and ATF agents standing around with devilish grins on their white faces. The scene resembled the horrid lynching of a black man.

She was approached by one of the officers. "I assume you're Ms. Thompson." he smirked. "Well, that's the name that came up after running a check on that beige car over there. We saw you remove a *Victoria's Secret* hand bag from the trunk last night after you and Mr. Wiley's return to your residence. Anyway, I'm Agent Booker."

Those muthafuckas been watching us all along. Alicia's mind raced as she recalled doubling back to retrieve the scarlet purple negligee she wanted to surprise Tone with. She had told him she was returning to the car to get her clutch purse. She soon burst into tears.

"Not again," she said to herself, "not again!"

"Here's the keys to his father's car, even though we know who it really belongs to. But since we can't confiscate it, you might wanna sell it and send the money to fund his books. He's gonna need the entire commissary he can get for the next fifteen to twenty years," Agent Booker snickered as he tossed Alicia the keys. She watched as they departed with her man, leaving her standing in the driveway as her tears dried on her cheeks.

CHAPTER 19

"Phillips!" An officer shouted from the 13th floor of downtown Chicago's Federal Holding Center.

Phillips turned from the television and yelled back from section two. "Yeah!"

"You got an attorney visit!"

Phillips stepped out into the foyer area to wait on the elevator. He sighed. *I wonder what's going on. He was just here yesterday. Nothing could've possibly changed that fast,* he said to himself. When he finally made it to the visiting room, he was surprised to see Agent Bradley along with his lawyer. He snapped.

"I thought I told you I don't have anything to say?"

Bradley waved his hand, "Have a seat Mr. Phillips. We're not here for that right now. This has to do with your son, Doc."

"You son of a bitch! I told you my son has nothing to do with this shit; so keep him out of it. You got that Agent Booker?!"

"I wish I could believe you, but we know he did have something to do with every dirty trick that his no-good cop father did. But that's neither here nor there. In fact, your son was trying to help you and himself before we found him dead last night."

"Dead?!" Phillips' heart sank. "Naw n-n-not my boy. No! I don't believe that shit. How?!" he screamed. Phillips stormed from his seat in a wild rampage. He was immediately restrained.

"Calm down Phillips," ordered Agent Tinley accompanied with Booker.

Phillips remained in his seat sobbing in disbelief. "Nooooo. Not, Doc. He was a good kid. Wh-what did ya'll do to him?" he skeptically asked.

"It's nothing *we* did Duke. His remains were found in a scorched building." Booker paused for a few seconds and allowed Phillips to take it all in. He could tell that he was distraught and weakened. *Time to go for the jugular;* he thought.

"Now, if you could think of anyone who might've wanted to murder him, let us know. Or, you can help us. Assist us by bringing in Captain Bullock, and we'll release you. You could have your job back. That way, you could personally oversee the investigation surrounding your son's murder. All you gotta do is implicate Bullock in front of a Grand Jury. If you don't want to do it for us, then do it for yourself; do it for Doc. Just ponder the thought. We'll come back tomorrow."

Mr. Jeffreys, Phillip's attorney, patted his shoulder. "Give me a call Duke." He exited the room with both agents.

Phillips was crushed. As soon as he heard the door close behind him he fell to his knees in pity and cried his soul out. As he poured his tears of repentance and regret over his folded hands, he heard the jingling of keys. Phillips quickly wrapped up his prayer and stood so the officer wouldn't see him in a vulnerable position.

"Let's go Mr. Phillips." The officer escorted him toward the elevators. He clicked his walkie-talkie. "Visiting room to control… pick up from 8 to 13."

Choice and Simmons immediately noticed the look of gloom written all over Phillips' face when he returned. Choice spoke up first.

"What's up Sarge?"

"Those sons of bitches just came trying to get me to cooperate again. I told 'em to suck a dick, of course."

Simmons chuckled, "That's right sir. Fuck them! They ain't got nothing on us. I bet ya'll a flat, well-done steak from *Ronnie's* that they don't indict us." Choice interjected. As Phillips walked away, he whispered to Frank, "But why the Sarge looking so shocked if that's all that really went on down there in the visiting room?"

"He's probably tired. You know he's up there in age."

Choice shook his head, "Naw. I've been around him long enough to know when something's bothering the old man." He turned and yelled, "Hey Sarge!"

Phillips stopped in front of his cell and turned. He sighed and stepped back to the section three telephone area. "What is it now?" he asked aggravated.

"Sir, it looks like something's bothering you. Did they find some new evidence or something?"

Phillips broke down, "Naw. Somebody murdered my son."

"Who? Doc?! Hell, no! Someone's gotta pay!" Simmons exclaimed.

"Did they tell you who it was?" Choice asked.

"Nope. They just said his remains had been found in some burned-down building out in the south hundreds. But right now, I'mma go and get some rest; alright?" Phillips walked off to his cell.

"What have I done to deserve such a thing God? Why did you take my son? I'm an old man now. Why not me instead?"

Phillips wrestled with himself. He searched for the answers to the confusing questions, deep within. But his conscious mind was drowned out by the laughter of his demons.

I can't take this no more, Phillips mumbled to himself as he stared into the small wall mirror. He turned and snatched his bed sheet from the mattress and tied one end of it around the bar on the top bunk. He tied the other around his neck.

The corrupt Sergeant wanted to join his son in a place where they could be together once again; a place where they both would be free. After Phillips made sure that everything was secure, he rolled of the top bunk. Guards later found his lifeless body dangling midair.

CHAPTER 20

After being arraigned by the Magistrate Judge, Tone went through two long continuances in court before the Grand Jury indicted him on conspiracy charges; along with some of Chicago's corrupt police officers.

His first thoughts were that the entire thing had to be some type of gimmick the government was playing. They couldn't catch him red handed. But after receiving the Grand Jury statements with Doc's name all over them, he knew they had finally gotten him dead to the right.

Tone had been on the 15th floor in the *Metropolitan Correctional Center* for nine months. He witnessed all the underhandedness going on with the Feds; guys lying on their best friends, and even their parents, just to go home. He'd seen the hardest criminals fold to duck the time they faced; talking to agents and prosecutors and negotiating deals.

For over four and a half months, Tone stayed on his attorney to get a move on things. He was ready to get to the joint and begin his time, especially knowing Doc had sealed his fate. If it hadn't been for his signed confession, the case against Tone would have failed just like the other ninety-nine percent of blacks and Latinos who had been wrongly convicted for ghost drugs or hearsay. As Tone lay in his cell, he prayed he would be the one percent who got a good shake.

Man, I wonder what would've happened if I hadn't had Doc whacked? He asked himself.

"Mail call!" an officer shouted. He proceeded to randomly call out the names of various inmates.

"Right here C.O.!" Tone yelled, upon exiting his room. "I'm Wiley. Pass it back." After grabbing his mail he rushed to his cell to read it. He was excited to see a letter from Alicia…

Dear Tone,

How are you babe? I hope you're in excellent spirits and health. As for me and the kids, we're fine. My no-good ass baby daddy came by my old house with a few gifts for them. He told my cousin and them that he's back on track, following God and all.

Anyway, I talked to your lawyer. She talkin' 'bout you facing ten to life. That's a long time daddy; time that I can't wait on. You know I love you, always will, but that's just too long. I'll finish paying your lawyer. I took the rest of the money to your mom, and kept the rest for myself. I'm selling the condo so the people won't take it for taxes or something like that. I'm moving to Nebraska somewhere.

I hope you forgive me baby. I'll keep in touch with you; okay? Look me up. Keep your head up and stay strong, sweetheart.

Love always-n-forever,
Alicia

Tone was sick. "That bitch!" He couldn't believe what he just read. He wondered why she didn't tell him what she had written in person when she visited last. "How could she do me like this after all I did for her?"

"Fuck it!" he said out loud as he balled up the letter. As soon as he tossed it into the trash can his homey, Jaymo, stepped into the cell.

"What up, kidd!"

Tone grabbed the chess board and said, "Nothing Joe. Just chillin'. What up? You wanna get trunked or somethin'?"

"I don't think they make trunks big enough to hold my black ass." Jaymo chuckled. "Oh yeah here's yo' legal mail. Somehow it came with the other mail today. I grabbed it when I saw yo' name and brought it up since you had already stepped off after the C.O. called your name."

As Tone opened his letter, Jaymo set up the pieces on the chess board.

Dear Mr. Wiley,
Your court date has been pushed up to Tuesday at 1:30 pm. See you there.

After Tone read the news he turned to Jaymo, "Yo', what's today?

"Monday. Why, what's up?"

"Man, I got court tomorrow afternoon according to this docket letter."

"Well, you better go shower and get some rest tonight?"

Early the next morning Tone was up waiting to be transferred to the court building, but he wasn't taken with the 7:30 a.m. court run along with everyone else. So he went to the C.O. with the letter his lawyer sent to show her that he was supposed to be in court.

Officer Hicks was in her late fifties with short and honey blonde weave sewn in her hair. "I'mma call R&D and see what's going on for you young man."

"Thanks Ms. Hicks." Tone waited patiently for a response.

A few minutes later, Ms. Hicks hung up. She turned to Tone. "You'll be going down for court at 9:30 a.m. young man. You should know that."

Tone felt offended by the spirit in which she delivered the message. He knew what she insinuated. Only the snitches go to court between 9 and 10 a.m. He snapped.

"Look, I ain't on that period C.O., you better ask somebody. I'm not that type of guy; straight up!"

"I really hope not young man. There's too many of you hanging, banging and slanging hardcore together until the police step into the picture."

Yeah, tell me about it. Tone thought as he headed to the T.V. area to check out the news until it was time for court. He knew he was already waiting to turn down another plea agreement. The prosecutor, Mr. Tussman, refused to give him eighteen years since he wasn't willing to testify on Officers Choice and Simmons, whom he didn't even know. Even if he did know them, he wouldn't trick. That would be a cold day in hell.

When it was finally time to go, Tone stepped into R&D from the elevator. There were two Marshals already waiting with shackles, cuffs, and chains in hand.

"Let's go Mr. Wiley. We didn't have you on our list this morning." One of the Marshals said as he and his partner connected the iron restraints around Tone's legs, wrists, and waist. Once their prisoner was secured, they led him toward the elevator. They got off at the dock area and hopped into their Grand Marquis.

Thirty minutes later, one of the agents wished Tone luck as they took him from the Marshal's custody, escorting him to the holding cell outside of courtroom 3303, at the *Dirkensen Building*. After locking him in, they went to inform his attorney, Darice Walker, that her client had arrived.

Several minutes later, a gorgeous woman sashayed her way through the bullpen door. She stood 5'7, 135 lbs. with a 34-24-36 inch frame. Her hair was reddish brown, cut into a sleek bob. She also had creamy, beautiful skin; just like Mariah Carey or Alicia Keys.

"Good morning Anthony," she said perkily, and stood in front of his cell. "How are you?"

Tone grinned. "I was a bit down until I saw you. God definitely sent one of his prettiest angels as my protector." he flirtatiously replied.

Her rosy cheeks broadened. "Aw, that's sweet. Anyway, I have some good news for you today."

"And, what might that be Mrs. Walker? Am I about to be released or somethin'?"

"I wish you were Anthony. But it won't be long for you if you like this new plea agreement." She pulled documents from her portfolio.

"Oh. That punk ass prosecutor changed his mind and brought down the time; huh?"

"No. It wasn't that at all. He got pulled off your case somehow and was replaced by a friend of mine. Her name is Melissa Sternberg. Just so happens, I work at her father's firm – Sternberg and Wilson

– with whom your father had relations with for years. I pleaded with her on your behalf and since their star witness was found dead a few months ago…"

"Yeah," Tone interjected. "That dude was my homey. I looked up to him. I would have never guessed he worked for the DEA."

"It happened when they arrested his father, Duke Phillips, of the 7th District and the other two dirty cops they were trying to get you to implicate."

"That was his pops huh?" Tone asked, acting as though he was new to the whole thing.

"Yes. He hung himself right after he found out that Doc was dead. Now, as you already know, the federal system has a ninety-nine percent conviction rate. If you take this to trial and lose, you'll be facing a ten-to-life sentence. Nevertheless, we've been blessed with a loop before. The government knows you can possibly win in trial – with everything going on with the Apprendi Case Law. The decision you have to make is all yours because this is your life; not mine. You're the one who will have to do the time."

Tone sighed, "I know all that Mrs. Walker, but what's the point?"

"Well, as I was saying before, Assistant U.S. Attorney Sternberg and I have reached an agreement to where you won't have to cooperate at all."

"I'm feelin' that," Tone anxiously responded. "How much time is this prosecutor talking?"

"She says that she'll drop the conspiracy if you would plea out to a buy and sell charge that happened only one time between you and Doc."

"Why would I plea for something that took place with a dead man?"

"Because they have you on tape, audio, and video. It turns out that Doc's Hum V had a recorder and camera installed, strictly for the purpose of setting guys up so he could walk and also get his father a lower sentence as you read in the statements. So, they've got you red-handed making the deal, and Assistant U.S. Attorney Sternberg said that they could prove you were purchasing the kilos for two other unidentified males. Now, the camera didn't capture them in return for their excellent service over the years".

"But she's also told me that if you take the ninety-six months she's offering in this plea and waive your appeal rights, she'll make those tapes disappear. What do you say Tony?" she asked hoping he'd agree.

Man, these people might try to superimpose that videotape, see Robby grabbing the work and possibly supersede indict me along with Robby if I go to trial, Tone reasoned with himself as he weighed his options.

"What do you say I do?" he asked unsure.

"As your attorney, I would advise you to accept the agreement because it's too much of a gamble to go to trial with a bunch of dirty cops who are fighting murders and all. However, if you decide to go to trial, I'll fight with everything I've got Anthony, I promise. Again, the choice is all yours." She straightened her documents. "So think on it a couple of minutes and let me know what you decide when I come back here to speak with you before going in front of the judge." She got up from the rotating chair and headed to the courtroom. But before she could get to the door, Tone called out to her.

"Mrs. Walker!"

"Yes, Anthony."

"I won't be enhanced for my background or anything like that would I?"

"No, she's put on 11 c/c cap on the deal. I've done the research on the whole thing from bottom to top, and you'll have the opportunity to review it yourself before signing it. The judge has also agreed to accept it today if you're willing to plea out."

"If you think it's the best decision, I'll take it then Mrs. Walker." Tone affirmed.

"Okay, I'll get you called right out so we can look over it, then get you sentenced before the end of the month," she smiled. "And good luck Anthony."

"Thank you, 'cause I'mma need luck or something since I'm signing my life away for the next few years."

Forty-five minutes later the bailiff announced, "All rise for the Honorable Judge Samuel Fuqua!"

The Judge took the bench and said, "You may be seated." He

glanced in Tone's direction. "I see Attorney Darice Walker reporting on behalf of Anthony Wiley. Uh, where's the U.S. Attorney?"

"She notified the courts stating she'd be a few seconds late due to finishing up her closing arguments in front of Judge Monday, your Honor." Sandi, the court reporter, confirmed. Just then a long legged, round-lipped, blonde female stepped into the courtroom. She was dressed in an extravagant white *Cantarelli* pantsuit.

When Tone saw her over his shoulder he smiled ear to ear. He was happy to see his late night creep, Jennifer. She was in the house to show her support. But when she opened her mouth and spoke her words completely took him by surprise.

"Sorry I'm late, your honor, but I had a trial going on. For the record, I'm U.S. Attorney Melissa Sternberg here on behalf of the United States."

"Okay, Ms. Sternberg, have you and the counsel reached an agreement?" The Judge asked.

"Yes, we have, your Honor." Attorney Walker exclaimed. "My client and I would like to take a moment to look over the plea sir. Then we'll be good to go."

"Very well. We'll take a five minute recess." Judge Fuqua responded.

Tone stared with his mouth agape. Melissa Sternberg, aka Jennifer, winked her eye at him as she made her way over to him. Then she passed him and his attorney a copy of the initial plea bargain.

"Hey, Melissa." Darice said, "Can I have a quick word with you?" Both attorneys stepped off to the side to converse.

Tone sat there trying to figure out what the hell was going on. He had been tricked, and the one who tricked him was now in court offering him some time in prison. He sighed as he flipped through the pages of the contract. Before everything began to register, he stumbled across a folded letter that had, "Read Me" on top of it. He remained inconspicuous and slowly unfolded it.

Hey there Tone. I know this may be somewhat shocking, but I tried to warn you and tell you they were coming. But you never answered your phone that evening of your 'retirement party' neither did you answer the following morning.

I'm sorry I lied about my true identity and occupation. I felt if you knew the truth you wouldn't have wanted anything to do with me. However, even if you don't forgive me, I understand.

I took the liberty to call in a few favors to get your case, so I could give you this 72-month plea. Please take it baby. I'll be here waiting once it's over if you find it in your heart to forgive.

Love always & forever,
Melissa! xoxoxox

P.S. Rip this up and flush it once you get back in the holding tank.

Darice took her place again next to Tone just as he had finished reading the small note.

"So, what do you think?"

"It's perfect. Seventy-two months? Yeah. I can go fo' that."

Darice smiled slyly. "I just bet you can. Melissa said, after reviewing your criminal history with the Presentence Investigator, they placed you at a level twenty-four, category two. This only carries sixty-three to seventy-two months. The judge agreed to hit you with the high end because he doesn't like you getting off with a smack on the wrist. But he's a Democrat who also owes her father a favor."

"Thank you all, Mrs. Walker. I really appreciate it. Could you also make sure to thank the prosecutor for sparing me?" he smiled.

"All rise. Court is now back in session!"

"You may be seated," the judge stated firmly. "Now what's the agreement between both parties?"

Mrs. Walker stood adjusting her beige conservative, *Collette Dinigan* skirt suit. "We have accepted a plea for seventy-two months your Honor, with a term of thirty-six months supervised release. Also with the condition that Mr. Wiley takes drug treatment while in B.O.P custody." She turned in Melissa's direction.

"That is the agreement your Honor."

"Okay, well, in the case of U.S. vs. Anthony Wiley, you have waived your right to a jury trial, do you understand?" The judge asked Tone.

"Yes, your Honor, I do." Tone replied.

"By understanding these stipulations do you still wish to waive your rights?"

"Yes, I do, your Honor."

"Then, we here in the Eastern District of Illinois hereby accept the plea of guilt from Anthony Wiley, and sentence him to seventy-two months in a Federal Bureau of Prisons, a one hundred dollar court assessment fee, which he must pay via the work program inside the prison. Upon his release the defendant is to serve three years' supervised release. Now, Mr. Wiley is there any particular place you would like to go?"

"I would like to be designated somewhere close to home your Honor."

The judge picked up his gavel. "Well, with that said, I now turn you over to the custody of the B.O.P. This court is now adjourned." With that sentence, the judge banged the wooden mallet.

CHAPTER 21

One month after sentencing, Tone found himself in the *Manchester Federal Correctional Institution.* As he left R&D with the several others being escorted to their designated housing units, he was approached by an older guy wearing a pair of platinum and wood grain *Cartier* frames. He had 360 degree brush waves in his hair, tapered in a low cut, with random strands of gray. Tone recognized him right away. He smiled.

The guy stepped up and greeted him, "Hey. What up, lil' homey! My boy told me you were coming down."

"Big Shawn! What up nigga?!" Tone cheerfully replied. "Yeah, I hollered at him right befo' I left the building. He told me I would be straight, 'cause you were here."

"No doubt. I just hope his lil' ass be cool so he don't end up here with us. This the big leagues boy." he assured him. "Now, before we go any further, I need to see your paper work to make sure you not hot."

"Come on Shawn."

"I know lil' man, but the rest of the Chicago car don't. We've seen the best of 'em break down when it came to these people."

"Believe me, I understand." Tone replied as they rotated throughout the unit.

Shawn immediately began explaining how the movements worked. "Beginning of the ten-minute recreation move!" A female voice stormed over the intercom.

"Let's ride! We only got ten minutes to make it to wherever our destination is on the compound." Shawn yelled. "I want you to meet the rest of the guys."

"Aight." Tone dashed into the neatly kept cell they placed him in, and dropped his bed roll onto the empty bunk. Afterwards, he dashed out again and followed big Shawn to the gym.

"Man, this bitch is big!" Tone exclaimed, observing the gymnasium as they walked in.

"Yeah. Hardball is on Mondays and Fridays. We also hoop on Tuesdays and Thursdays."

"Hold up Shawn! I gotta handle somethin'." Out of the blue, Tone rushed away.

"What you talkin' bout?" Shawn asked, but his man was already in midstride heading directly toward a five-foot-nine slim brother with brush waves.

"What up now muthafucka!" Tone yelled, advancing on the guy. "You ain't so tough without yo' pistol; nigga!"

Rocko thought he was in a nightmare. "Ma – man, Tone. Let me explain!" he pleaded.

Shawn caught up to his man right away. "Tone! This ain't the time, nor the place," he said sternly. He locked his arms around Tone's body to prevent a scene.

"Let me go Shawn. This punk ass stud tried to kill me about a year ago! Let me go!!!"

Shawn looked young, but he was knocking on forty. "Rocko, gon' back to your unit and I'mma holla at my man. When I'm finished, I'll come get you so all three of us can discuss this shit together." After Rocko stepped out of sight, Shawn released Tone.

"Man Unc.. Why you ain't let me fuck playboy up? He shot at me and my broad. Thank God my car was bulletproof or we both would've been dead. Next time I see that fake ass gangsta, it's going down!"

"Naw, lil' bruh. It ain't going down like that at all. Straight up!"

"What?!" Tone had a hard time believing that he was talking to the same Shawn Bradley who had paved the way for him and his sons to walk up the block safe and sound. He snarled.

"Fuck that Moe. I didn't come to jail to get soft," he boldly exclaimed.

"Neither did I lil' brother. But this is how it goes in here. By us being so far from the crib, we gotta ride together. The whole East coast, South, Midwest and West coast sticks with people from their regions just in case something jump off.

So whatever differences we have amongst each other from the streets, or wherever the beef fueled, we squash them in the Feds. Believe me. I know how you feel, but there's only so many of us brothers. When you get out, you can do whatever you want. But here in my house, it's not happening; understand? Like I said, ain't nothin' but a few of us from the city and we need to stay bonded; aight?"

"Yes, sir, Shawn. I got you," Tone humbly replied.

Shawn exhaled relieved. Then he patted Tone on the back. "Now, we gonna get Rocko out here. Sit back and nip this old gang bangin bullshit in the bud. Truth is, neither one of our organizations was formed for that purpose. It was supposed to be to uplift our communities. But once the dope flooded Chicago's neighborhoods, it started wars for more territory. That's where the greed came in," Shawn preached.

"I had heard about what happened between ya'll out there. They say his boy, Shane, was the only one who got hit up; huh?"

"Yeah. He got what he deserved, and that other bitch ass stud gon' get his once I'm out," Tone growled.

"Man Tony. I don't think he wanted that shit to happen. From what he told me, he said Shane pulled a pistol on him tellin' him to pull around. He really didn't have a choice in the matter. He did put strong emphasis on how he strongly regretted what happened, and how he forgave whoever was with ya'll for blazin' him up."

"Why you say ya'll?"

"'Cause when he said a black Nav, it dawned on me that he was describing my son's truck. I just stayed quiet and listened to the story. You know I wasn't gonna expose my baby boy under no circumstances. But, what I did do was tell Robby to get rid of that hot ass truck," Shawn confessed. They took a seat on the bleachers near the baseball field.

Tone grinned, "I see you still keepin' yo' ears to the streets like you never left."

"That's my job. I got three sons besides my godsons Brian and Brandon to worry about out there," he sighed. "Now look, I'm not saying you have to forgive Rocko, but at least hear the brother out. Sooner or later, one way or another, you gotta put this shit behind you."

Minutes later, the movement bell rang. Rocko returned to the recreation yard outside, holding his cooler in one hand, while smoking a *Black and Mild* cigar with the other. Shawn spotted him and waved him over.

Rocko saved his sagging grey pants from falling down to his knees as he walked toward them.

"What's the deal fammo?"

"Nothin' much gangsta," Shawn replied.

Rocko immediately turned to Tone. "Man…fam…I apologize for everything that's taken place Chali. Straight up. I tried to tell Shane to leave that shit alone, we gettin' money. But he was being a hothead, telling me to come back around," he paused. "I can't lie Tone. That was the worst mistake I ever made in my life. Now my brother from another mother is dead. I caught this case in Kentucky for fear of my peoples wanting to violate me sayin' I left folks for dead by his self fo' the second time. But, that's neither here nor there. Anyway, I apologize my nigga. And if you're willing to leave the past behind us, let's do it; aight?"

Tone stood there holding back with all his might. The thought of dealing with the same dude that killed his homey Flye and tried to kill him as well, just didn't feel right. However, for the sake of being where he was, he opened his mouth.

"Rocko brotha, I understand where you comin' from. I'm cool. My bad for comin at you like that earlier." He stuck out his hand to seal his word with a shake.

"Recall! Yard recall!" The female announced over the intercom. It was time for the inmates' 4p.m. institutional count which was operated all over the United States Bureau of Prisons.

"Let's ride Tone. Aye Rocko, we'll holla later on after court or somethin'." Shawn dapped hands with Rocko as he and Tone detoured towards their housing units.

"You in the cell with homeboy One Hand Mike from Cleveland. He tight, so take it easy on him; aight?" Shawn grinned. "I'm just kiddin', bruh. But dude is good peoples. You'll learn a lot from him, too."

"If you say so," Tone casually replied as he stepped inside the unit.

"After count, lil' brother." He shook hands with Tone and they parted towards the directions of their cells.

Stepping into his cell, Tone could see the genuine interest his cellmate held with Big Shawn. He was well-groomed, wearing crispy creases in his beige khaki uniform, stroking his hair with a brush. He introduced himself right away when he saw Tone.

"What's the deal, homey? My name is One," he smoothly introduced.

"Nothin' much. I'm Tone."

"Okay. I see you from Chi Town," One supposed. The numbers 424 at the end of Tone's inmate I.D. shirt tag gave it away.

"Yeah, man. Unfortunately, that's where I'm from."

"You know my homey, Big Shawn?"

"*Do I know him*? He watched me grow up. Me and his sons were raised with each other. He's like an uncle to me. We was just together."

"Yeah, that's cool fam. But look, my nigga, befo' we start rotating I need to see yo' paper work." One referred to Tone's pre-sentence investigation report that verified whether or not he was a snitch. "It ain't nothin' personal."

"I know how it is," Tone replied, "I also need to see yours too playboy."

"You ain't said shit but a word," One turned to his locker searching for his legal envelopes. They exchanged papers and glanced over each other's work. Both were satisfied.

"Man, Chi Town, you never know about people these days; straight up."

"I know what you mean, especially after the shit I just went through."

"We all go through that shit, lil' homey. Those snitches will get what they hands called for. Believe that."

"Yeah, but it wasn't only the snitch in my case 'cause he ended up dead. So they dismissed the conspiracy."

"Right. I peeped that in your papers."

"Ain't no question. Anyway One, I had this chick I met when I was eatin' with my ex-broad. I'm talkin' 'bout she could suck a pool ball through a *Twizzler*," Tone joked. "But anyhow, I'm fuckin this broad for a while then I catch this case and..."

"And let me guess," One interjected, "She wrote you talking bout she can't do the time, but she loves you."

"Naw, that's another hoe. I was talking about my ex. We'll talk about her later on. Anyway, I go to court for my pleas and this broad turned out to be the prosecutor."

"Hell naw, nigga!"

"I'm not lyin'. This bitch was the prosecutor brother and I never knew it. Straight up kid. I wish I did know 'cause shorty could've been laundering all types of money for me. On the real," Tone continued. "When I met her, she had lied about her name and all. Although I never really asked her much about herself, I did wonder how she could always afford those expensive ass rooms at the *Drake* downtown. She was a snow bunny, so I automatically assumed she just had a good job. Not to mention how much of a sex maniac she was."

One laughed. "The chick was a bunny; huh?"

"Yeah, and I let my dick get the best of me," Tone said remorsefully.

"I know you don't regret fuckin' with the white girl; do you?"

"Naw, 'cause if our relationship was genuine, love wouldn't carry no colors. As I look back at all my past relations with sisters, they've all abandoned me throughout hard times. But I figured since shorty worked with the government that's always against us, I say fuck that hoe. Then she had the nerve to write a letter and stick it inside my plea agreement talking 'bout how sorry she is and how much she loves me."

"Yeah," One responded sarcastically, "her ass should've freed you if that was the case. These broads always talkin' 'bout that 'love' shit. They don't realize love don't love nobody. It's about stayin' loyal and true nowadays."

"Who you tellin'?" Tone agreed.

"Damn though, Chi Town, that's the craziest shit I've heard since I've been down. You should write a book on everything you just told me," One suggested.

"Come to think of it, I had started writing one while I was in the state joint, but I never got a chance to finish it. So, I might tell my mom's to send me my old project so I can finish it up."

"It'll damn sho' be a cold-blooded story fo' real Chi Town." One bragged. Just then, Big Shawn stepped into their cell.

"Hey, what up youngstas? I see ya'll got past the formalities."

"Yes, sir." Tone replied.

Shawn snatched a joint from the inside of his sock, right above the ankle. "Good. Let's get out and smoke one before them bitch ass C.O.'s make their rounds." He lit it and One sparked a *Black and Mild* cigar to help camouflage the marijuana's aroma.

"Welcome to the big house Tone," Shawn said, talking between puffs. "Just rotate with the guys and all will be well Moe; aight?"

"I got you, bruh. Don't even trip."

Shawn felt a heavy buzz coming on. "Man Tone, what you think my boys up to?"

"Ain't no tellin' what them cats on." Tone couldn't imagine what it was like for Shawn to be doing a life sentence with sons who referenced the streets for guidance. Tone cleared his throat.

"But the last time I talked to Robby, he had enrolled at *Columbia College* to be a producer."

Shawn smiled ear to ear. "Yeah, boy! I show do hope my baby boy becomes one of those Diddy type cats; straight up! Then he can pull some strings to get his pops outta here."

"Yeah, I hope so too Moe. I hope so too." Tone replied with sincerity resounding in his voice.

DEDICATIONS

This book is in loving memories to all those who past away in spirit yet their Souls Survive continuously through me and our loved ones - my brother Cedric (YaKo) Wiley, Grandma Warrine Wiley (Great Grandmother) Dartee, My shining star Martha (Big Momma) Jackson, Dennis, Aunt Earlene, Uncle Nick, Auntie Elaine, Linnette Stubbs, Ethel Butler, Ken-Ken, Lil Luke, Meechie, Terrell (Chilli T.), Lee-Lee, Otis, Shon Franklin, Mookie, Johm, Willie (Baby Squirrl) Triplett, Marcus (J. Rock) , June (J. Town), Maurice (Kriss Kross), Money, Larry, Melvin, Lance (Lotion), Shavon Dean, Dantrelle Davis, R. Black, Robert (Yummy) Sandifer, Black Shake, Black Jermaine, Dontae (P. Dubb) Brown – Antwon (Moochee) Brown, Rino – Dino (Dwins, Eric (Forty), Jimme, Brandon Baity, Wayne & Lil Terrell, DeAndre Williams, Charles (Maine) Young and his son Diontae Young, Glen (Pimp) Tatum, Lil Dontae, Eula (Grandma) Young, Dwight Jones, All the lives of those who were victims in the tragic accident at E'2 Nightclub, The September 11th, attack, and those who didn't survive Hurrican Katrina, Ofc. Charles Dickerson, Ofc. Thomas Worthman and Chicago Police Officers who died in the line of duty K. Bull, D. Boxdale, Flukey and Willy (Wimp) Stokes, G. Red and son, P. Ames, Antionette (Toni) M. Wiley, Auntie Beverly, Stephen and Dawon Bailey, Crawford Davis, Andrew (Man-Mann) Powell, last but not least My Big Brother Ronald D. Wiley (Ronny Moe). The only reason your name is last is because I still can't believe you gone!!!

SOULS SURVIVING

Malik, Larry Hoover, Keeta. *Antwon(G.B) Mason you keep me rooted from the outside still looking in!* Gregory (Fridge) Brown, G. Ranger, Damien (Lil-Mo), Spook G, Shorty Rough, Omar Andrews, Putt, Nuke, Alden Banks, Anderson Bey, Jerri Louis Bey, B. Matlock El., Clarence (Booky C.) Hankton, Will (G.I.), Deatrick Banks, Johnny F., Reggie Golden, Jeremiah (Jaymo) Smith, Emanuel, Tone-Tone, Patches (Bad Twin), Kevin Turner, Sam Peeples, Charles (E. Smooth) Smith, Michael (One Hand) Stubbs, Clint, Will (Off The Ave.), Lil Smoke, Ant Green, Sambino, Big Dock, Nino, Geno, Kethon, Don Ho, Lil Amen (OH), Chino (N.Y.), Messiah, Short (Louisville K.Y.) Old-man Doc. (Memphis TN), Vegas, Jamar (J. Billa) Bailey, Breezo, Big Ghost, Sabu, Gaine, Biggs, Rocko G., G. Black, B. Rubb, Smutt, Edwin (Lil Stokes), Dex (Maniac), Fresh (OH), Alfred Span, Mike G. Old Man Breed, Old Man Arthur, Mook, Rump, Be-Be, Thomas (Doo-Doo), Diego, Chinaman, Big Ru, (IN), Lee (GI) Ralph-Smalls (WI), Tyrell (Nut-Nut) Mason, Brandon Anderson, Brandon Bl, Darren (Boo-Man) Young and those whom I didn't name you are not out of sight nor out of mind just don't give up hope cause real dreams becom reality. Keep your minds free!

WE <u>ALL MUST</u> <u>COME TOGETHER</u>
IN ORDER TO <u>MAKE A DIFFERENCE!</u>